HOW MY HEART

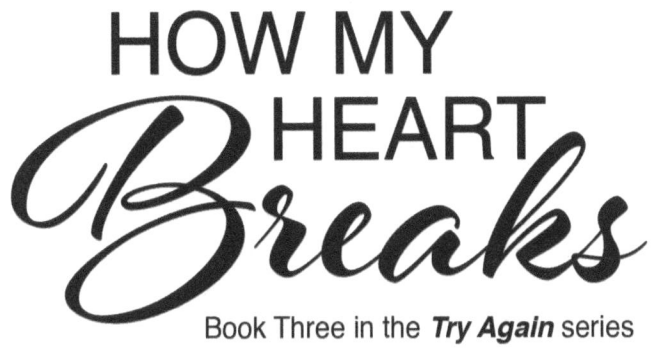

Breaks

Book Three in the *Try Again* series

I0461034

Stephanie Smith

How My Heart Breaks
Book 3 in the *Try Again* Series
Copyright © Stephanie Smith 2015

Editing by Lauren K McKellar
www.laurenkmckellar.com

Cover Art by Hang Le of By Hang Le
www.byhangle.com

Interior Design by Stacey Blake of Champagne Formats
www.ChampagneFormats.com

ISBN-10:0994242735
ISBN-13:978-0-9942427-3-0

Other Books

The Try Again Series
Wherever You Will Go
Whatever You Do

Dedication

To all military personnel who serve here and overseas, and to
all the families they leave behind.
Thank you for the sacrifices you have made for our freedom.
You are our heroes.

They shall grow not old, as we that are left grow old:
Age shall not weary them, nor the years condemn.
At the going down of the sun and in the morning
We will remember them.
Lest We Forget

*"A soldier doesn't fight because he hates what is in front of
him. A soldier fights because he loves what he left behind."*
– unknown

Chapter One

Jake

All I see are flames. I'm easily a mile away, and the large licks of fire sweeping through the dark night sky make it seem as though I'm driving into the pits of hell.

Glancing at Hallie in the backseat, I start to question whether dragging my five-year-old out in the middle of the night to a house fire was a smart idea.

Even still, I knew I didn't have a choice. When Brad had called to tell me there was a fire a few minutes from my house and he needed me urgently, how could I say no? He was one of my best friends. My brother. We had served in the Army together for more than ten years and had been deployed together four separate times.

Driving up to the inferno I think was once a house, I see

Brad on the side of the street, waving me down. Pulling over, I jump out of my truck and lock the door behind me as I leave my sleeping princess in the backseat. Tension knots in my stomach as the roar of flames fills the night air. I hate that I had to bring her here, but what other option did I have?

Since her mother's passing nearly four years ago, it's just Hallie and me, so it's not as if I could've left her home alone. Fuck, this better be important.

Stalking towards Brad, his eyes are wide, his face pale, and if he wasn't standing in front of me, I would be sure he had stopped breathing.

I lift my arms in question. "What's going on?"

"There was a fire."

"Clearly," I snap.

"I was just visiting . . ." He pauses, his eyes shifting around the area. "A friend," he finishes.

I raise my eyebrows at him, pushing him to continue and wondering what in the hell he is talking about.

"We smelt smoke, and as soon as I glanced out the window, I could see flames coming from next door."

A choking cough pulls my eyes across the street to a young woman lying on someone's front lawn.

"What the hell?" I yell as I run across to the woman lying still and unmoving. Why the fuck has she been left alone?

Dropping to the ground, I lift her limp upper body so that her head is in my lap.

"What the fuck is going on, Brad?"

"I went inside the building . . ." He rubs a shaky hand over his face and begins to pace. "I was sure she was the only one inside, so I pulled her out. Callie has already called emergency. The fire and ambulance are on the way."

The woman in my arms sputters again, and I can hear the soot rattling in her chest. God, I hope the ambulance comes soon.

"I have to go." He scans the area.

"What?" I yell, frustrated that I can't make any sense out of him.

"I can't be here, Jake. Sheryl can't know I was here."

I look up to the man I have known most of my adult life. The man who stood by my side while we entered some of the most dangerous situations we have ever been in. Narrowing my eyes at him, I study the emotions on his face. I can normally read him like a book, but here tonight, in this fucked-up situation, I am struggling to see what's going on.

Glancing at the woman across the street, I only now notice that she is holding a barely there silk robe around herself, and she clearly doesn't have pyjamas underneath. Looking back at Brad, I can suddenly see all the emotions flowing out of him.

Guilt, shame—*fear. You've got to be fucking kidding me.*

His eyes widen as the sound of sirens peak in between the swirling of flames. "Please, Jake. I can't be here."

"What do you want me to do?" I snap.

"Say you were driving past and saw the flames. Say you carried her out." He gestures to the woman lying limply on my lap.

"Are you fucking serious? You dragged me out for this? I've got Hallie in the fucking car."

He glances down the road to my truck with worried eyes and pinched lips.

"Fuck," I yell into the night sky. I should have never answered my phone. This is not my problem. This is exactly why I do nothing but work and stay home with Hallie. I don't need this fucking drama in my life.

Glaring at him with his shirt inside out and zipper undone, I tell him, "Put your dick back in your pants and go home to your *wife,* Brad."

"Jake—"

"Go," I seethe, my voice lethally quiet.

Brad doesn't even look back as he runs across the road, jumps in his Toyota Camry, and spins his wheels down the street. The silk-wrapped woman stared dumbfounded as she watched him go before turning her glance my way.

"Fuck," I mutter, looking down at the woman on my lap, not wanting to encourage the practically naked woman across the street to think I'm open for her to come over.

I mentally run through my first-aid training and gaze over the woman checking for other associated trauma. Bleeding, fractures, head injury, and respiratory distress. I don't notice any physical wounds but gently lay her head back to open up her airways. I then shrug my jacket off and lay it on her.

Closing my eyes briefly, I shake my head in frustration. I want to go and check on Hallie and make sure she is still sleeping peacefully, but I can't really leave the woman lying unsupervised on the grass. I shake my head again as I remember that's exactly what Brad did when he left to greet me in the street.

Fucking Brad.

I can't believe this shit. In reality, without the Army, I'm not sure if Brad and I would be friends. He's not like me at all, his actions tonight solidifying that thought.

It doesn't matter, though. We are brothers in arms, and I have his back. I would do anything for him. Even if it means involving myself in this messed-up situation.

Movement on my lap draws me from my thoughts. The woman is quietly moaning in pain. Rubbing my hand over her head in comfort, I finally take stock of her. She is beautiful. Stunning, even. Shiny, long red hair that glows under the street light and is clearly natural and a face free of makeup.

I pick up some of that long wavy hair, feeling the softness

between my fingers. It's been a long time since I've had my hands in a woman's hair, and in this moment, even with the chaos around us, I can't think of anything else.

My eyes follow the spackle of freckles that sprinkle her nose. Other than that, her skin is flawless. With the reflection of the flames on her face, she looks like an angel. Her skin, so creamy and pale, and so in contrast with her plump pink lips.

Just as my focus rests on those full lips and I think about what they would taste like, they open and she starts to choke again. This time the choking is fierce, and I hear her struggling to breathe. Wide bright green eyes pop open and I'm momentarily shocked still until she starts clawing at my chest, trying to sit up.

I push her into a sitting position just as the fire and ambulance vehicles pull up in front of her house. We are across the street and down a bit so I call out to the ambulance crew. They hear me immediately and run towards us, carrying their large medical bags at their sides.

They don't delay as they begin working on the woman. I'm shoved back and out of their way, and they don't acknowledge me at all. No questions, no *what happened* as they take care of her.

"What's your name?" I hear the female paramedic ask.

"La. . ." she chokes. "Lana."

"Hi, Lana. I'm Susie, and I'll be taking care of you, okay?"

Lana. It's not a common name and suits her uncommon looks perfectly. Her red hair, green eyes, and pale skin make the most beautiful combination I've ever seen on a woman.

While the paramedics look her over, I quickly go and check on Hallie, pausing a minute to take in my perfect princess. I smile as she snores lightly, her blond hair ruffled and falling on her face. She's my world. My everything. What would I have without her? Nothing, that's what. Nothing but a meaningless existence.

By the time I lock the truck up again and make my way back to the scene, the ambulance crew are repacking their bags as they give Lana instructions on how to take care of herself. The male paramedic gives me a curt nod before they make their way back to their ambulance and leave the scene much quieter than they arrived.

"Shouldn't you be going with them?" I gesture to the ambulance.

Lana sits on the grass sipping on a bottle of water, her face pale and sickly.

"No, I'm okay."

"You don't look okay," I say, narrowing my eyes and searching her face. Is she about to pass out?

Just as the thought crosses my mind, she sways from side to side and I crouch down to steady her shoulders.

"You're not okay. You were in a house fire. You must have smoke inhalation. What did the paramedics say? You need tests and X-rays," I ramble all my thoughts as they come to me.

"They checked me out. They said there were no signs of smoke inhalation, and that I must have got out early."

I narrow my eyes, not sure if she's being honest with me or not. "But—"

"Did I?" she interrupts.

"Did you what?"

"Get out early?"

"I don't know, I just . . ." I pause, realising what she's asking. "I think you should go to the hospital." I avoid her question. "Is there anyone I can call for you? Drop you off at the hospital?"

She bites her lip in thought as her eyes wander to the sky. "No, really. I'm okay. I'll just call a cab."

"You can't take a cab," I snap and scold myself when her eyes widen in surprise.

"It's okay," she says as she glances around the grass, as if she's looking for something.

"What is it?"

"My phone." She looks longingly at the house the firefighters have just now contained. "I guess it's in there."

"You can use mine." I pull it out of my back pocket. "But please, not to call a cab. I can take you anywhere. Drop you off wherever you want to go."

She doesn't take my phone as she gets to her feet, standing on legs that are shaking with shock.

"A ride to the Royal Inn would be great, thanks." Her voice is hoarse and quiet, and I'm not sure if it's the remaining smoke in her lungs, the shock, or if it's always like this.

"You can't go to a hotel," I say, trying to hold back the sharpness I used last time.

She rocks on her feet again, and I grab her elbow, steadying her.

Her head flies up and we make eye contact for the first time since those piercing green eyes popped open. It's as if she's only just realised that I'm here.

"What happened?" she whispers.

I go to open my mouth but pause as I think about what Brad asked me to do. *Fuck.*

Lana sways on her feet again, and I grab her once more, wrapping one arm around her waist as I lead her towards my truck. Holding her against me feels so natural that it unnerves me for a second.

"We'll still be here a while dealing with the fire and police. Why don't you sit in the truck and rest while I deal with it?"

"No, it's okay, I can do it," she mutters even as she continues

7

towards my truck.

"You need to rest, Lana, and you need to do it off your feet. You can barely stand and I'm worried you may pass out again." I unlock the truck as we reach it and open the passenger door. "You were out for a while."

"What happened?" she asks again. She stares into space as she asks me, and I'm reconsidering the idea of getting her to a hospital.

She's in shock. This shouldn't worry me. I have seen it many times before—worse even—but for some reason, I feel a protectiveness over her. As if she has no one else. Why would she want to go to a hotel? Doesn't she have family she can call?

I set her down in my truck and even have to lift her legs and place them inside the cab. She stares blankly through the windshield and I pause, hesitant to leave her alone for even a minute. Glancing into the backseat, I check on my sleeping girl before closing the door, locking the truck once more, and making my way back over to the police and fire crews, hoping to get this over with quickly.

I run the lies through my head before I stand there with a straight face and relate them all to the expecting officers, just as Brad wanted. I was driving past, saw the flames, stopped to help, found Lana inside and carried her out.

My gut churns—what I'm doing and why I'm doing it goes against everything I stand for. Everything I ensure to live by. Everything I try to instil in my daughter. Everything I want her to come to expect in life.

The police buy all the lies and don't even question why I was '*driving around*' after midnight with my five-year-old daughter in the car.

After chatting with the fire crew and organising to speak with them tomorrow about the cause and damage of the fire, I make my way back to my truck.

Settling myself inside, I look around the cab to see Hallie still sleeping peacefully and find that Lana has joined her. Her head rests on the seat back, her body and face turned towards me.

I relax in my seat and watch her. I watch long enough to see that her lips are slightly parted as she takes light easy breaths. I watch close enough to see her eyelids flutter with dreams. My gaze once again follows the line of freckles over her nose, and I reach out with my finger to follow the trail as well.

Pulling back before I make contact, I realise what I was about to do. Turning in my seat, I shake my head, secure my seat belt, and start the loud truck before taking off down the street.

I don't even think as I make my way to my house. She cannot stay in a hotel for the night. She needs monitoring. Hell, she should be in the hospital. I briefly consider turning left towards the hospital instead of right towards my home, but the thought crosses my mind that she will just check herself out and I continue on to my place.

Pulling up into my driveway, I turn off the truck and glimpse at my two sleeping passengers, contemplating the best way to do this. I decide to take Hallie in first and then deal with Lana.

Hopping out of my truck and opening up the back door, I unfasten Hallie's child restraint and lift her in my arms. She begins to stir and I 'shhh' her while kicking the truck door shut and making my way inside.

While walking down the hallway to her bedroom, her eyes flip open to meet mine, and she smiles.

"Are we going out again, Daddy?"

"No, darlin'." I laugh. "It's back to bed."

"Oh, that's good," she says in a sleepy voice.

I smile as I lay her down in bed, her tight grip around my

neck pulling me down with her. I chuckle as I pry her arms off me and then pull up her quilt, tucking her in.

Running my hand over her hair, I place a soft kiss on her forehead.

"I'm so sorry. I didn't realise you had your daughter with you."

I turn at the voice and find Lana standing in the doorway to Hallie's room. Her eyes leave mine to roam around the space, and I wonder how she knows Hallie is my daughter. Hallie's room is not like your typical little girl's room. With pale green walls and sports posters hung all about, I wouldn't hold it against Lana if she'd assumed I had a son. I guess growing up with only a daddy will do that to a girl.

Lana bows her head and looks down at the ground, making me realise I have just been staring at her for the past few moments without answering. She fidgets with her fingers as she shifts her weight from side to side.

"I'm sorry for just bringing you back here." I stand and make my way out of the room. Lana follows me down the hall and into the living room.

"Please, take a seat." I gesture to the brown leather couch.

Lana sits on the edge, another show of her uneasiness, so I head to the kitchen and fill a small tumbler of scotch.

Carrying the glass and the bottle back to the living room, I find Lana standing in front of the wall plastered with photos, her eyes gazing at all the different pictures. Most are of Hallie and me, with a small amount of Hallie with her mum, and a few family shots with us all.

"You should really be sitting down," I tell her.

She drops her head to stare at the ground, avoiding my gaze. I would give anything to be able to see her face and read whatever emotions she is trying so hard to hide.

Chapter Two

Lana

I startle at the strong voice and try to hide all the emotions I am feeling. Not only the unexplainable jealousy I feel at looking at this picture perfect family, but the shame of being caught snooping around. Snooping around some strange guy's house. A strange guy who pretty much kidnapped me. I should probably be more concerned than I am at my current situation.

I probably should've bolted down the street when I woke up in an unfamiliar car, but instead, I just invited myself inside, searching the house until I found him. What choice did I really have? My house had just caught on fire. I may no longer even have a house. God, I may no longer have anything. My furniture, my clothes. Oh God, all my parents' photos and possessions. It's hard to see the extent of the fire and damage when the flames are as big as they were.

"You need to rest," he says, interrupting my thoughts and gently coaxing me to the couch.

I blindly follow him in a daze as realisation dawns at all I could've lost. I sit on the edge of the couch as he hands me a tumbler full of amber liquid. I can't help but take in the man who rescued me properly for the first time. My white knight. My saviour. He is gorgeous. Untouchable gorgeous. The type of gorgeous you only see walking around with a blonde supermodel on his arm. My mind briefly flits back to the pretty blonde in the family photos.

Family photos. God Lana, how can you even be thinking about how hot this guy is after what has just occurred?

"You'll need that," he says, picking up on my hesitation and gesturing towards the glass. His warm brown eyes meet mine and I can't help but look down to my glass.

Having this tall, strong man standing in front of me, looking down at me expectantly, there is nothing I can do but throw the drink back. Again, taking a drink from a guy whose name I don't even know is probably another dumb decision, but his strong chocolate gaze has me stupefied.

His body seems huge, and even though he can't be that much taller than my own 5'10" height, the pure size of him makes me feel as if I'm two feet tall. Even in a relaxed stance with his arms dropped by his sides, there is power there, with thick veins running down his forearms and roped muscles wrapped by golden skin.

I notice his large hands, rough and dirty from hard work. "You a mechanic?" I gesture to his dry hands with the tumbler that rattles in my shaky grip. The black worn into his skin tells me he works with grease. It reminds me of my grandpa's hands after he had been working on his car.

"Yeah." He breathes out slowly, his shoulders dropping. "A diesel mechanic."

"You work on semis?"

"Some." He pauses. "Army vehicles. I'm a staff sergeant in the Army."

"Oh." I nod, looking back down to his hands. "Makes sense."

"What makes sense?"

I still at the words I didn't mean to say out loud being repeated back to me. "Well . . ." I pause. "Look at you." I bark a short laugh.

The corner of his mouth tips up in a grin, and I find I can't stop. Looking at him that is. Something about him captivates me. Keeps my thoughts from drifting back to the hell that tonight has been. A perfect distraction from all I may have lost.

He has short brown hair, a typical military cut that I think, if grown longer, would be a gorgeous sandy colour. Add that, and his huge body covered in worn jeans and a tight grey T-shirt to his stoic face, and I should've guessed Army.

"I'm Jake, by the way."

"Lana." I give him a nervous smile.

"I know."

Quirking an eyebrow at him, he explains, "I heard you tell the paramedics."

"Oh, of course."

We stay in an uncomfortable silence before once again, remembering the events that led to me being here in the first place.

"What happened?" I ask him.

He releases a deep breath as he sits himself next to me. His presence up close does nothing but enhance the power he seems to exude. Bowing his head and rubbing his fingers across his brow, he takes a moment before answering.

"I just happened to be driving by and I saw the flames." His voice hitches and he pauses once more. "Once I reached your place, the flames were pretty big, but I figured someone was probably inside." He shakes his head as though he's angry with himself. I can't imagine why. He saved me. I don't even want to think about what could've happened. "I could only find you. I carried you out and called for help."

"Jake, it's okay," I soothe him. His strong, stoic face is beginning to crack, and I see his own frustration about that. I would be willing to bet that the hard façade he wears never wavers. "There was no one else in there."

His eyes shoot to his arm, and I realise I've placed my hand on it and am now rubbing my palm up and down his soft skin.

I snatch my hand away and clear my throat. "I'm so sorry you had to find me. Was your daughter in the truck the whole time?" I didn't notice her in there; I only remember staring out of the windshield in a daze before I must have fallen asleep.

"It's okay. She slept through it, and I doubt in the morning she'll even remember we left the house."

"What *did* you leave for?" I wince at my rude and intrusive question. "I'm sorry, I just meant, well, couldn't you leave your daughter with your wife?"

Yeah Lana, because that's a heap better.

When I'd seen her in the photos, seen her bright smile and blue eyes, my jealousy had spiked. She was just like all the girls in high school I envied. The type of girl I once wished I was. They had gorgeous curvy bodies, beautiful faces, and big breasts. They always seemed to have it all, and I'd been an emotional teenager who wanted what I thought they had.

I eventually grew up to love—well, not love, but accept who I am. Accept my tall and lanky figure, my wild red hair, small breasts, and an array of freckles.

"I don't have a wife. She passed away," he says matter-of-factly.

"Oh . . . I . . ."

"It's okay. We were separated when it happened, and it has been a long time. It's just Hallie and me now, and we're doing okay."

I nod. "You seem like you're doing more than okay." I smile at the thought of Jake tucking her in and caressing and kissing her head. His love for his daughter filled the little girl's room.

A small smile touches his lips as well, and we just stare at each other for a moment. Part of me wonders if he knows just how good looking he is. If he puts on the strong and stoic bravado just to add effect to his hard and handsome look.

Jake pulls me from my daydream. "Did you want to take a shower? The smell of smoke must be bothering you, and you are covered in soot." He gestures to my face.

"Oh my God." I swipe at my cheek. I hadn't even noticed the overpowering stench of smoke before he mentioned it. Too busy distracted by the perfect that is Jake.

I run my gaze over his flawlessness once more. "I'm not the only one." I gesture to the soot on his pants and the bottom of his T-shirt.

Jake chuckles, reaching forward, his hand cups my face as his thumb glides along my cheek. I nuzzle into his palm, my body reacting without thought.

"You missed some," he whispers.

"Oh," is all I can say as I stare deep into his warm eyes.

The clearing of his throat as he stands pulls me back to reality and has me fidgeting in my seat.

"The shower is just down there." He gestures to the hallway where Hallie's room was. "There are clean towels on the shelf, but I'm sorry, only Hallie uses that shower so there's only her strawberries and cream shampoo and bodywash."

15

"That will be fine, thank you." I give him a shy smile.

Jake just nods. "I'll get some sheets for the couch. You can sleep in my bed; you'll be much more comfortable in there."

He leaves the room and descends the opposite hallway to where Hallie's room is before I can respond.

I mentally berate myself. What did I think was going to happen? He was going to carry me to his bed? With him?

Sighing, I shake my head. I watch *way* too many daytime romance movies when it's summer break.

I've never been the girl who gets swept off her feet. Never the one who gets what she wants. In college, I had a crush on the quarterback, but somehow, I ended up marrying his best friend. All I have to show for that is a bastard of an ex-husband and a baggage-load of hurt.

Jake enters the living room carrying an armful of blankets and a pillow. I shift off the couch and he begins to set up his makeshift bed. The smell of freshly washed linen floats through the air as he shakes the sheets open and lays them over the cushions.

There is something so sexy about a domesticated man. A domesticated man who also carries women out of burning buildings.

I take another moment to really look at him. God, he's good looking. Not just normal good looking, but really, really, really good looking. I wonder what he's like underneath that hard exterior? What would it be like to kiss him, to make love to him? Would his hard shell soften or would it be rough, raw? Either way, I think it would be unforgettable.

I swallow the lump in my throat caused by my wayward libido when I realise I have just been watching him for minutes on end. "I'll just go grab a shower."

"Here." He hands me a pair of shorts and a T-shirt. "Your

clothes are covered in ash."

"Thanks." I give him a quick smile and then hustle off to the bathroom.

When I'm all showered and dressed, I make my way back to the living room to find Jake still fiddling with the sheets but now dressed in his own pair of shorts and T-shirt.

"Jake, I can take the couch." *As much as I would love to be wrapped up in your sheets.* "I feel terrible. You have already done too much, and I couldn't put you out more."

"No," he says firmly. "You need to rest. You have been through a lot tonight. A lot that I don't think has actually hit you yet." He narrows his eyes at me, as if waiting for me to answer that. "Besides . . ." he returns to setting the sheets, "Hallie wakes up early, and I don't want her to wake you."

"Okay," I whisper. I think he's right. Besides the nonstop shaking hands, I don't think it has actually hit me yet that tomorrow morning I could be waking up with nothing.

He nods in agreement, a wide smile lighting up his face. God, he is sweet. So in contrast to the vibes that pour off him.

I step towards him, and without thinking, I lay my hand on his forearm. He freezes, his eyes shooting to mine.

"Thank you." It seems lame after everything he has done for me—you know, carrying me out of a burning house and all—but I don't have any other words right now.

A small smile tips his lips and we stare at each other, our eyes roaming each other's faces. My gaze skims his light stubble and all I want is to feel it. Run my fingers over it.

So I do.

Without thinking, my hand reaches up and I graze my fingertips along the edge of his jaw. He gasps at the contact and I consider pulling away.

But I don't.

I am always the careful Lana. The cautious Lana. I don't do anything without thinking it through first. Making lists of pro and cons. I never take risks. I never put myself out there.

Now, in this moment, doing something I want to do without any thought for the consequences has my heart racing. Blood is pumping so fast through my veins I think I may faint.

My hand shakes as I go to move it off Jake's skin, but he grabs my wrist and holds my hand to his face. He wants this. Well, he's not opposed to it. Why shouldn't I do this? People have one-night stands all the time. It's not as if I'll ever have to see him again. Plus, I almost died tonight. If that doesn't make you grab life by the horns, then what will?

I tighten my grip on his cheek and step towards him, lining up our bodies. Jake slides his hand behind my neck and then runs it down to my lower back before pulling me harder into him.

I'm doing this.

Leaning forward, I press my lips to his. Hard and unforgiving. Probably harder than I need to be, but once Jake returns my enthusiasm, I'm lost to it.

His kiss is warm and comforting and soon our lips are tangling in a mess of lust and passion and it's not much longer before our hands are joining in, Jake's running over my back, mine holding his face tight, the stubble on his jaw scratching my palms.

The sensations his touch exudes are new, like nothing I've ever felt before and I find it hard to control my reaction, pushing myself harder against him. His hands glide to my hips and pull me even tighter against him until I feel his own reaction up against my stomach.

I gasp as he lifts me and I wrap my legs around his waist, never breaking our kiss. Cupping my ass, he carries me down another hallway opposite to the one Hallie's room is.

When we step into a room, he pulls back, both of us breathing heavy. I glance around to see he has brought us to his bedroom. Looking back at Jake, his eyes search my face, and I know he is looking for confirmation. Confirmation that this is okay. That this is what I really want.

I don't even think when I give him the only answer I have. Smashing my lips against his, I pour everything I have into the kiss. He meets my ferocious need and I melt into a puddle of euphoria.

Moving towards the bed, Jake lies me down in the middle of it, his body still between my legs as he looks me over.

"Jesus, Lana," he breathes. "I don't know if this is a good idea."

My heart stops. *I thought he wanted this too.*

"If you don't want this . . ." I lean forward to sit up, shame and embarrassment washing over me.

"No, fuck." He grabs my shoulders to stop me and then quickly pulls his hands back. "I want this. My God, do I want this," he says, as his eyes roam my body from top to toe. "But you could be in shock. I don't want to take advantage of you. That's not why I brought you back here."

"Why *did* you bring me here?" I lean up on my elbows.

"You had just been in a house fire, Lana. I couldn't leave you alone. Drop you off at some random hotel." His fierce gaze meets mine, and then I see a flash of something before he closes his eyes and throws his head back groaning, "Fuck."

"What?" I sit up, panicked, and grab his hands.

"You've just been in a house fire, Lana." I see it. The resignation on his face. I'm losing him. He is going to put a stop to this.

My need for him is overwhelming, and as concerning as it

19

is, I don't have to time to focus on it as I vie for all his attention on me.

Linking my fingers through his hands that I'm now clutching, I lie back and pull him with me. "It's been way too big a night to be thinking so hard."

He narrows his eyes on my face, and I realise I need to take control here. For the first time in my life, I need to be the dominant one. The one calling the shots.

I lean forward and take his lips with my own. He pauses briefly before returning my affections, and the kiss is so raw I think it shocks us both. Jake leans back on his heels and runs his eyes down the length of me before following the path with his hands. His touch is intoxicating, and even though we are both still fully clothed, I know it's a sign of what's about to come.

"Jesus, Lana," he breathes. "It's been a long time for me."

"Me too," I whisper. Even longer since it's felt like this. *Has it ever felt like this?*

"Let's just take it slow, okay?" His voice is calm, but I feel the unsteadiness of his touch as it glides up my ribs.

I nod, losing any form of speech as his thumbs brush the underside of my breasts. The touch feels so sensitive and close, and I soon realise it's because I'm not wearing a bra. Of course I'm not; I was carried out of my bed. Sleeping peacefully before my house caught on fire.

Oh my God, my house caught on fire.

I don't have time to come back to reality as Jake leans down and takes my nipple into his mouth. I gasp and arch my back as he sucks hard, the cotton T-shirt rough against the sensitive tip.

He growls and moves back to rip the T-shirt over my head, not needing my assistance at all.

Leaning back down, he takes the other breast in his mouth, switching between sucking and biting.

So much for taking it slow.

I reach down and tug at the hem of his T-shirt. Leaning back, Jake pulls the collar at the back of his neck and slips his shirt over his head, throwing it on the bedroom floor. My eyes go wide as he reveals his upper body.

It's not as if his tight black T-shirt hid much, but in all my wildest dreams, I couldn't imagine a body like this. It's like something from a men's fitness magazine. I don't need to ask to know he spends a lot of time on his body. This isn't an *'I have a physical job'* kind of body. This is an *'I sweat my nuts off to look like this'* kind of body.

My fingers, aching to touch him, reach out and run down the front of him. Scars and marks are scattered all over his chest and my hands trail a path, running over every single one. It's as if I'm not controlling them at all as they graze over every curve and crevice that lines his chest and stomach. I didn't know there was such a thing as an eight-pack.

Jake throws his head back and groans, and I'm delighted with the knowledge that my touch is what's causing this reaction.

My eyes drift down to the large erection tenting his sports shorts, and I swallow hard as nerves hit me for the first time. It's been a long time since I've been with anyone besides Craig, my ex, and even before him, there weren't a lot.

My need and want overpower my nerves, and I run my fingers over the bulge in his pants. When his eyes shoot open at my touch, I see the question in them.

I make quick work of slipping my hand inside, palming his hard, hot length and I whimper in need. *God, I want this.*

"Lana," he growls. "I'm not going to last very long with you touching me like that."

"Jake," I moan in response.

Sensing my urgency, he moves back and slips his shorts

down my legs, taking my panties with them.

"You are so fucking beautiful," he whispers.

Doubt enters my mind and I quickly squash it as he hops off the bed and makes quick work of his own shorts and briefs before sliding back between my legs.

Leaning down, he trails soft, wet kisses from the corner of my mouth, across my jaw and down my collarbone. I arch my back as he makes a path between my breasts, down my stomach and across my hips.

Grabbing his shoulders, I pull him up and into me as I kiss him hard. Jake follows and we are soon a tangle of lips, tongues, and limbs rolling around his sheets until I'm under him again and he presses his tip against my entrance.

We still at the contact, our eyes meeting and never moving as he pushes inside me, inch by slow inch.

God, has it ever felt this good?

Chapter Three

Jake

Once I'm deep inside her, we both release long sighs. She feels like heaven. Tight, hot, silk-wrapped heaven.

I lean down, pushing her wet hair to the side and press kisses to her neck, shoulders, and chest. *Have I ever tasted anything so sweet?*

Lana is something I have never experienced before. She is a shy beauty who screams innocence and naivety. But behind those fierce green eyes, I see experience beyond her years. Hurt and pain shine through.

I don't take my eyes off hers, as I start moving inside her. Long, slow strokes as she clamps around me, pulling me in and begging for more.

Speeding up my pace, I brace myself on my elbows as I

move above her. She moans and grabs onto my biceps. The pain of her fingernails piercing my skin only spurs me on and I close my eyes as I give her everything I have.

"God . . . Lana . . . fuck, you feel so good," I breathe. "I'm not going to last long."

Not wanting to leave her hanging, I grind my hips into hers as I thrust and groan when she whimpers at the contact. I continue this rhythm until I feel her tighten around me, her moans getting louder and more intense.

My body is tight with the strength it's taking me to hold off, and once Lana is shaking beneath me, repeating my name over and over again, I let go. I push into her until she is limp, and I ride out my own release.

Not wanting to squash her under my weight, I roll over and take a sated Lana in my arms until she lies languidly on my chest.

Our breathing is fast and erratic but somehow matches, as our chests move up and down together in a rhythmic pattern. Holding her tight, I kiss her head as I breathe in her scent—well, Hallie's scent, as strawberries and cream fill my nose.

The smell of Hallie sends my mind in overdrive. Guilt tightens my chest as I realise what a sham I really am. Only earlier, I was pissed as hell at Brad for his late-night antics and here I am, pretending to be some kind of hero and then taking advantage of a traumatised woman. Fuck.

Silence descends upon us as our breathing slows and our bodies still. I don't want to think about what a prick I am. I don't want to think about anything but her.

"Go to sleep, Lana. You've had a big day, and there will be a lot to sort out tomorrow."

She sighs deeply and her body relaxes against my own. My eyes drift shut and I go to sleep in the early hours, feeling peaceful and content for the first time in a long time. Maybe ever.

What has she done to me?

I'm cold. The sheets are still wrapped around my waist, but there is no longer a soft, sweet-smelling Lana warming me. I reach out to see if she moved away from me during the night but don't feel anything. The mattress is cool to the touch, so she hasn't been here for a while.

When pans clatter in the kitchen, my eyes pop open and I wait for more noise. I hear giggling and shoot out of my bed. The last time Hallie didn't want to wake me and tried to make breakfast herself, I was cleaning flour, eggs, and sugar for days.

Not even thinking, I run into the kitchen, hoping I don't have my own house fire started.

"Daddy!" Hallie squeals as I run in, sliding to a stop as I find her and Lana. "Daddy, where are your pants?" She is now covering her eyes with both her hands as she giggles.

"Shit." I cover up my junk, not taking my eyes off Lana. She stands by the stove, setting up a frying pan.

"Daddy!" Hallie shouts again, and I quickly retreat out of the kitchen, but not before seeing the cheeky smile on Lana's face.

"I'm going, I'm going," I shout as I head back down the hallway to my room to find some pants, the girls' burst of laughter following me.

Not wanting to waste any time before I get back in there and see what's going on, I find my shorts from last night and throw them on, sans underwear, while picking up my T-shirt off the floor as I leave.

I pull it over my head as I make my way into the kitchen.

Lana is now standing on the other side of the breakfast bar next to Hallie, who is stirring something in a bowl. Both sets of eyes shoot up to me as I enter and I still in the doorway, taking them both in. I didn't notice before, but Lana is wearing one of my way-too-big-for-her sweatshirts over the shorts I had given her last night. *Fuck, that's hot.* It's been a long time since I've seen a woman wearing my clothes. A long time since I've seen a woman in my kitchen, for that matter.

"That's better," Hallie says, breaking my moment. "What were you doing?"

"Well, I heard pans banging and was worried we had another pancake incident." I grin.

Hallie looks up at Lana with a sheepish smile and my grin fades. She's already trying to impress our guest. I didn't think it through very well when I thought about bringing Lana here.

God, I hope Hallie didn't see us in bed.

I should know better than this, to act this way with Hallie home. I guess it's something I've never had to think about. Since losing Jamie four years ago, I haven't had a woman here. Hell, I've barely *had* a woman. There have been a couple of regrettable finds at a bar when Hallie has been with her grandparents or my sister, Marley, but other than that, it's just us. And that's how I like it.

"Well, actually . . . " Lana interrupts my thoughts, "Hallie here has done most of the work. I'm just following her instructions." She looks down at Hallie, giving her a warm smile, and Hallie's face lights up at the attention. *Fuck, this isn't good.*

"She tells me chocolate chip are your favourite," Lana says, not taking her eyes away from Hallie's proud grin. I can't blame her—that kid has an infectious smile.

"Yeah." I clear my throat. *Fuck, what's wrong with me?*

"I told you," Hallie says to Lana, her attention going back to stirring the bowl in front of her. "Daddy says I know him better than anyone ever has." Lana's eyes shoot to mine, giving me a questioning and sad look. "Isn't that right, Daddy?"

I don't break our stare. "Sure is, princess."

Hallie giggles at my nickname for her, and Lana shakes her head as she stands up straighter and places a hand on Hallie's shoulder. "Well, we better start cooking this up. Your dad looks famished."

"He does." Hallie nods with a concerned look on her face as she hops off her stool.

Lana grabs a dining room chair and carries it over to the kitchen bench. "Hop up, babe." She gestures to Hallie.

Hallie's face lights up as she climbs onto the chair and stands on it, watching Lana closely.

"Can you set the table, Daddy?" Hallie asks, turning around on the chair to look at me.

Lana smirks at me, and I realise I'm leaning against the door-frame just staring at them with a dopey smile on my face. "Sure, princess," I answer Hallie and go to collect the settings.

Is this what being a family feels like? Everyone working together to make breakfast on a lazy Sunday morning? A beautiful woman wearing my clothes with rumpled hair and a satisfied smile?

Because if it is, I fucking like it. I like it a hell of a lot.

By the time I've set the table with place settings, cutlery, condiments, and juices, the girls have finished cooking the pancakes and are carrying a plate full of them.

Lana sets the plate down in the middle of the table as I pull Hallie's chair out for her.

"Ladies, thank you for breakfast. This looks delicious."

Lana gives me a shy nod, and Hallie gives me one of her signature toothless grins.

We eat in a comfortable silence. Well, I eat in silence as Hallie talks Lana's ear off, asking her all sorts of questions. I should tell her to let Lana eat in peace, but the truth is that I want to know the answers too.

Lana is patient and answers all Hallie's question with what seems to be sincere honesty. Even the tough questions are answered thoughtfully. If it were me, I would just avoid the questions altogether.

"You'll need to drop by the fire station sometime today to get the details of your house. They should've written up a report by now," I tell Lana. "I could take you before I drop you off . . ." I leave my comment open wondering where I will be dropping her off. Does she have someone to stay with?

"No, that's okay. I mean, I will go by the fire station, but I can call a cab to come get me." Lana doesn't look at me as she pushes around the pancakes on her plate. Does she think I haven't noticed she hasn't taken one bite?

"Lana." My voice is stern. "You can't stay at a hotel. I doubt the house is liveable, and it could be months before it's safe to return. By the time insurance is paid out and you get renovations started . . . Christ, you have insurance don't you—"

"I'm not staying at a hotel," she blurts out, probably trying to stop my diarrhoea of the mouth.

"Why would you stay at a hotel?" Hallie asks, and I silently chastise her for interrupting right before I found out where Lana plans to stay. "And why are you going to the fire station? I went to the fire station once. We had a preschool excursion there. I didn't get to see much though because Bobby Frankel threw up when he climbed to the top of the fire truck ladder and we had to leave and go back to preschool so we could wait for his mum."

"Oh no, that's not good," Lana says to Hallie, avoiding the question. "I hope Bobby was okay."

"Who cares?" Hallie scrunches up her nose. "We didn't get to see anything, and I never got to go back."

"Hallie," I scold her. Lana bites her lip, trying to hold in her laughter.

"What?" she asks, innocence lacing her tone.

"You know," Lana says gently, still trying to hold her laughter in, "I'm sure Bobby didn't do it on purpose. How would you feel if you got sick and people said that about you?"

Hallie drops her head at Lana's words. "Sad."

"I'm sure Bobby was sad too," Lana says. "And hey . . ." She nudges Hallie, who lifts her eyes back to Lana. "Maybe you could ask your dad to take you to the fire station when they have one of their family fun days."

"Oh my goodness, could we, Daddy?"

"Sure, princess," I answer her but don't take my eyes off Lana while Hallie rambles on about the fire station. Who is this woman? She's just come out of nowhere and infiltrated this house. Sitting here with her and Hallie, it's as if we have done it a million Sundays before.

Lana bows her head and looks at me through lowered lashes. The thought of dropping her off today sends a stinging sensation through my gut.

What the fuck am I thinking? I barely know the woman. It must be the guilt. The guilt of not only lying to her and pretending to be some kind of saviour, but then for taking advantage of her. Fuck, is that what I did? I'm going to hell.

"Why are you staying in a hotel?" Hallie asks again, her question not forgotten.

Lana looks at Hallie and exhales deeply. "Last night, my house caught on fire." I see the emotions flit through Lana's eyes, almost as if she had forgotten. Forgotten what had happened and forgotten why she was here in the first place.

"A fire?" Hallie exclaims, her eyes going wide. "How did your house catch on fire?"

"That's what I have to go speak to the fire department about," Lana explains. She is so patient with Hallie. If I hadn't seen her leave that house alone, I would have assumed she had kids of her own. I wonder why she doesn't have kids. Why there is no husband.

"So you're staying in a hotel?" Hallie asks.

"She's not staying in a hotel."

Lana looks at me, frustration shining in her eyes before she turns back to Hallie. "No, I'm not staying in a hotel—"

"Oh, that's good." Hallie nods. "Grandma says hotels are breeding grounds for thugs and hookers."

I shake my head, not at all surprised at what her grandma has told her. Jamie's parents live close and still see Hallie at least once a month. They love her fiercely, and I make a point to make sure we visit them often, no matter how much damage control I always have to do after she's seen them. Only last term at preschool, Hallie had told the teacher her grandma had said she needed to use deodorant and some nasal clipping wouldn't go astray.

"So are you staying here?" Hallie asks excitedly.

"No," Lana and I say at the time.

"Why not? You stayed here last night." *Shit.*

"Last night it was too late to call anybody, and since your dad carried me out of the fire, he was just looking out for me."

"You carried her out of the fire?" Hallie's head whips around to me. *Oh fuck.*

"Yes, I did, but now isn't the time to talk about it. Go get washed up and dressed." I try to end this conversation, but Hallie isn't having any of it.

"You carried her? Like a knight coming to rescue his prin-

30

cess?" *Double fuck.*

"Hallie, what did I ask you to do?"

"Fine, fine, I'm going," she mumbles as she gets off her chair, singing 'Someday My Prince Will Come' from *Snow White*, making me smile and shake my head.

"I guess you did ride in and save me," Lana says, and my face instantly drops. There it is. . .that guilt.

"Hardly." I plaster on a fake grin as I stand from the table. Fuck. I feel like a scammer. Being thanked for something I didn't do. Thank God, Hallie didn't say anything about why the hell we were driving around in the truck in the middle of the night.

Clearing our plates from the table, I carry them over to the sink. Keeping my back to Lana, I rest my hands on the counter and stare out the back window, gripping the edge until my knuckles are white.

I'm no hero. I'm a fucking liar and a fraud.

"Jake, I—"

"I'll just get Hallie dressed, and I'll drop you wherever you need to go. You're not catching a cab." I don't give her a chance to respond before I'm walking out of the kitchen without even so much as a glance in her direction.

Once Hallie's dressed in her chosen attire of a green polka dot skirt, a rainbow T-shirt, and pink-and-blue striped knee-high socks, we make our way to the kitchen.

Lana still sits in the same place at the kitchen table when we enter, but she looks forlornly out the kitchen window. Her face is pale, her eyes shiny with tears. My heart stills at the sadness flowing out from her.

She turns in her seat to look at us, and her face lights up when she looks at Hallie. "Oh my goodness, Miss Hallie, you look beautiful."

"Do you like my skirt?" Hallie asks, as she twirls around in the middle of the kitchen.

"I love it. I wish I had a skirt like that."

"You could probably get one." Hallie scrunches her face in thought. "Dad, could you take Lana to the boring shops where you got my skirt?"

Lana bites her lip, a smile still creeping in, and raises an eyebrow at me. "Boring shops?"

"Daddy says that girls spend too much time at the shops and it's boring. He said we need to learn to get in, get what we need, and get out."

"Does he?"

"Yeah. He begs Aunt Marley to take me to get clothes."

"Come on, ratbag." I ruffle Hallie's hair as I push her towards the front door. "Let's get you in the car."

I pause slightly in the entryway as I leave. I don't want Lana to go. But that's ridiculous. I don't know this woman; I don't l know anything about her.

I'm securing Hallie's seat restraint when the front door shuts and I turn to see Lana walking towards the driveway. She stops awkwardly by the open truck back door and wrings her fingers.

Once Hallie is secured, I kiss her head, closing the door behind me. Lana gives me an awkward smile as I open the truck for her and she slides into my truck. Closing the door, I pause for a moment as I take in the image in front of me. Lana, sitting in my car, is a fucking nice sight.

I make my way around to the driver's side and settle myself inside. Lana gives me directions to a café in the city, and Hallie is asleep in the first five minutes of the trip, no doubt tired after last night's interruption to her sleep.

The next twenty minutes pass in silence as I contemplate what I'm going to say to get Lana to see me again. I used to be good at this. Really good, actually. I never had an issue talking to women.

This situation is different though, and I don't want to force myself on her. Something about her tells me to be gentle with her. To tread carefully where she is concerned. Should I even try to see her again? Our first meeting was a sham, a fucking lie. It's not a big deal if I don't ever see her again.

When Lana points to a parking spot in front of a café, I decide it's do or die time.

"Lana, about last night—"

"Last night was a one-time thing. I get it. I don't normally do stuff like that either." She looks away as a light blush covers her cheeks. "My head was in a crazy place."

The way she writes it off, as if last night was a stupid teenage mistake, is like a punch to the gut.

She glances to the backseat at the still sleeping Hallie and smiles. "Thanks for everything, Jake. For everything."

There is a hidden message there, but I don't have a chance to ask as she smiles at Hallie once more and then jumps out of my truck.

I watch her go and she turns back to look at the truck once more before she opens the café door and slips inside. And with that, my angel is gone.

Chapter Four

Three months later

Lana

"Another round?" Tate asks, and everyone cheers his or her approval as Tate makes his way to the bar.

Tonight is my brother, Tate's, big renovation re-opening at our family café. He's been running it since our grandfather passed but has been working here helping since he was little. Well, we both did until Mum and Dad passed away when Tate and I were only young. We then went to live with our grandparents, spending most of our spare time here with them.

Maurice squeezes my shoulder, and I give him a forced smile as he passes me on his way to the bar to help Tate carry all the drinks. Although we have suffered through the loss of our parents, and more recently our grandparents, Tate and I are blessed to have our grandpa's best friend, Maurice. He has worked at my grandfather's café since it opened almost fifty years ago, and still to this day runs the kitchen for Tate.

Glancing around at the café, I admire all the changes that have occurred during the past three months. My brother and his gorgeous girlfriend, Harper, have been working tirelessly to get everything together for the opening tonight.

Well, his gorgeous *fiancée* now. Tonight, my baby brother made a big song and dance, literally, on stage and proposed to Harper. They've only been together for six months, but I have no doubt the punk rock couple are perfect for each other. Harper brings things into Tate's life we only dreamt of after losing our parents. And she brings those things into my life too.

Looking across the table to my soon-to-be sister-in-law, who's giggling like a schoolgirl with her friend, Brooke, I can't help but smile.

Harper and I didn't have the most conventional start to our friendship. After finding me at Tate's in only a towel and thinking the worst of my brother, she was embarrassed to find out I was actually his sister and was staying with him because my house had caught on fire.

My house. My beautiful, simple, modest home. My classic old house that had wiring so dated it sparked and caught my roof on fire.

I miss it. I miss having all my own things. I miss having some privacy. Don't get me wrong, I love my brother, and living with him and Harper has been a blast. Harper and I have become as close as I imagine real sisters to be, but they are a newly in love couple. They moved in together the same week I came to stay, and stay I have, for the past three months.

I try to keep out of their way, but it's not as if I have a tonne of friends to go hang out with. When I met my ex-husband, Craig, in college, he slowly pushed any friends I had out of my life. He did it gradually, without me noticing, until it was too late. In the end, I preferred it that way. I was too ashamed to have people see me living the way I was with him. Now that I am finally rid of him, I am trying to rebuild my life. Well, at least I was trying to until my house caught fire. One step forward, two steps back.

Someone slips a drink in front of me and I smile up at Saxon in thanks. Saxon is handsome in a traditional sense. He is tall with dark hair and when you add that to him wearing a suit to work every day, it equals hot. He is also Brooke's fiancé, and they are another wonderful addition Harper has brought into our lives. The two girlfriends couldn't be more opposite, with Brooke's classic dark beauty and Harper's edgy modern style, but their friendship knows no difference.

Before Harper came along, Tate and I only had each other and Maurice, and now we have Harper, Brooke, and Saxon too. We are our own little dysfunctional family.

Harper's snort brings my attention back to the group, and I sip my cocktail. I have no idea what I'm even drinking anymore. We started the day off slowly and have been here drinking since early afternoon, but now that the café has emptied out and we are the only ones left, along with the catering staff who are packing up, things have taken a turn.

Harper snorts again and sways in her chair. I'm sure she's going to fall, but then Tate secures an arm around her shoulders to steady her, and she looks up at him with adoration in her glassy eyes.

I wonder what that must feel like. To feel so safe in someone's arms. To have someone you can count on and trust implicitly. I've never had that. Not even with Craig. I think I knew from the start that things weren't right there. Even before things turned bad once we were married, I knew it wasn't the healthiest of relationships.

I should've known better than to marry him. I had been surrounded by happy marriages all my life. My mum and dad, my grandparents . . . I should've expected more, demanded it. But I was lonely. My grandparents had just passed, leaving Tate and me alone, and I'd just wanted to feel safe. To feel as if I had someone I could rely on.

My brother catches my eye and winks at me. The happy bubble surrounding him makes my heart soar, and I give him a huge smile. He deserves this. After everything we have been through, he has earned it. I am so happy for them. I almost can't believe it—my baby brother, engaged to be married.

Being a few years older than Tate, I have always been the one to look after him. I would walk us to school, making sure he got to his class okay. I taught him how to tie his shoelaces and ride his bike without the training wheels.

When Mum and Dad died, I took on even more responsibility—helping him with his homework, sticking up for him in the schoolyard when some dumb little snot would say something about us being orphans, and buying his first pack of condoms. I silently giggle when I think about how I sat him down and tried to explain to him how to use them. He just blew me off with his hysterical laughter.

I'm not sure when things turned around, or how it came to be Tate looking after me. Tate saving me from my marriage and helping me leave in the dark of night when Craig was "working" late. Tate helping me to use my inheritance to purchase my own place. Tate securing restraining orders when Craig decided he wasn't willing to let me go. And now, Tate letting me live with him while my house is being repaired.

I wonder if I'll ever go back to being the strong woman I

once was, or if I'm permanently broken. Even as a teenager just starting out in college, I was more in control of my life. More confident in the decisions I made. Now, I'm thirty years old and have no idea what I'm doing.

My eyes wander over to the other two women sitting at the table. I know the struggles they have been through, and the challenges they have faced. We have spent many a night drinking cocktails and sharing stories. Hearing their tales, I barely recognise the women sitting in front of me. They are confident, strong, and secure. None of the issues they held, and somewhat still do, show through in them. Do they just hide it well, or is there hope for me to move on, to build back up to who I once was?

"So, Lana, are you excited to be starting work on Monday?" Brooke leans forward, resting her elbows on the table.

"What are you doing?" Saxon asks.

"Still teaching, but I've been given a permanent position." I can't help but smile. This is the start of rebuilding all I've lost. "I'm starting with a new kindergarten class at the elementary school."

"I'm so excited for you." Harper smiles.

"Me too. Finally, no more substituting. I can't wait to get in there and be able to plan things as I want."

"Something to keep your mind off the house." Brooke nods.

"How's that going?" Maurice asks.

"Yeah, okay," I mutter. "Actually, I didn't get to tell you . . ." I turn towards Tate. "I went to see Lou today, and he showed me around the house. I think enough has been done that I can move back in a few weeks and finish off the rest while I'm living there."

Tate narrows his eyes at me. "I told you that you can stay with us for as long as you need. I don't want you living in a half-finished house. Especially alone."

Here we go again—my baby brother looking out for me.

"I have been with you for three months. You are recently engaged . . ." I wink at Harper. "And the house is nearly finished—"

"It's far from finished."

"I want to do most of the work myself, so it's easier if I'm living there while I do it."

"Lana," he warns.

"Tate, the house has a roof, doors, and is secure. I'm moving back home. Stop it with the overprotective brother; you have someone else to protect now." I smile sweetly at him as I try to change the tone of our conversation.

"Yeah, but who do you have?" Tate mutters under his breath. I'm not sure if we were meant to hear it or not, but the whole table goes quiet. The sharp pain cuts through my chest as the truth of what he said hits me. I have no one.

"So, have we picked a date?" Brooke asks, her voice high with excitement and I'm thankful for the diversion.

Harper laughs. "Give us a break. We've only been engaged for about a minute. Besides . . ." she looks pointedly at Brooke, "you're one to talk."

"Well, actually . . ." Saxon smiles and wraps his arm around Brooke, pulling her close, "we've set a date."

The table is silent once more as we all look around at each other. Is he joking?

Brooke and Saxon have been engaged for nearly a year. I know they were holding off on the wedding until Brooke's ex-mother-in-law came around and accepted their relationship. It meant a lot to both of them that she would be there. I didn't get why; she sounded like a witch to me.

My eyes glance from Saxon to Brooke, and once I see her

beaming smile, I know he isn't joking. They've set a date.

"So you've spoken to Jeanie then?" Harper asks, her eyes wide with surprise.

Brooke's face drops. "No, we haven't." She looks at Saxon with a sad smile, and I assume they must be doing it with or without her.

"So, when is it?" I ask, trying to divert the conversation.

"November fifteenth," Saxon answers.

"That's only a few months away," Harper screeches. "How are you going to plan that with all that's happening at the gallery and with Saxon's investment work?"

"Rachel," Brooke says simply. Rachel is Brooke's oldest and dearest friend. I have spent a lot of time with her during the last few months since we've all been hanging out together.

"Oh, good." Harper nods. "I'll give her a call fist thing in the morning and see what she wants us to do."

Saxon smiles down reassuringly at Brooke and her cheerful grin returns.

Will I ever have that? A man whose smile has the power to turn my whole mood around? The power to tell me that everything is going to be okay with just a quirk of his lips?

I think of Jake. *What else is new?* He is all I have been thinking of since he saved my life three months ago. I think of the beautiful smile, the smile that didn't grace his stoic face nearly enough. I think of the sincerity in his eyes, and the way they softened when he looked at me. The lust that filled them when we were together.

Laughter from the table breaks my thoughts, and I look around to find Tate's eyes narrowed on my face. I give him a small smile and excuse myself, making my way to the kitchen.

I try to busy myself, filling the sink with hot soapy water while I collect the dirty plates and cups scattered all around the kitchen.

I should just use the dishwasher but washing the dishes gives me a moment to clear my thoughts. Well, that's not true. It lets me stew on them without anyone noticing I've zoned out at the table.

"You know I've paid people to do that tonight."

I jump at the unexpected presence and then turn to my brother who's standing in the doorway to the kitchen, his arms folded across his chest. I force a smile on my face and, judging by my brother's grim reaction, it must be an awkward one.

"What's wrong, Lala?"

Panic fills me with Tate's use of my childhood nickname. He uses it so rarely now that I know he's about to get serious on me.

I return my attention back to the dishes in front of me. "Nothing's wrong. Just thought I'd help out."

"Uh-huh," Tate says, his tone telling me he doesn't buy that for a second. "Everything will work out."

My eyes shoot to his, alarm and panic running through me. How does he know about Jake? I never spoke a word about him to anyone. Well, except my friend Georgia.

"With work and the house," he interrupts my thoughts, somehow reading my mind. "You are going to kick ass as a permanent teacher." He smiles. "And the house? Well, I'm here. I'll take care of it."

My shoulders drop in relief, and I smile at my baby brother. He makes his way over to me, and I throw my arms around him.

"You're getting me all wet and soapy," he teases, wrapping his arms around me. "It's going to be fine." He chuckles, rubbing my back as I hold on for dear life.

"I know. I'm not worried about any of that." And I'm not. "I'm just so happy for you."

"Thanks, Lala."

41

"I just can't believe my baby brother is getting married. I'm so happy for you, Tate. You deserve all the happiness in the world. You both do."

"You do too, you know."

I pull back, holding his shoulders and smile warmly at him. "Who would've thought you'd be the one getting married and settling down?" I tease, pushing him on the shoulder.

"And what about you?"

"What about me?" I scoff. "In case you've forgotten, I just got out of a marriage. Remember? You had to sneak me out in the middle of the night?"

Tate narrows his eyes, not at all amused by my bad attempt at humour. "How are you doing?"

"I'm good."

"You know what I mean," he says, his voice tight with frustration.

"I don't know what you mean." *I know what he means.*

"Have you heard from him?"

I think of the blond-haired, lying scumbag. "No, not for months. I actually ran into his sister the other day at the market. She said he moved interstate for work."

I want to change the subject, but I don't know what to say, so I turn back to the sink and continue washing the dishes. I don't want to talk about Craig. I don't even want to think about him.

"Mum and Dad would be so proud of you," Tate says as he grabs the dishtowel and begins drying the dishes. "What it took for you to leave. How strong you are."

"They would be so proud of both of you." Maurice stands by the door, smiling at us, his eyes soft. He makes his way over and wraps an arm over each of our shoulders, pulling us into a group hug. "Your grandparents would be too. You have both grown up to become wonderful adults, and I know they would all be so proud of you because I am."

Maurice kisses us each on the tops of our heads, just as he has done since we were little, and Tate and I laugh.

This right here is all I need. Family, friends—I don't need a man. He'd just be another person in my life for me to be attached to, only to have him taken away.

I know that's what *he* would be for me, and I don't need that. I don't need *Jake*.

Chapter Five

Lana

I can't breathe.

Smoke fills my lungs and I can't see anything but darkness. Are my eyes closed? Is it all the smog?

I can smell fire, the scent of burning, but I don't see any flames. My heart beats so fast that blood pounds in my ears. Come on eyes, open.

I'm floating, floating through the air. A heart beats next to my ear, and I know it's not my own. Strong arms hold me and I rest against a hard chest.

My eyes finally cooperate. Opening, looking, searching for my saviour as he carries me out the front door. There is no face, no sincere eyes, no sharp nose or hard jaw. Just a blank face.

But I know it's Jake. I can imagine his stoic expression, his serious chocolate brown eyes and the light stubble that covers his jaw in the morning. I can picture it without seeing it because it's all I've thought about for the past three months.

My eyes fly open and I struggle to catch a breath.

It's as if God is trying to torture me by replaying that night over and over but not letting me remember any of it. The only memories I have are of what happened after I woke up on my neighbour's front lawn, and the small glimpses I get in my dreams.

At first, I didn't have any dreams after the fire, but during the past month, they have become more frequent. Each one adding a little more detail than the one before. Except a face. In all the dreams I've had, Jake has never had a face.

Yes, God definitely is trying to torture me.

The alarm clock reads six o'clock, and I decide to get up rather than spend another morning lying in bed, staring at the ceiling and thinking about Jake.

Knowing Tate is probably awake and already at the café, I text him to have a hot coffee and a breakfast bagel ready for me. I tiptoe around the apartment, trying not to wake Harper. I can't wait to be back in my own place.

I shower and get ready for my first day back at work after the summer break. My first day with a permanent position and my own class. I smile for the first time this morning just at the thought. My fresh start.

When I enter the café, it's as quiet as it usually is this early in the morning, with only a few stragglers coming in on their way to work. In an hour, it will be bustling with customers, barely any standing room as people pick up their breakfast orders.

A smiling Tate greets me as I slump onto a stool at the bar. He doesn't say a word as he places my takeaway coffee in front of me.

"What are you smiling about?" I mumble.

"Life." He chuckles. "Why are you so grumpy?"

"I'm not grumpy. I just couldn't sleep."

"Nervous?"

"I guess." *Sure, let's go with that.*

"You have no reason to be nervous." Maurice walks through the kitchen door carrying two brown paper bags.

"How much time do you spend spying on us and then just waiting for the perfect moment to jump out?" Tate asks him.

Maurice chuckles, shaking his head, and walks over to us, placing both bags on the counter in front of me.

"Your breakfast." He smiles. "I also made you lunch."

I grin up at him as I push to my tiptoes and lean over the counter, laying a smacking kiss on his cheek. There are some things I will miss when I go back home.

"See you boys later." I wave as I turn and walk out.

During the thirty-minute drive, anticipation pulses through me. I feel off today. Just not quite myself after that dream, and especially after stewing over it for the last thirty minutes. I can't wait to be back in my house; my house that's five minutes down the road from the school in the quiet suburbs.

Spending the summer in the city living with Tate and Harper has been fun, but it's time to get back to reality. Honestly, I can't freaking wait.

Entering the staff room today sends a thrill through me. Even though I have done it a hundred times before, something about today is different. I don't feel like an intruder anymore. This is *my* staff room. The staff room where I'll make plans and lessons for *my* class.

I spot Georgia across the room chatting with another teacher. When she sees me, she waves frantically and then practically skips over to me.

"Oh my goodness, are you excited?" she squeals. Georgia

46

and I have both been substituting here for a couple years and were both offered full-time positions here at the end of the last school year. I was given a kindergarten class, and Georgia was given a fourth-grade class.

"So excited," I tell her. "I have so many great ideas."

"Yeah, yeah, that's great. So tell me, how did your holidays go? How was living with your brother?"

"Well, actually. He got engaged over the weekend."

"Oh my God. Really?" Disappointment fills her voice. "Isn't he, like, twelve?"

"Twenty-six." I laugh.

"Twenty-six. He's practically a baby. I'm thirty-two, and I don't even have a boyfriend."

"Neither do I."

"Oh my God, it's so depressing. I'm going to die alone," she says, ignoring my comment.

"Oh, Georgia." I laugh. "Dramatic much? You have lots going for you. Look, a new job."

"Yeah, well, that's one thing going right in my life," she mutters.

I frown at her tone. "Georgia, don't be ridiculous. It's 2015. We are strong, independent women. We do not need a man to define us." I nod, happy with the point I'm trying to make.

"That's easy for you to say. You're getting it on with hot GI Joes."

"Georgia," I scold. "I'm going to my classroom. You've clearly lost it."

"Having sex and not even giving me the details," she calls across the staff room as I make my way to the door. I shake my head but keep walking, refusing to look back at her or the other twenty staff members who are probably staring at me now.

Unlocking my classroom door, I switch on the lights and

smile. The room is bare—plain white walls with nothing on them, desks empty of books and stationary—but all I can see is the potential. All the fun activities we are going to do that will eventually cover the walls. The small pots of markers and coloured pencils that will line the tables. The smiling faces that will start arriving soon and sit facing me with their toothless grins for the rest of the school year.

Yes, this is my fresh start.

I busy myself with setting up seats, stationery, and an art-and-crafts area. Before I know it, an hour has passed and children are beginning to arrive. I make a point to introduce myself to all the parents to put them at ease, as they can be just as nervous as the children are on the first day.

My name is called from the doorway, and it instantly draws my attention. It's the first Lana in a sea of Miss Washingtons, so I look over the shoulder of the parent I was chatting with and my heart stops at the sight in front of me.

Hallie stands in the doorway to the classroom, a huge smile on her face. My heart must have started beating again because, as my eyes roam upwards and meet Jake's wide stare, I can hear the blood rushing in my ears.

What. The. Hell.

I excuse myself and make my way around the parent I was talking to. Standing in front of Jake, I place my arm around Hallie's shoulders as she smiles up at me.

"Angel," he breathes.

"What are you doing here?" I whisper, although I don't know why.

"Miss Washington?"

"Yeah." I draw out the word.

"Hallie's in this class."

Oh. My. God.

48

My heart has dropped into my stomach and taken any form of function with it—my words, my thoughts, my movements. I just stand there with my mouth hanging open as I stare at him.

"Lana?" He chuckles.

"Yeah?"

"Are you supposed to show us around or something?"

"Oh yes, sure, come on." *Back to work, Lana.* I turn around, still holding Hallie under my arm as I straighten my shoulders and make my way across the room.

"This is your table, Hallie." I kneel down in front of her, not looking at Jake, though I can sense him hovering over us. How did I not recognise her name on my roll? "See? I've put your name on the desk. This is also your pot of pencils and stationary." She smiles widely and her excitement seeps through me as well. "You have scissors, a ruler, and some glue as well."

Hallie nods eagerly, and I glance up at Jake to find him staring at me.

"Did you bring her covered books?" I ask Jake. I'm as formal and professional as I would be with any other parent, and I inwardly high-five myself.

"Yes." He nods and pulls them out of her *Frozen* backpack. There is something so hot about a man comfortable enough in himself to carry around a pink bag.

Jake hands me the books, and I raise my eyebrow at him. The contact he has used to cover Hallie's books is completely wrinkled and bubbled. I don't think one small part is covered smoothly.

"When they told us in the parent handbook to cover the books, they didn't mention it would be practically impossible." Jake pouts, and I smile widely.

"Daddy threw the book across the room and said the plastic was a piece of shit."

49

"Hallie," Jake reprimands.

"What? You did."

"Okay." I laugh. "Maybe we just keep this between us. I think I have some spare princess slip covers if you want them?"

Hallie gives me her huge smile and I melt. As shocked as I am to see Jake, and no matter how much I wish he were not going to be a parent in my class, I can't wait to have Hallie every day. Her happiness and innocence are contagious, and I already know seeing her in class is going to be a highlight for me.

I show them where her bag goes and then tell Jake to feel free to hang around and stay a while. I have set up various activities around the classroom to give parents some time to settle the kids before they leave. It also gives me a chance to make it around to all the parents, introduce myself, and answer any questions they may have.

Leaving Jake and Hallie at the painting table, I head back to my desk to get some slips out of my drawer before I forget. When I turn to go mingle with the parents, I hit a very hard, very nice-smelling chest.

Jake grabs my shoulders to steady me, but I pull away. Rejection fills his eyes when I do, but I don't care. I already know I do stupid things when he touches me, and this is not the place or time to make a fool of myself. Not on the first day in my new class, which is still full of parents.

"Lana, I wanted to talk to you —"

"No, Jake. We are not talking about that. It was a fluke. What are the chances? It's not our fault. We do not need to talk about it."

"I don't want to talk about that. I want to ask you out."

"What?" I screech. His voice is confident, his eyes are fierce, and he now stands in front of me with his arms crossed over his chest, daring me to argue.

So many thoughts fly through my head that I can't correlate them. I think about how I've thought of Jake nonstop for the past few months. I think about how I recently left a volatile marriage. I think about our night together and the connection I felt, about how I don't have it in me to love and lose again. And I think about how I could get fired for dating a parent. Well, I don't know for sure if that's true, but that's what I decide to go with.

"I can't date you, Jake."

"Why not?" he asks me, almost pleading. "I know we started off unconventionally, but I would like to —"

"Jake, stop. It has nothing to do with any of that. I can't date you because it's against school policy." Again, I'm not sure if that's the case, but I now think out of all my thoughts, it was the most genius.

"Lana." His eyes are soft and warm and it reminds me of the way he looked at me that night. God, I have to get away from him.

"Jake. I need to go chat with the other parents. Feel free to stay as long as Hallie needs you."

"You won't be pushing me away that easy," he mumbles as he turns away from me to return to the painting table, and I stare daggers into his back. *Cocky bastard.*

The time goes quickly, and it's not long before the parents are saying their good-byes. I reassure them as they leave the classroom, some in tears, and remind them that the kids will be fine. I smile at Jake as he passes my desk to leave, but he turns his head away from me as he strides to the door. I frown at his rudeness and then see a hand go to his face and brush his cheek. Did he just wipe away a tear?

Holy shit. My heart beats in double time, and I have the urge to run over to him and throw my arms around him and console him. I didn't get that urge for the other parents who were upset to leave their kids for the first time.

But the other parents aren't Jake. The other parents didn't lose their wife when their daughter was one and had to raise her on their own for the past four years.

"Lana, can we play on the playground yet?" Hallie draws my attention to her with the use of my first name. Shit, how am I going to deal with this one?

"Hallie, it's Miss Washington," I say as gently as I can.

Her smile drops into a frown and her eyebrows scrunch up in confusion.

Shit. This is exactly why teachers should not get involved with parents. And with that thought, my decision to steer clear of Jake Weston is cemented.

Chapter Six

Lana

We don't waste any time before we dive into the curriculum. We begin the day learning our first sound of *A*. The children love the actions and the songs that go with the sound, and I realise I have a class full of bright students as they grasp the concept quickly.

Before recess, I take the class on a walk through the school, showing them the basics they need to know. The excited chatter that surrounds me as we walk through the library, the computer room, the music room, and even the cafeteria sends pleasure through me. I am so going to enjoy watching these children grow. I'll be with them from their first day when they have no idea what to expect, all through the year as their learning, their confidence, and their self-esteem continue to grow. I already feel a special connection to them, as if they belong to me. As if it's my job to protect and care for them, as well as teach them.

It's such a different feeling to substituting, where you have no idea where you are going to be each day and with what students. Not in any class long enough to build an attachment.

We fill the rest of the day with handwriting, math, and even some time on the playground. The hours go by quickly, and I notice before the bell how tired and worn out they all look. It must be a big day for them.

I decide to finish off with an educational program on the TV so they can rest while they wait for their parents to come. It also works as a great tool to keep them occupied while I chat with the parents, each one eager to know how their child's first day went. I wonder if I'll worry that much when I have a child.

If I ever have a child.

The parents begin straggling in and I chat with each one. Most of the children had a wonderful day, but of course, there are a few who were upset at times, some who were scared of going out at recess and lunch, and some who didn't interact with the other kids.

I know many teachers would just lie and tell all the parents that their child did great, but I have a one hundred percent honesty policy with parents. It doesn't matter how much it will upset them, they deserve to know how their child really coped so they can handle it accordingly at home. It doesn't help anyone to hide or deny the issues.

Jake's the last parent to walk in the classroom, and judging by his smile, I think it was on purpose.

"Hey."

"Hi." I smile and my cheeks heat. *Pull it together, Lana. He just said* 'hey'.

"How did she do?" he asks, smiling over at Hallie who is lying on the mat, still engrossed in the TV.

"She did great. She's quite the social butterfly." I laugh.

"Yeah. I guess, being an only child, she kind of craves other kids' company." He frowns momentarily, and I can read the guilt in his eyes. What would he have to feel guilty about? "Anyway . . ." He shakes his head. "I'm glad we have a minute."

"Jake—"

"I want your number, Lana. I should've gotten it from you the morning I dropped you off. I want it. I want your number, and I want to use it to call you up and ask you out."

"Jake, I am Hallie's teacher. It's highly inappropriate for us to start something."

"But we're not starting something, are we?"

I frown in confusion.

"We are not starting anything because we started something months ago."

"Jake . . ." I plead. I don't know how much longer I can fight him on this. How do you keep saying no to the man who saved you from a burning building?

"Daddy!" Hallie screams, excited as she jumps up from the mat and comes running over, throwing herself into her dad's arms.

"Princess." He picks her up. "How was your first day at school?" He kisses her forehead and smiles at her. God, that's so hot. I think my ovaries just combusted.

"It was so good, Daddy. I got to see all the places. Do you want to see all the places?" Hallie talks so fast with exhilaration that Jake and I both laugh at her.

"And what places are there?" he asks her.

"The library, the cafeteria, the office. Can I take you to the office, Daddy?"

"Sure, princess, we can go to the office." Jake kisses Hallie once more on the forehead and then places her feet back on the ground. "Grab your bag and we can go."

Hallie skips off to the bag area, and Jake turns to smirk at me. I wonder why and then I realise I am sitting at my desk, my chin in my hand and smiling like a loon at the scene that just played out in front of me.

"You . . ." I clear my throat. "You better hurry. The office ladies get cranky if they have to stay late," I tell Jake as I quickly stand from my table and head over to the sink, pretending to clean some paint equipment.

"See you tomorrow, Lana," he says. I don't turn to look at him.

"You're not allowed to call her that anymore. It's Miss Washington," Hallie tells him.

"See you tomorrow, Miss Washington." I can hear the sarcastic tone in his voice and can imagine the mischievous smile on his face, so I'm glad I have my back to him as heat rises in my cheeks.

How am I going to do this for the rest of the school year?

I stay at school as late as I can and grab dinner on the way home to give Tate and Harper a bit of privacy. In truth, I'm trying to avoid them without having to lock myself in my room all night thinking about Jake. I know if I sit around chatting with them, then they'll know something is up with me, and I just don't feel like going into the details with them.

Luckily, arriving home late works, and I don't stay around to chat about my day. But I do end up locked in my room thinking about Jake for most of the night.

I tossed and turned all night running through every Jake scenario since the night we met, and even some new ones I made up. Analysing every gesture, every word spoken. Now I'm running on three hours sleep, which is never easy, but especially so when it's only Tuesday, and the reason for my sleepless night will be waiting for me at school.

I arrived at school early this morning since I wasn't sleeping anyway and have already set up the class activities and programs before I expect the children to arrive.

So, of course I am shocked when Jake and Hallie enter my classroom well before the bell has rung. Judging by the huge grin on his face, again, this isn't a coincidence.

"You're early," I snap at him, running my hand over my hair hoping every piece is in place.

"I just wanted some extra time to settle Hallie in," he says, trying to feign innocence but still smirking at me.

"Mmm hmm."

I can't help but watch as Jake helps Hallie put her bag away, place her drink and diary on her desk, and then leads her over to the cutting table.

Once Hallie is seated and cutting, Jake turns and stalks towards me. I fidget in my chair, wondering where I can run to.

Don't do it, Jake. Don't ask me again. I don't know if I can keep saying no. I wonder if I put my head down and pretend to work if he'll go away.

"Sleep well?" he asks.

My mouth drops open, and I stare at him with wide eyes. How does he know I was up all night?

Jake answers my unasked question as he places both his hands on my desk and leans so close to me I flinch, wondering if he's going to kiss me. He doesn't. And I'm glad about that. Aren't I? He then whispers, "You look like you slept as well as

I did."

My breath catches and I lean back in my chair, my mouth frozen and my thoughts vanished.

"Lana, I can't stop thinking about you. All I can think about is our night together and the chemistry we had. I want to explore this further. I want to take you out."

"Jake—"

"I understand this is your job, and I would never be so unprofessional if I didn't feel so strongly about this—"

"You're the parent of one of my students. It just can't happen. I'm sorry." My voice comes out much steadier than I feel, and I'm proud of my strength and professionalism. I choose to ignore the connection I know he is talking about. I can't go through that again. Loving someone only to have them taken away from me.

"I understand." He stands up from my table. "And that's why I told myself if you said no again this morning I would leave you alone."

What? I narrow my eyes, unsure if this is a ploy.

"I am a parent and you are the teacher, and we have to work together for the rest of the year. I don't want to make you uncomfortable or create an awkward situation. I'm sorry, Lana."

I stare at him for a moment, my mouth opening and closing while I think of what to say. "No need to apologise. Thank you for understanding, and I look forward to working together in the best interest of Hallie."

He nods and turns to head back to the cutting table where Hallie sits, still occupied with cutting pictures out of magazines.

A small pang of remorse floats in my belly, but I push it away, pretending it was never there in the first place.

Jake left this morning with nothing but a small nod on his

way out. I hate how much that bothers me, and I hate that it's all I've thought about for the past six hours.

Today has dragged on, and for this last lesson, I have given the kids free rein of the art cabinet. Glue, paper, felt, pipe cleaners, glitter, and cardboard cover every surface, but the delight on the children's faces makes it worth it. Plus, it has allowed me to just sit at my desk and stare into space while I think about Jake.

Just the thought of seeing him at pickup in a few minutes has my heart racing. How does he do that? How does he affect me so much? I've never met a man who can curl my toes with just the memory of him.

It's that connection. That chemistry. I've never had it with anyone else before, and instead of embracing it, I am running scared. I know that's what I'm doing. My heart is running, terrified at even the thought of giving myself over to another person. Another person who I could potentially lose in the long run.

I glance over at Hallie's table and watch her giggle at Ben, who is making underarm farts.

Two people I could potentially lose in the long run.

Another ten minutes of daydreaming about Jake, and the parents begin to arrive.

My heart thuds, my hands shake, and heat warms my body with excitement. Excitement to see Jake. *Calm down, Lana.* I shake my head at myself and greet the first lot of parents, telling them how their child's second day went.

Pickup time is much more frantic than drop-off. Trying to talk to parents, helping the children pack up their things, and finding their misplaced items keeps me running around like a headless chicken.

I'm looking for Maddison's lost sweater when a dark-haired woman walks into the classroom, glancing around as though she's looking for someone. The woman looks vaguely familiar to me, but she's not one of the parents.

"Aunt Marley!" Hallie squeals and runs across the classroom, jumping into the woman's open arms. *Aunt.*

"Hey sweetie, how was your day?"

I make my way over to them and smile curtly. "Hi, I'm Miss Washington."

The beautiful woman, who I'm guessing is in her late thirties, smiles warmly at me as she holds Hallie tightly. "Hi, I'm Marley, Hallie's aunt. I'm her dad's sister."

His sister. No wonder she looks familiar. On closer inspection, I notice she has his eyes. The same shape and the same chocolate brown. Marley's are softer, though. More open and more accepting.

"Where is he then?" My eyes widen at my tone at the same time as Marley's do. She is polite enough to ignore my abrasive and rude attitude and embarrassment fills me.

"He's back at work. He took yesterday off for Hallie's first day but from now on, we will be sharing drop-off and pickup duty."

"Oh," is the only word that comes out of my mouth. My heart aches a little at the fact that I'm not going to get to see Jake every day, and the absurdity of my feelings just frustrates the hell out of me.

Except for that one night, that one unforgettable night, I barely know him.

Chapter Seven

Jake

I dodge in and out of the traffic as I race to Marley's house. I can't wait to see Hallie and hear how her second day at school was.

I've barely pulled up to the curb when I'm switching the truck off and heading inside, without so much as a knock on the front door. "Hello."

"Daddy." Hallie comes barrelling down the front hall, and I step back as she crashes right into my legs, groaning when her head hits my groin. She's at that awkward height where I should constantly be wearing a cup.

"Hey, princess." I pick her up. "Wow, you are getting too heavy to lift." I fake a groan and pretend to drop her.

"Daddy," she squeals, hanging onto my shoulders.

I laugh and secure her in my arms once again. "How was

your day?"

"Great. We had to draw a picture of our favourite thing, and I drew a football field. Lana . . ." She purses her lips. "I mean, Miss Washington said it was the best football field she had ever seen."

"I bet it was, princess." I kiss Hallie's forehead and pull back to see my sister leaning against the wall, her arms crossed and her eyebrows raised. *Great. What does she have to say?* "Why don't you go out back with the boys for a little while? I'll come get you when it's time to go."

Putting her down, she runs off down the hallway grumbling, "I'll show Thomas how a real girl throws a football."

I chuckle and shake my head as I watch her go to show her eight-year-old cousin. She'll show him, alright. Growing up with a single dad and three male cousins, Hallie has had no choice but to learn how to compete and hold her own.

I avoid my sister's scrutinising gaze as I pass her and head for the kitchen. "Where's John?"

"What was that about?" she asks, not letting me escape.

"What was what about?" I sigh. Having an older sister is tough. But having an older sister when you're a single dad, and the rest of your family lives away, is almost unbearable.

"Hallie calling the teacher *Lana*? How would she even know her name? She introduced herself to me as *Miss Washington*."

The tone she puts on Lana's name is almost condescending, and it bothers me. "Stop saying her name like that."

"Jake, what's going on? She acted really weird today when I picked Hallie up."

"Who?"

"The teacher."

"What?"

"It's like she was pissed you weren't there or something."

I release a deep breath and sit myself at the kitchen table, needing to tell someone. Marley pulls out her own seat and sits with her legs up on the chair. Her eyes are wide, and she has a huge smile on her face. This is what happens when you become a stay-at-home mum—even the smallest possibility of gossip from the outside world has you sitting on the edge of your seat.

"Lana, Miss Washington, is the woman from the house fire."

"Fuck off," Marley blurts out.

"Mummy, you said a bad word," Marley's three-year-old son Dylan says as he comes in from the backyard, breathing heavy.

"Oh, I'm sorry baby." She jumps out of her seat, rushing over to him. "Mummy was having an adult conversation with Uncle Jake. What do you need?"

"I'm thirsty."

She practically runs to the kitchen sink, filling up a huge glass of water, before she's shooing Dylan back outside and sitting in front of me once more.

"Oh my God, Jake. Hallie's teacher is your *'best sex of your life'* one-night stand?"

I groan. This is what happens when you're a single father, and between work and caring for your child, you don't spend any time in the real world making friends with anyone other than your sister.

"Yes."

"Fuck off." She stares at me with wide eyes, her mouth hanging open. I guess that was my reaction too. "Oh, Jake, it's like fate. It's meant to be."

I roll my eyes. "Not quite. She doesn't want to see me again. She wants to keep our relationship *professional*."

"You told her you didn't?"

"I told her I wanted to see her again."

"What did she say?"

63

"She practically recited the school's policy on teachers dating parents."

"Oh." She frowns, looking out the back window, her brows pinched in thought. "That's really weird because it's just not the impression I got from her today."

"What does that mean?" I lean forward in my seat.

"Well," she says thoughtfully, as though she wants to get her facts straight, "she seemed disappointed that I would be doing a lot of the drop-off and pickup."

"I doubt it, Mar. You're reading too much into it. She made herself very clear. I mean, I asked twice. It was practically on the verge of begging." I stand from the table. I don't want to get my hopes up.

But as I collect Hallie, say good-bye to my sister, and buckle Hallie in her car seat, I can't deny it. My hopes are up.

I can't help it; a huge grin takes over my face at the possibility that Lana might be feeling the same way I do. That maybe she feels the connection between us, and maybe, just maybe, she *is* willing to give us a go.

The grin stays plastered to my face all night and well into the early hours of the morning as I think about Lana Washington.

As much as I want to take Hallie to school and see Lana, I drop her off at my sister's house early, as I have PT first off and then I have to finish an engine rebuild on a tanker by mid-morning. What would I say anyway? 'Hey, Lana, even after what you said, I want to ask again, just in case, because my sister thinks she read some kind of emotion in your face yesterday, and now I'm hoping there's a chance you might change your mind about us'. *Yeah, good one, Jake.*

After working on a few hundred engines over the years, I can rebuild one now without much concentration. This, of course, frees up my whole day to think about Lana.

64

Life was so uncomplicated before her. When it was just Hallie and me. Before dickhead Brad called me out to that fire.

But I don't want uncomplicated. I don't want it always to be Hallie and me. I want Lana. I want her fucking bad. Something about her calls to me. Something about the connection I felt with her that night.

I pull my cell out of my overalls pocket, dialling and waiting for an answer.

"Hey, what's up?" Marley answers on the third ring.

"Hey. I don't need you to pick up Hallie today."

"Really? Everything okay?"

"Yeah. I'm just going to leave early and go grab her myself."

"Oh, I see." All the concern that had laced her voice before vanishes in a heartbeat, and I can virtually hear the smile in her tone.

"What? I'm just getting off early." I'm sure my annoyance is clear in my own tone.

"Sure, baby brother. When have you ever just *'gotten off early'*?"

"Today," I snap and hang up on her before she can laugh at me.

My hands grip the steering wheel tight as I drive to the school. A woman has never made me so nervous before. Before I met Jamie, I had no troubles with the opposite sex. I'd had my fair share of the high school female population by the time I'd left for college. I was in no way a player, but I was the football star and the class captain. And now I'm just a single dad who hasn't dated in nearly ten years. Fuck.

I don't give myself time to rethink it as I fly into the parking lot and rush into the school. I'm not going to overthink this. I'm going to take what's mine.

The classroom door is open, and I stalk straight to Lana's desk. "I know what I said yesterday, but I've decided . . . fuck it."

"Jake." Her eyes are wide with panic.

"No, Lana. I have not been interested in a woman in a long time—a *very* long time—and I am interested in you. I want to get to know you. I'm only asking for a date."

"Jake." Her tone is urgent, but I ignore it.

"Only one date. Please. If things don't go anywhere, then what's the harm of one date?"

"Jake," she finally snaps and halts my rambling.

"What?"

"I'm in class, for goodness' sakes. The bell hasn't rung yet."

Lana looks out to the classroom and my gaze follows hers, meeting the eyes of twenty-something silent, five-year–olds, mouths open and eyes wide. When my mouth drops open in imitation of theirs, they all crack up laughing. Hysterics ring out around the room and I come back to myself, smile at them, and wink.

"So . . ." I turn to Lana with a cocky grin. "How about it?"

"Yes," she blurts out, her voice breathy. I'm not sure if she meant to say it or not, but I'm not letting her renege.

"Well, then." I smirk. "I'll let you get back to it." Turning to leave, I give the kids a small wave, and Hallie a little wink as their laughter continues.

Once I have patiently waited for the bell to ring, I re-enter the classroom and try to look busy while all the other parents file out. Some giving me disapproving looks on their way passed. I guess word travels quickly.

When I finally catch Lana alone again, I invite her to the football game on Saturday. Hallie and I never miss a week, and

I think a casual date, just hanging out, might not be so scary.

For either of us.

"Daddy," Hallie yells before poking her head into my bathroom. "Are you ready yet? I don't want to be late for the game."

I flick my fingers through my hair, adjusting the waxed pieces a couple more times before sighing, shaking my head, and deciding it'll do. Fuck, I'm nervous.

"Daddy, come on," Hallie whines.

"Alright, princess. Come on, let's go."

Hallie smiles, and she races out of the bathroom and through the front door. I follow, grabbing my wallet and keys off the side table at the entrance.

"Have you got everything?" I call out to her. She's already climbing into my truck.

She waves her foam thumb in one hand and her team's red and white scarf in the other and winks at me. Well, Hallie's wink is blinking with both eyes twice, but I get the gist. I laugh as I lock up the house and join her in the truck.

As much as I argued, Lana insisted on having someone drop her off at the game rather than letting me pick her up. She said she was currently living in the city and didn't want me to have to drive all the way into town and back out again, and she could get her brother to take her. I would've driven anywhere if it meant I had her sitting in my truck again, but I didn't want to push her too much after her finally agreeing to come out with me.

Luckily, the drive to the field isn't that far from our house because Hallie decides it's a great time to play twenty questions.

"Do you think Miss Washington likes football?"

"I don't know, princess—"

She barely takes a breath so I can answer. "She liked my drawing of the field."

"Yeah—"

"Do I still have to call her Miss Washington when we aren't at school?"

"Maybe you could ask her—"

"I wonder which team she wants to win?"

"I'm not sure —"

"Is Miss Washington your girlfriend? Brax and Danny said she was your girlfriend. They said she would be my new mum, but I told them I don't have a mum. They laughed at me, and I punched Brax in the stomach. He cried like a girl and then told on me."

"Hold up, hold up, hold up." I hold one hand up, signalling for her to stop. She takes a deep breath and then sits patiently, waiting for my response. I'm sure she's expecting some profound answer. The kind of answer a good dad should have. But I have nothing. Nada.

"Miss Washington is not my girlfriend," I tell her, and she frowns. "She is our friend and wanted to come see a game with us. No big deal." Hallie nods, as if encouraging me to continue. Christ, sometimes I'm sure she's five going on fifteen. "You already have a mum, Hallie—she just isn't here anymore. It doesn't mean you stopped having a mum. Your mum is just in Heaven."

She nods again, her thoughtful gaze turning out the window.

"*And,*" I say, reaching back to put my hand on her knee, bringing her attention back to me, "it doesn't matter what anyone says to you. You can't go around punching people. You know that." What I really want to tell her is next time Brax is a smartass, kick him in the balls, but I don't.

"Dylan punches me all the time," she whines.

"He's three. He doesn't know any better."

Hallie crosses her arms and pouts as I pull into the stadium parking lot.

Parking the car, I get out and walk around to the back, opening her door. "Come on, Rocky. Let's go."

She soon forgets her sulking as she grins up at me and jumps down from the truck. I hope she's this easy to placate when she's a hormonal teenager. Somehow, I doubt it.

We make our away around the large stadium, fighting through the hordes of excited fans to get to the front gates. After scanning the crowd for quite some time, I see Lana standing by the ticket booth. The small smile she flashes me turns into a megawatt grin when her eyes land on Hallie.

I love that she likes my kid. I want her to love my kid. I want her to love her so much that she can't imagine her life without us. Am I crazy?

"Lana," Hallie screams, finally noticing her standing in amongst all the people trying to get inside the stadium.

"Hi, Hallie." Lana smiles as we walk to her, getting down on her knees to greet Hallie.

"Can I call you Lana if we're not in school?" Hallie hasn't forgotten her list of questions. Let's just hope she doesn't voice them all. Especially the one about Lana being my girlfriend.

"Sure, Hallie. You can call me Lana outside of school. Just make sure to keep it our secret, okay?"

"Yeah, because all the other kids will want you to be their daddy's girlfriend so they can call you Lana too."

Lana laughs. "Exactly."

I love how genuine she is. She doesn't laugh at Hallie just to appease her or to do the right thing. She likes kids. Really likes them. You can see it in every interaction. Fuck, I like that about

69

her too.

"Hi." I smile, trying to keep eye contact, but I can't help it as my gaze roams over every inch of her face and body.

"Hey." She smiles up at me from underneath her lashes.

When Lana stands, I finally take note of the sports top she is wearing. "Wrong team." I gesture to her sweater of the opposing team, with the blue and yellow stripes and the picture of a lion roaring.

She laughs. "The *only* team."

Hallie frowns up at Lana's top but chooses not to say anything.

"Shall we?" I nod towards the gate. Lana smiles, and Hallie absentmindedly grabs her hand and pulls her along.

Chapter Eight

Lana

Jake finds our row in the crowd and after pushing through a few rowdy teenage fans, we slide into our seats.

"I'm next to Lana," Hallie shouts and pushes Jake over a seat so she can squeeze between us. I laugh as Jake shoots her a mock glare.

"We've still got a little while before it starts. Want some food or snacks?" Jake asks, his eyes on me.

"Just get me the usual, Dad," Hallie says, not taking her eyes off the players practising on the field.

"And what's the usual, princess?"

"Ummmm . . ." She thinks about it. "A hot dog, some nachos, some fries, and a cherry Coke."

"You have a death wish?" He raises his eyebrows at her.

"That sounds great. I'll have the same." Jake's eyes go wide as they take me in. "Oh, and some popcorn for us to share."

Hallie nods in agreement, and Jake chuckles as he shakes his head and stands to leave.

He goes to pass us, and I stand up and lean back to give him room, but his thighs brush over mine. I gasp, yet he doesn't flinch. He just keeps walking out of the row and up the aisle, but I see the corner of his mouth twitch.

I flop back down into my seat, releasing a breath. An imaginary warmth covering my skin where his hard and thick thighs touched. The feel of him brings all kind of memories flooding back and my body breaks out in goosebumps just at the thought of it. I shiver and cross my legs, trying to ease the ache that the thought of Jake alone has stirred.

Hallie interrupts my erotic thoughts, and I remember that I'm sitting at a family football game and that this is not the time or place to be fantasising.

"Are you my dad's girlfriend?" she asks with a serious expression.

My mouth opens and closes as I stutter for an answer, but Hallie continues. "Brax and Danny said you were my dad's girlfriend, and you were going to be my new mum." *Jesus.* "I told them I didn't have a mum, and they laughed at me so I punched Brax in the stomach. He cried like a girl and then tattled on me to the music teacher." I nod, trying not to freak out. "My dad says that I do have a mum, she's just in Heaven." My heart breaks for this little girl and a frown mars my face. "My dad says—"

"What does your dad say?"

Hallie and I both turn to find Jake standing at the end of our row, a young boy in stadium uniform behind him, both carrying trays full of food.

"Nothing," Hallie singsongs, and I have a feeling she probably was not supposed to tell me any of that.

I am so thankful for Jake's interruption that I give him a huge smile. He narrows his eyes in confusion but doesn't ask. This time when he passes me in the row to get to his seat, the tray he is holding in front of him keeps our bodies separated and I frown on the inside, a little disappointed I didn't get another small feel of him.

The young boy hands me the other tray, and I lay it across my lap as Jake starts divvying up the food.

We sit in silence for the next ten minutes or so while we all stuff our faces, watching the crowd of people slowly filling the stadium.

"Have you been to many games?" Jake asks me, popping the last bite of hotdog into his mouth. "You're obviously a fan." He gestures to my top.

"No, this is actually my first one."

"No way," Hallie says, both her and Jake turning to look at me with disbelieving eyes.

"What?" I laugh. "I've just never had the opportunity."

"Fair enough." Jake smiles. "Well, we are glad you are here with us today. Hallie and I come as often as we can."

"We never miss a home game," Hallie adds, her mouth full of fries.

I smile down at her. "Lucky you live so close." She nods, shoving another handful of fries in her mouth.

"How long have you worked at the school?" Jake asks.

"I've been there for a couple of years doing substitute work, but this is my first year as a permanent teacher."

"You enjoy it then? Your job?"

"Yes, I love it. More so now that I have my own class."

Jake nods. "Hallie is really happy there."

"She's had a great first week, Jake. She has settled so well."

"I'm glad. She likes you." He stares into me, his warm brown eyes glimmering in the sunlight, almost as if he's willing me to read his internal thoughts. *God, how I wish I could.* What I wouldn't give to know what he was thinking.

"How about your work?" I ask, trying to put him in the spotlight. I want to know everything I can about him.

"It's great. I always wanted to be a diesel mechanic. To be able to do it to serve my country is just icing on the cake."

"It's very admirable. I know there's not a lot of money in it. You could have your own business and be earning a fortune."

"It's not about the money. It's about doing my part for the greater good. And if I can do that while doing what I love, well, all the better."

I stare at Jake. Just stare at him. I have absolutely no words for what he just revealed. My shock must be obvious as a flush creeps up his cheeks and he smiles sheepishly at me before turning his attention to the field in front of us.

Clearing my throat and thoughts, I ask, "You don't tour?"

Jake turns back towards me. "Not since it's been just Hallie and me. I work solely on base now."

"Oh. It's great that you can be there for her."

"I enjoy being involved. I don't want to miss the school events and the special occasions." A sad smile touches his face as he ruffles Hallie's hair. "I miss enough as it is just trying to being a single dad and working."

"You're a wonderful father," I whisper. My eyes widen. Why does my stupid mouth have to speak aloud my inappropriate thoughts? Jakes grins at my embarrassment then schools his features.

"So, you're living in the city now?" he asks, and I'm thankful he let my comment slide.

"Yeah, just while my place is getting fixed up. I'm staying with my brother and his fiancée."

"They still working on your house? It's been over three months since the fire."

"There were a few issues." My laugh holds no humour, and Jake stares at me intently. I can tell his controlling side wants to ask me what has been happening, but he does well to rein it in. "I'm hoping to move back in the next few weeks actually, if all goes according to plan."

"That's great. If you need a hand moving or anything, I'd be happy to help. I don't work on the weekends, so Hallie and I will be around."

"I can help you decorate," Hallie pipes in, letting us know she is still listening to the conversation.

"That would be wonderful. Although, I need to paint the walls first."

"Paint? Aren't the builders doing all that?"

"Well, I didn't want to wait any longer. It's ready enough for me to move in, and I'm just going to finish it myself."

"How ready?" Jake narrows his eyes.

"Ready enough."

"Painting a whole house is a lot of work, Lana."

"Lucky I have a lot of time." I smile sweetly at him and see the restraint on his face. His jaw is tight and his mouth grim. I try not to laugh out loud. Really? Another overprotective alpha male? As if I don't have enough of those in my life. Better than the alternative, though, I guess.

Instantly, thoughts and visions of my life before bombard me. Harsh words, derogatory name-calling. A life with no choice. Nothing but orders and demands. I'm transported back to a time when the words *slut, whore, bitch,* and *cunt* were used more than any other words. No *thank you*s; no *I love* *you*s.

Yes, an overprotective male is definitely better than the alternative.

"Are you okay?" Jake has a hand resting on my shoulder, giving me a slight nudge.

"I'm sorry." I shake my head.

"We lost you for a second there." Jake gives me a warm smile and squeezes my shoulder where his hand still rests.

I grab a fry from Hallie's bucket. "So, what else do you guys do together?"

Jake leans back in his seat, taking the warmth of his hand with him, but I feel the heat of his stare on my face as I look down at Hallie for an answer.

"We go to the park near our house. It has a big plastic blue seat that spins around and around. Daddy will sit on it and spin us as fast as he can go."

"Wow; that sounds like fun."

"It goes very fast because my daddy is so strong, but I don't get scared. Do I, Daddy?"

Glancing up at Jake, I find him staring at me, his eyes fierce and tumultuous.

"You must be brave." I smile down at Hallie, having to break eye contact with Jake. His stare is so intense, as if looking at the sun.

"I am." She nods with a serious expression on her face.

We eat in silence for a bit longer, all three of us seeming to somewhat zone out into our own thoughts for a while.

Once the game has started, the tension around us fades and we are back to the light-hearted fun we came here to have.

Hallie screams at the umpires, with Jake laughing and egging her on. Hallie's only a hair's breadth away from knocking other spectators over the head with her huge foam thumb.

This is the most fun I've had in a long time. In fact, it could be the most fun I've ever had.

Chapter Nine

Jake

"So, shall we go and grab some dinner?" I ask as we make our way out of the stadium. The other fifty thousand spectators are pushing and prodding us, so I hold Hallie in my arms as Lana walks alongside us.

"Eat? Again? You guys haven't stopped eating since we got here," Lana says.

Hallie and I look at each other and then laugh. I turn back to Lana. "Yeah, so? You wanna come eat with us or what?"

"I guess so." She sighs, but there's humour in her eyes and she gives me a slow smile.

I love that smile. I could say it warms me from the inside or something more eloquent like that, but the truth is that it makes me want to kiss the shit out of her. Kiss her so hard that her already plump lips soften and bruise.

My daydream is cut short as Lana is pushed from behind and almost topples down in front of me. She rights herself and stands straight, but her eyes are wide with panic.

Moving Hallie into one arm, I grab Lana around the waist with the other, pulling her tight against my side. I hold onto her and she smiles up at me, relief washing through her emerald green eyes.

Her reaction *does* warm me from the inside this time. It's been a long time since I've felt protective over someone like this. More than a father to his daughter. More than a brother to his sister. I don't know what it is—it's just more.

It scares me and excites me all at the same time. I'm not opposed to meeting someone. I'm not opposed to settling down. In fact, I would love to find someone for Hallie and me. But it has been a long time since I've dated. Even longer since I've had anything even close to feelings like this.

What happened with Jamie hasn't scarred me or left me jaded. But Lana—she carries something. Baggage that seems to sit just below the surface. As if she carries the world on her shoulders.

I want to take that baggage from her. Carry her burdens so that the smile I enjoy so much comes more often, so that the light in her eyes shines brighter.

We finally make it out of the stadium and the crowd thins as everyone goes in different directions. Lana pulls out of my grasp and I frown as the warmth of her body disappears.

"I can walk now," Hallie says, shifting in my arms, trying to get down. I place her feet on the ground and she immediately grabs Lana's hand and pulls her along until they are walking more than a few steps ahead of me.

I stroll behind them, taking in the view. Not even the sight of Lana's ass in those tight jeans can distract me from the picture of Lana and Hallie, walking hand in hand while chatting and laughing together.

My stomach flips and my chest aches. I want that. I want it for Hallie and for me. We fucking deserve that. We have been alone long enough.

Lana and Hallie stand by the front of the truck, giggling, while they wait for me to unlock it. I press the fob and Lana holds Hallie's door open while she gets in, and I make my way around to the driver's side.

"What's so funny?" I ask as I slide inside and the girls are giggling again.

"Nothing," they respond at the same time, giving each other mischievous smiles.

"Yeah, right," I mumble, starting the car, but I can't help my grin as I stare straight out the windshield.

It's only a short drive to the diner Hallie and I usually go to, and before I can even get out of the truck, Lana is out, has Hallie's door open, and is helping her down. They hold hands again as they make their way inside, finding a booth at the back and sliding in together.

"I may as well not even be here," I say, as I slide into the booth opposite them.

"Well, who would drive us around if we didn't bring you?" Lana teases.

I wink at her and glance at Hallie who is watching us closely. "What do you want, princess?"

"Ice cream, please."

"What flavour?" Lana asks.

"Umm . . ." Hallie looks up in thought. "I can't decide."

"How about you, Daddy, and I get one flavour each and share?" Lana raises her eyebrows at her.

"Oh, can we, Daddy?" She plays me like a violin, knowing

I can't say no to her when she pouts and blinks those big puppy-dog eyes at me.

"Sure, princess." I shake my head as her and Lana smile in delight, and my heart warms once again at the sight.

"What can I get you guys?" The waitress interrupts the girly laughter.

"Can we please have three sundaes? One strawberry, one chocolate, and one caramel, please," Lana orders. "Oh, and can we get sprinkles on the strawberry and chocolate and nuts on the caramel?"

"Sure, hon." The waitress smiles.

While we wait for our ice cream, Lana tells Hallie all about what she has planned for class. The two chat between themselves and even though they have barely acknowledged me in the last hour, it's still the best date I've ever been on.

"Here you go, guys." The waitress places the sundaes down onto the table and Lana hands them out—strawberry to Hallie, caramel to me, and chocolate for herself—and we all dig in eagerly.

"We're going to do a special pets day at school. Do you have any pets?" Lana looks at me now as she takes a bite of her ice cream. "I don't remember seeing any when I was at your place."

"No." Hallie pouts.

I close my eyes briefly, rubbing my hand over my head. Fuck, I know where this is going.

"I want a dog, but Dad says we can't have one."

"Why not?" Lana frowns.

"Because dogs take a lot of work and commitment. We have never been in the situation to get one," I say.

"Your dad is right; dogs are hard work," she says to Hallie.

Hallie just nods, her frown deepening as she stares down into her ice cream.

"Switch!" Lana yells, catching us off-guard as she pushes her chocolate sundae towards me and then grabs Hallie's strawberry from her, not waiting a second before she takes a huge spoonful. I follow suit and push my caramel sundae to Hallie. She grins at Lana, probably thinking this is the funniest thing she has ever done. Kids—so easily entertained.

Lana winks at me and it throws me for a second until I realise what her plan was. Distraction. That's another thing about kids. So easily distracted.

I nod my thanks at Lana, and she returns her focus to Hallie. I watch her lips as they wrap around the silver spoon, sucking the cold ice cream off. Her tongue runs along her bottom lip, cleaning any trace of ice cream before she brings another spoonful to her mouth.

I imagine those lips wrapped around me, and I swallow hard and shift in my seat, my jeans suddenly too tight. Watching Lana innocently eat ice cream may be the sexiest thing I've ever seen. Fuck, I can't even imagine if she were trying to be sexy.

That's the thing about her. She doesn't have to try to be sexy—she just is. Her doing something as simple as eating a sundae has me wanting to jump across this booth and bite that plump bottom lip before licking all traces of ice cream off it.

A throat clears, and I look up to meet Lana's wide eyes. I shrug, not even trying to deny what she caught me doing.

"Switch!" she yells.

Distraction.

Chapter Ten

Lana

"I'd walk you upstairs, but . . ." He nods towards the backseat where Hallie is singing to herself.

I smile. "I'm sure I can make it on my own." Times like this make me really wish I were back in my own place. I could invite Jake and Hallie inside. Make them dinner and maybe watch some worthless TV. We could put Hallie to bed in the spare room and maybe they could stay the night.

Whoa. Slow down, Lana.

"As much fun as I had today, I'd really like to take you out . . ." he pauses, lowering his voice, "just you and I."

"I would really like that."

Jake's face breaks into a huge smile, and I can't help but return it. We sit there smiling at each other like two goofy idiots, and as much as I don't want to, I know I eventually have to get out of the car.

"Well, I should get going." I give Jake a small smile and hop out of the truck. Closing the door and popping my head back into the window, I grin widely. "I had the best time."

I walk away before he has a chance to say anything, and the last thing I see is his huge smile. Butterflies float in my stomach as I think of his excited and hopeful eyes.

After today, I am certain I want to see where this could go. Because something low in my stomach tells me it could go somewhere wonderful.

When I enter the apartment and shut the door, two heads come flying up from the other side of the couch. Tate and Harper both have wide eyes, wayward hair, and guilty looks on their faces.

"Is it safe for me to walk away from the door?" I ask them.

"Mostly," Tate mutters as he fumbles with their clothes. God, I can't wait to move back home. Maybe get a little couch action of my own. *Jesus, Lana, get a grip.*

Harper jumps up off the couch, practically skipping over to me, and Tate follows us into the kitchen area. I potter around, trying to look busy while I grab everything I need to make a coffee.

"So, how was your day?"

I know Harper is trying to sound nonchalant, but her bright eyes and high-pitched voice give her away.

"It was good." I don't turn to look at her.

"Just good?"

"I told you it was no big deal."

"It's a single father from your school," she exclaims at the taboo of it.

"Exactly. It's practically work."

Harper's stare burns the side of my face, and I shrug as I pick up my coffee, blowing some steam off before I can take a sip.

"I'm going to my bedroom. Give you two some *alone* time." I purposefully don't look at Harper as I leave the kitchen, giving Tate a wink on the way past.

When I'm in the comfort of my temporary bedroom, I sit down at the small table in the corner that looks out the window. There's not much of a view except for old city buildings, but I stare out at them as I sip my coffee as if it's Niagara Falls.

My day spent with Jake and Hallie was . . . overwhelming. Not only have I never had so much fun, but also I have never felt so . . . content.

It was comfortable, yet still exciting. Relaxed, yet still exhilarating.

Being with the two of them just felt . . . right.

I'm lowered down onto the floor, which feels like grass underneath my sweaty palms. Everything is in darkness once again, but I hear a voice. Am I dreaming?

The voice is panicked and having a one-sided conversation. He is pacing now, his voice getting louder, but nothing at all about it is familiar to me. I don't know this man and my heart speeds up as panic sets in.

I gasp as my eyes fly open. My lungs are heaving with heavy breaths and my heart pounds like a stampede of elephants are running rampant inside my chest.

Another dream.

"Ughh," I groan, trying to slow my breaths. When will they end? What are they trying to tell me?

Rolling over to my side, I stare at the cream wall, afraid to close my eyes again. The dreams aren't scary. I don't dread thinking back on that night, and I don't suddenly have a fear of fire. But something about the dreams bothers me. Something about them sits heavy on my heart and throws me off whenever I have one.

I stare into space for a moment longer before I drag myself out of bed to shower. I'm catching up with Georgia for a coffee today. I have decided not to tell her about Jake. She knows about my one-night stand with the guy who saved me from the fire, but I just haven't gotten around to telling her about Jake and Hallie entering my classroom on the first day of school.

Okay, so it wasn't that I hadn't gotten around to it, I just never planned to tell her.

After yesterday, things feel different. I know this thing with Jake isn't going to fizzle out anytime soon. I want to tell someone. I also want to get someone's opinion on the whole thing. Well, someone's unbiased opinion. If I just wanted an opinion, I'd ask Harper.

Once I'm showered and ready, I head downstairs to the café. This is one positive of living with Tate and Harper—I don't have to go far for food or entertainment.

Thankfully, the café is pretty quiet on a Sunday. I don't feel like shouting the details of my love life across the loud chatter that normally fills the place on a weekday.

Another bonus of it being a Sunday is that Tate and Maurice are trying to cut back the amount of time they both spend here, so they are now having the day off. I guess with it being so quiet, they felt they could let go of their control somewhat on a Sunday. *Men, pfft.*

I find a small table in the back corner so the staff can't overhear my conversation with Georgia. Having family try to stick their nose in my business is more than enough.

"Hey, sorry I'm late. Traffic was a bitch." Georgia sighs, frustrated, as she takes her purse and hangs it over the back of her chair.

I glance out of the large glass windows that fill the front of the café and watch the eerie desolateness of the street.

I look back at Georgia, who has now taken her seat, and raise my eyebrows.

"Fine," she huffs. "I had a late night and I slept in past my alarm this morning."

"A late night, hey? What did you get up to?" I tease.

Her face drops and her shoulders slouch. "A *Pretty Little Liars* marathon."

Georgia and I stare at one another until a few seconds pass, and then we both laugh our asses off. The hysteria only grows until we are both wiping tears away.

"Shut up," she gets out between her laughter. "I doubt you did anything more exciting."

"Well, actually . . ."

Her face drops, and her laughter immediately ceases. She narrows her eyes on me as if trying to read my face and determine whether I'm messing with her or not.

"Go on," she says sceptically.

"I have something to tell you." Her eyes flare. "I should've told you earlier, but I didn't think anything would come of it. I was also a little shocked, so I guess I just wanted to keep it to myself. I honestly didn't think anything would come of it —"

"Come on, Lana, spit it out already."

"Okay," I breathe. "Remember Jake?"

"The hot Army guy who carried you out of your burning house, only to take you home and burn it up between the sheets?"

"Okay, so you remember him," I deadpan.

"Heck yeah, I do."

"Well, he rocked up to my classroom on the first day of school. I have his daughter, Hallie, in my class." Georgia nods slowly, taking it all in. "He kept asking me out for the first couple days and I kept turning him down. But then I decided, what the hell. We went out yesterday, and to be honest, I had the freaking best time of my life."

Georgia's eyes are now wide as she keeps nodding. "Okay." She drags the word out. "All I can think is, what the fuck, Lana?" I flinch at her words. "He is a scumbag piece of shit, and I can't believe you would even consider talking to him again, let alone *dating* him." The disdain in her voice leaves me speechless. "What a dirty, cheating —"

"What?"

"What?" she repeats after me.

"Cheating?" She nods. "No. Oh my God, Georgia. Jake is a single dad. It's just him and Hallie. Has been for the past four years."

"Holy fuck, Lana." She releases a deep breath, holding her hand over her heart, which I assume is now beating double-time. "Holy fuck. I thought I was going to have to give one of my best friends the *'stop being a dirty home-wrecking whore'* talk."

I crack up laughing as Georgia just shakes her head in dismay. "A home-wrecking whore?"

"Yes." She nods firmly.

"Well, I'm not."

"Well, I'm glad. Now tell me what's been happening." She leans forward. "Wait. Let me get a double shot of espresso to calm my nerves before you start."

"You think a double-shot espresso is going to calm you?"

"Hello, it's me."

"Okay." I laugh as I get up to go make our order.

By the end of our catch up, Georgia has downed two double-shot espressos and her whole body is shaking. I'm not sure if it's all the coffee or all the laughter. My stomach is painfully sore with the overuse of those muscles today.

"Lana, I'm just so happy for you," Georgia says as we walk out of the café two hours later.

I told her everything, from the house fire until our date yesterday. I opened up completely to her about my feelings for Jake and Hallie; how I thought this could be something.

Georgia listened attentively, offering advice, encouragement, and pure elated excitement. It felt good to get it all off my chest and have someone validate my state of mind. Have someone tell me I wasn't totally crazy for feeling this way already about a gorgeous man and his beautiful daughter.

After Georgia and I say our good-byes, I know more than before that I want to see this thing through with Jake and Hallie.

I want it to work.

I need it to work.

Chapter Eleven

Lana

I brush my long red waves down my back. I have never gone to so much trouble for a man before. Never really cared that much about how I looked. I'm confident in my looks. I'm in no way stunning, but I'm pretty enough to gain some attention.

But tonight, I don't want to be just 'pretty enough'. I want to be gorgeous. To look so good I knock Jake's socks off. I want to be the most beautiful woman he has ever known. When he sees me, I don't want him to be able to think of other females. I want to be all he sees.

I take stock of my more glamorous than usual makeup. Dark smoky eyes and bright red lips. I chose to forgo the blush. I'm sure my constant awkwardness will keep my cheeks rosy enough.

Voices float through the apartment and into my room. I rush to my door and fling it open to find Harper and Tate standing in the kitchen talking to Jake, who is standing on the other side of the counter. All three sets of eyes turn to me, but I only meet one of them.

Jake's face lights up when he sees me, and I give him a huge smile. His eyes travel down my body and back up as I make my way over, and his throat moves as he swallows.

"Angel," he breathes. "You look beautiful."

Just as expected, no blush needed.

"I hope this is okay?" I gesture down to my knee-length red silk dress. The dress is a seamless mixture of casual and dressy with the style of a button-up dress shirt, only longer.

"Perfect."

I raise an eyebrow at Jake as I take in his jeans and dress shirt, sleeves rolled up to his elbows.

"Perfect," he says again, his expression unwavering.

A throat clears, and Jake and I both turn to Tate and Harper, who are now just staring at us. Tate's eyes narrow in suspicion, and Harper's face is bright with excitement.

"So you met my brother and his fiancée?"

"We introduced ourselves." Harper smiles.

"Good, well, we should get going," I tell them, not looking their way once as I head straight for the door.

"Nice to meet you both," Jake says, and I see him in my peripheral vision shaking hands with my brother.

I wait just outside on the step and Jake soon follows. Before I'm able to close the door, I hear Harper say, "Well, he seems nice," and my brother grunt in response.

Shaking my head, I shut the door and lead the way down the stairs to Jake's truck.

I love my brother, and I know he has my best interests at

heart. I know he has seen me go through things no brother should, but I'm stronger now. Does he think I'd really fall into that trap again?

It bothers me that he won't give Jake the benefit of the doubt and probably already hates him. Will any man ever be good enough? Especially now after Craig.

Jake opens the passenger door to his truck and I smile, trying to forget about Tate for tonight. I'll deal with him tomorrow.

Wearing a dress probably wasn't a good idea for climbing in and out of Jake's truck. I place one heeled foot on the step and grab onto the handrail inside. I jump in surprise as Jake's hand lands on my lower back. As I pull myself up into the seat, his hand slides over my ass and down the back of my thigh. Jake doesn't react to the touch and just shuts the door and makes his way around the front of the car.

Holy shit. Goosebumps cover my skin, and I'm sure my face says it all. Above the surprise and shock though, sits excitement. I can't remember the last time a man touched me like that, and I don't think it's ever felt so good.

Just the thought of Jake's soft touch running all over my body makes me squeeze my thighs together. Even though we've had sex before, and I've had his hands all over me, this is something different. Those moments in life you can't even explain once you've experienced them because they are so powerful.

Jake jumps in the truck and winks at me as he starts the engine. I turn to stare out the window, trying to keep my nerves in check. When I'm wired up like this, it's likely that I'm going to embarrass myself.

After a few minutes of driving in silence, we are on the main road out of town and Jake reaches across the centre console to grab my hand. I turn to look at him, and his face is reassuring as he links our fingers together. I release a deep breath as my body relaxes and he grins at me. That gorgeous grin doesn't leave his face the whole time we chat on the way to the restaurant.

"Wait here," he says as he pulls into a parking spot in front of the restaurant.

He makes his way around the front of the truck and opens my door. I didn't know men could still be so chivalrous.

Grabbing my waist, he lifts me out of the truck and places me on the ground with a chaste kiss to my lips. The corner of his mouth tilts up, and I give his cheek a peck. Jake locks the truck and takes my hand, leading me into the restaurant.

"Good evening. Welcome to Taboo's." The hostess greets us.

"Good evening. I have a booking for Weston."

The waitress glances down at her paperwork before smiling brightly at Jake. "Right this way, sir."

The restaurant is dimly lit; the only sources of light are the sets of candles used as centrepieces on each table. The tables are set far apart, and there are different screens and separators throughout the small room. This place is definitely made for romance, and I'm almost surprised Jake picked it.

Once the waitress has sat us down at our table and read the specials, we order drinks and settle in.

"This is a beautiful place. Come here often?" I ask, fishing for information.

"No." He chuckles. "They don't exactly have a kid's menu here."

"You only buy your dates kid's meals?" I tease.

"Date? I've only dated one girl since my wife."

"Oh." I frown.

"Hallie." He laughs.

"Oh. I'm surprised. Didn't you say your wife died four years ago?"

"Yes," he says, his face expressionless.

"Oh." My eyes go wide.

"Oh." He smirks.

Jake reaches across the table and entwines our fingers again. Holding his hand has quickly become my favourite thing to do. I think I could probably spend the rest of my life happy just holding his hand.

The waitress returns for our orders, and Jake asks if he can order on behalf of us both, not even glancing at the menu.

"If you haven't been here before, then how do you know the menu by heart?"

"Someone from work suggested this place. They also recommended the meal." Jake frowns at that for a moment before straightening his features and smiling at me. I wonder what that was about but decide not to ask, wanting to keep tonight light.

Apparently, we both feel the same about that as we enjoy our meals and each other's company, keeping the topics of conversation general and light-hearted.

We speak about Hallie, our siblings, his sister's kids, our jobs, and even our childhoods, but neither one of us ventures into the other person's past. Jake doesn't ask about my previous relationships, and he didn't mention his wife. I think we both want to pretend this is a fresh start for us. Well, at least that's what I'm thinking. I don't want our tragic baggage weighing our first official date down.

I know we will eventually have to deal with all that history, but even if just for tonight, I want to pretend we are baggage free.

Once we have stuffed ourselves with dessert and coffee, Jake requests the cheque, and we make our way out of the restaurant, his hand on my lower back.

As we step outside, a cold breeze blows past and I wrap my arms around myself, realising in my haste to get out of the apartment that I forgot to grab my jacket. Jake looks over at me and wraps a strong arm around my shoulders, pulling me tight against his side.

My body warms from the inside out at his closeness and the comfort of his embrace, and I bask in it all the way to his truck.

Jake only loosens his hold once we reach the truck and he has to unlock it. He opens my door for me and as I go to climb in, he grabs my arm and spins me around. His mouth is on mine in an instant, and he pushes my back against the truck.

His kiss is fierce, telling me all I need to know. And I know Jake Weston wants me. *Oh, he wants me bad.* It takes only seconds before I catch up to him and wrap my arms around his neck, pulling him down harder into me.

He doesn't break the kiss as he grabs both my thighs and lifts me up into the passenger seat, spreading my legs and pushing himself between them.

A moan escapes me as he rubs up against my core. His hard denim-covered cock rubs in all the right places to set my body on fire. Warmth and fireworks run through my veins, pushing me closer and closer to the edge as he swivels his hips while continuing the punishing force of his kiss.

Oh my God, he's going to make me come. Right here, in this dark parking lot with my skirt hiked up around my waist and my wet panties out for everyone to see.

And I don't even care.

Jake pulls back and nuzzles into my neck. We are both breathing hard as our bodies rise and fall against one another.

"Come home with me," he gets out between breaths.

"What?"

"Please. Please stay, stay with me tonight."

"What about Hallie?"

Jake pulls back to look at me. "She's at Marley's tonight. I don't have to pick her up until tomorrow."

He grinds his hips into me once more, rubbing in that perfect way, and I whimper. Jake's fierce gaze meets mine as he waits for an answer.

"Yes," I breathe, and his eyes light up.

Chapter Twelve

Jake

With the vibration of the truck, Lana's hand held in mine, and her scent surrounding me, I got no relief from my rock hard cock the whole way home. We sat in nervous excitement, the lust and fierce need from the parking lot dissipated, with neither one of us saying a word or making a move.

I held onto her hand, never once loosening my grip. I needed to keep her grounded, to keep her anchored to me. I could tell she was nervous, and I did not want her changing her mind on the ride back to my place.

Now she stands on my front porch, looking anywhere but at me as I unlock the house to let us in.

In the parking lot, the need between us was so high and spontaneous that I didn't have any time to second-guess myself or to fear rejection. Now, standing here, with the anticipation of what's to come, nerves have overtaken me.

Me? Fucking nervous?

I don't think I've ever been so tense, and I've travelled into war zones, for fuck's sake. Even though we have done this before, this time is different. The first time was impulsive, and we were never supposed to see each other again. This time it's premediated. I have thought about this moment for so fucking long. I care how it goes. I care what Lana thinks, and I want it to be so fucking memorable that she will never think about doing this with anyone else ever again.

Pushing open the front door, I step in and hold it open for Lana to follow. She enters and my gaze follows her as she stands in the entryway, wringing her fingers together.

I meander over to her, taking my time, trying not to scare her. She is a deer caught in the headlights, and I'm worried one small move will cause her to bolt. Grabbing her hand, I entwine our fingers, once again anchoring her to me.

"You're nervous," I whisper.

She nods, her throat moving with her swallow.

"I'm fucking nervous too."

Lana laughs and my whole body takes a breath as it relaxes, softening into her as I pull her into my arms and kiss her. This kiss is not like the others. It's not hard or punishing. I take my time. I build her comfort up as I kiss, nibble, and lick her lips.

Pulling back, I grin as Lana stands there, her eyes shut and a small smile on her face. I give her lips one last peck and then drag her down the hallway to my bedroom.

I place her in the middle of my room and take her in. I love having her here. I want her here on a permanent basis. When she's in here, I want to know she is mine and that I can do anything I want to her . . . and with her.

Kneeling down by her feet, I run my palms up from her ankles to the tops of her thighs. Her skin is soft and supple, and I groan at the feel of it against my calloused hands. My caresses continue over her hips and up her stomach, taking her dress farther up her body until I glide my hands over her breasts and shoulders. Lana raises her arms and I slide the dress over her head, letting the light silk material float to the floor behind her.

She stands in front of me in a black lace bra and matching panties. They are modest but sexy, and I have no doubt she is the hottest fucking thing I have ever seen. My cock strains against my jeans, and I adjust it to get some relief.

"You are so fucking beautiful."

Lana gives me a shy smile and then crosses her arms over her stomach.

"No. Don't do that." I grab her arms and pull them apart. "I have been dreaming of you for months. Dreaming of seeing you again, like this." I cup her face in one hand and step closer to her. Our bodies are in line and pushed up against each other in perfect sync. "It's fucking better than how I've been remembering it."

Leaning in, I kiss her mouth, her nose, and her eyes. Her lips part and she breathes heavily, her chest rising and falling harshly against my own.

I lead her to the bed and lay her down in the middle of it. Standing in front of her, I kick off my boots and tug at my socks. Reaching behind my neck, I pull my shirt off, dropping it to the floor, then strip off my jeans before I crawl over her, throwing her shoes off as I go. I rest my weight on one forearm beside her head. Her body is stiff and her expression is rigid.

"Tell me why you're nervous," I whisper into her ear before I lay a soft kiss underneath it, my breath flowing over her neck. She squirms beneath me. I know I affect her; it's not that she doesn't want this.

"I've only ever really been with my ex-husband. Well, besides some awkward drunken nights in college and . . . you."

"What?" I lean back to look at her.

She's biting her lip and staring at the ceiling, almost refusing to meet my gaze. "He said. He said—"

"He said what, sweetheart?" I can see the anguish on her face, and I already know I'm going to want to punch him in the face for whatever 'he' said.

"He said I wasn't very good at it." She squeezes her eyes closed, as if waiting for the blow.

"Angel." I smile, and Lana's eyes shoot open to meet mine. "You forget that we have already done this. Okay, yeah, it was under different circumstances, but it was still fucking unreal. Trust me, you are fucking good at this." I grab her hand and place it on my hard cock. "See just how good you are? See what you do to me?"

Lana gives my cock a squeeze, and I groan, nuzzling my head back in her neck as I kiss, bite, and lick every inch of skin.

"He was a selfish lover," she whispers, pulling me from my lustful haze.

I lean back again, not really wanting to hear this but giving her all my attention anyway. I want to know everything there is to know about this woman, and if this is when she decides she wants to talk, I am fucking going to listen. She meets my eyes this time, and I hope she reads everything they are trying to say. *'You can talk to me. You're safe here. I've got you'.*

"I'd never had an orgasm during sex before you and I, well, you know."

It takes everything in me to hide my shock. To make sure my face remains impassive. "You'd had orgasms before though, right?"

"Yeah." She bites her lip again. "Mostly self-induced."

My eyes do go wide this time. I can't help it. What the fuck? Lana is the most beautiful, sweet, caring, and sexy woman I know. How could you not make it your number one priority to please her? As soon as those bright green eyes had popped open on my lap that night, I knew I wanted to see them satisfied and content with pleasure after she had just come apart at the seams because of my touch.

I drag my hand from the base of her neck, between her breasts, and down her stomach. I lean up and follow the same path with soft kisses. "Oh, angel, I have so much to show you."

Chapter Thirteen

Lana

Jake's lips descend my body, his eyes laughing with me, leaving a trail of goosebumps as he goes. My body shakes as he slides my panties down my legs and he gets closer to my core. I knew exactly what those mischievous eyes were telling me.

Light kisses caress my pubic bone and I squirm underneath his touch. I gasp as he tugs my short landing strip of pubic hair with his mouth. "This is so fucking sexy," he growls. Warmth moves up from my chest, and I know my face is probably the same colour as the hair he just pulled. I've learned to love my vagina's individuality, but for the first time ever, I'm self-conscious about it.

Jake tugs it one more time before he lays kisses over my hipbone and down my thigh. I whimper as they trail farther and farther away from where I need them. He chuckles and whispers, "Relax, angel," as he licks and nibbles down my leg and back up again until his mouth is resting on my sex.

He breathes deeply against my skin before lathering me in sweet kisses. "Please," I beg, my body shaking with anticipation.

"No," he whispers against me. "I wanted to taste you so bad last time. I'm savouring it."

I moan in frustration and shift beneath him. Jake chuckles again, but before I can scold him for teasing me, his warm tongue glides delicately through my folds. He sweeps his tongue in gentle strokes up and around my core. My body trembles, and I hold my breath as the sensations tighten my whole body, his movements pushing me closer and closer to the edge without nudging me over.

This is not my first experience with oral sex. But in all the years I was with Craig, it never felt like this. He gave it a good go. Actually, I think he coined the phrase 'eating out', as that's what he seemed to be doing. After a year of trying and never getting anywhere, he finally gave up.

I had no idea it could feel like this. So torturous, so overwhelming, so . . . toe curling.

And that's exactly what I do. I press my heels into the bed as Jake circles my clit before he sucks it into his mouth. My hips arch off the mattress of their own accord, and I scream out in ecstasy, my body floating into euphoria.

Jake holds my hips down as I writhe against his mouth, which is now lazily stroking me, pushing everything out of this orgasm.

Who knew a self-administered orgasm could feel so different to one given by someone else? I don't think I'll ever be able to satisfy myself again after this.

Warm kisses line a path up my stomach to my breasts. Opening my eyes, I meet chocolate brown ones. Emotion shines bright out of their warm depths. They are soft, in awe, and a little smug. I give him a slow, satisfied smile, and he grins.

Kissing my neck and collarbone, Jake reaches under me and undoes my bra, pulling it off my arms and throwing it to the floor. He leans back and gazes down at my breasts. Goosebumps break out over my skin, but I keep myself from crossing my arms over my chest at his serious perusal.

He keeps staring as he leans down and takes one nipple into his mouth. His attentions are gentle at first, licking and suckling as he kneads the other breast, but they soon turn rough, needy, and demanding, with hard sucks and biting while he pinches my other nipple.

I had no idea you could come from breast-play alone, but just as I'm moaning and begging, that's what's about to happen. Jake groans against my skin and then his touch is gone as he shoves down his briefs, kicking them off his ankles.

A rush of air leaves me, my body taking the reprieve of his touch as a chance to catch my breath. But I don't want to catch my breath. If it means the loss of his touch, then I don't want to breathe properly ever again. I could easily live off his touch alone.

Jake leans over me, his body snug between my legs. The need to close my eyes overwhelms me, but his eyes boring into my own hold me captive. Manoeuvring his hips, he places the tip of himself at my entrance. This time I do close my eyes, the relief of it finally happening washing over me. It's almost as if I've waited a lifetime for this.

He moves into me slowly, and at first, I wonder what the hell he is doing, but then I gasp as he pushes in deep, burying himself inside me. He pulls back gently and I whimper at the loss of him, the head of his cock dragging in all the right places before he thrusts deep again. He continues this pace, and my mind is blown at how wonderful it feels. How he not only fills me so deeply, so wholly, but fills my heart too. Fills it with love, trust, and passion, and I know I've never felt anything like this before. Nothing even comes close.

The euphoric build begins again, and I'm climbing and climbing before an earth-shattering orgasm sets off inside me. Jake cries out his own release buried deep inside me and falls down onto my chest, every small thrust milking his orgasm and having mine continue to ripple through me with waves of consuming pleasure.

He lies on top of me, my body holding all his weight, and the aftermath of it all is so overwhelming that tears well up behind my closed eyes. I enjoy every piece of the moment, every detail. His warm breath flows over my neck as he nuzzles me, his fingers grazing the skin of my arm, rubbing up and down lazily, and a light sheen of sweat covers both our bodies.

Rolling us over onto our sides, Jake smiles down at me. "Are you okay?"

I frown in confusion at his concern. I'm pretty sure my expression says that I'm more than okay.

"I don't know why I'm asking. I just feel like I should. That was . . ." He pauses in thought.

"Amazing, wonderful, mind blowing." I suggest just a few of the words running through my mind. I hold on tight to the words that float along at the forefront but scare the absolute living shit out of me. *Love, forever, mine.*

"Yeah," he breathes. "It fucking was."

He pulls me into him and wraps his arms around me. His hold is so tight I struggle to catch a breath as he shoves me against his chest. Giggling, I turn my head to the side to find an air pocket through his arms.

"Sorry," he says sheepishly, his voice low. "I just . . ."

Jake doesn't finish his sentence, and I don't ask. I just wrap myself around him as I lay my arm over his waist and shove a leg between his. We lie in silence in our tangled mess of limbs, our fingers gently rubbing over each other's backs.

Even though we are together, it's as if we're in our own worlds. I can sense our minds both ticking over in thought. I would give anything to know what he's thinking. I would give anything to know what I'm thinking. I can't make sense of any of it as the last week and tonight just keep running over and over in my head.

We lie in silence for a while longer, and I bring my hand to his chest, rubbing light circles over it.

"What happened to your wife?" My voice, as quiet as it is, breaks the silence in our love bubble like a window smashing in a storm. Jake looks down at me, his eyebrows drawn, not answering immediately.

He then looks at the ceiling, his gaze going blank. I know he is taking himself back there, back to that point in time. Deep down, as much as I want to tell him all about my past, I hope he doesn't ask because I don't want to go back there. I never want to look back again.

"I left for a tour after Hallie was born. She was only three months old, and I knew Jamie was reluctant about it. I assured her as much as I could. She had support here—her family, Marley. I just don't think it was enough."

Jake looks down at me, sadness in his eyes, and I know I'm not going to like what comes next. "She sent me a letter. Told me she couldn't do it anymore. She felt trapped here with Hallie and was moving out and into her parents' house." His eyes shift from mine once more. "I think she resented me for leaving her."

"I'm so sorry, Jake." I place a small kiss on his chest.

"I don't think we had a strong enough foundation to survive. Jamie definitely wasn't suited for that lifestyle. Not that anyone is, but I guess some cope better than others do. She sacrificed, I know she did, but . . ." He sighs and pulls me tighter against him. "I thought being a father in the Army would be a benefit to our family. That being good at one only made me better at the other. I feel like I failed at both."

"Oh, Jake, you were doing what you thought was right."

His eyes meet mine. "I was. I believed in my mission, in serving my country."

In that moment, I see the soldier. The fierce determination in his eyes that I imagine was there every day while he was away. "People can't ask for more than that."

He gives me a sad smile. "I like to have people I can depend on, who are there for me. And I like that they can depend on me too."

I hug him tighter, just wanting to scream *'you can depend on me, Jake'*.

Chapter Fourteen

Jake

"You're loyal, Jake. Loyal and dedicated."

Her words slay me. *Look what it's making me to do to you, Lana.* My loyalty to a brother, causing my lies and deceit.

"See?" She waggles her eyebrows. "You really are a hero, not just saving me."

I feel sick. She thinks I'm a hero. I'm a fucking liar—no one's saviour. I push her away from me and jump out of bed. I'm going to be sick. Dashing to the bathroom sink, I turn on the tap, drenching my face with the cold water.

I sense Lana's presence before she speaks, and I stand up straight, grabbing the hand towel and drying my face, preparing for her questions.

"What happened after, Jake?"

Turning to look at her, I frown. I wasn't expecting that question. "After what?"

"You told me your wife was dead. I haven't seen her around, and Hallie rarely mentions her."

"She did die," I breathe, relieved that my hasty exit from the bed didn't draw any red flags for Lana.

I lean back against the bathroom counter and rest my hands on either side of my hips. "Towards the end of my tour, Jamie was in a car accident." Lana gasps and covers her mouth. "I was sent home early. And I've been here ever since."

"I'm so sorry, Jake," she whispers.

"Don't be sorry for me, angel. I didn't lose a wife; I lost the mother of my daughter. It's Hallie I worry about."

Lana's expression straightens, but her eyes speak volumes. They are soft, comforting. She steps towards me and wraps her arms around my waist, holding me tight. I pull her closer and rest my chin on top of her head.

I don't know how long we stand there until Lana finally breaks the silence.

"I like this," she says as she runs her palm over my left shoulder blade. I glance back in the mirror and see her fingers tracing my tattoo. She fingers all the tiny soldiers that together make the shape of a feather and then runs her touch over the words '*Lest We Forget*'.

"You said you're still in the Army?" She rests her chin on my chest and looks up at me.

I take her in for a moment, her expressive green eyes, the smattering of freckles across her nose and cheeks, those red plump lips. "Yeah." I kiss her nose. "I work on base now." I kiss her lips.

"Oh." She nods. I kiss her eyes in turn.

"Oh." I repeat, kissing under her ear.

No more words are spoken as I pick Lana up and carry her to back to bed, making love to her again. Except this time, it's not sweet love. It's not soft, or slow, or gentle. It's hard love. It's rough, and hot, and sweaty.

I hold her hands above her head and hold her body down with my own. There is biting, spanking, and sucking, and I'm sure even some bruising. It doesn't have to be sweet or slow all the time, but I can feel with her. Just be myself with her.

I'm jerked awake as Lana's body freezes in my arms. She whimpers and I shake my head, trying to wake myself up. Light shines through the edges of the blinds and the room is warm, so it must be early morning.

Lana whimpers again as she shakes her head from side to side. My mind goes straight back to that night, holding her on my lap, her scared moans and terrified sobs.

All those thoughts do is lead me back to what I did to her. What I'm doing to her. Lying to her about that night, why I was there, and what I did.

"Angel," I whisper in her ear, not wanting to startle her if she's having a nightmare. "Angel, I'm here."

Her eyes pop open, much like they did that first night at the fire. They are wide as they swing around the room, trying to anchor herself in reality. They finally meet mine and soften in realisation and relief; her panicked look disappearing.

"I'm here, angel."

She gives me a sleepy grin. "It's always you saving me."

My stomach drops and I hide my face in her neck, unable to look at her. "Do you have nightmares about the fire?"

"A lot recently." My heart skips a beat. "It's funny, though—it's never your face in my dreams." My body stills and I hold my breath. I should tell her. This is the perfect time to tell her and to explain the fucked-up situation Brad put me in. "Not that it's someone else's face. There's just no face. It's blank."

I close my eyes and breathe in her smell. Taking several deep breaths, I use her vanilla scent to calm me. I'm a fucking coward. I can't tell her. Not now. Not ever.

Lana's stomach rumbles, and in the silence of the bedroom, it sounds like a freight train just rolled through. She cracks up laughing, her body shaking against mine.

"Hungry?" I pull back to look at her. Her smile is relaxed, happy, and satisfied, and it's the most beautiful thing I've seen. So different to all the smiles I've seen before this. Smiles full of trepidation, caution, and sometimes even a little sadness.

I want to see this smile more. I want to be the cause of this smile. Every day. Every day for the rest of my life.

"Famished." She grins, rubbing her stomach.

"Can I make you breakfast?" I kiss her lips.

"I don't know, can you?"

I frown at her. "Angel, I'm a single dad. Of course, I can." Her eyes go wide in surprise. "Well . . ." I shrug, "I had to learn."

She laughs and I place one more smacking kiss on her lips before I hop out of bed. The warmth of her stare follows me all the way to the bathroom.

"You can take a shower while I get breakfast ready, if you'd like?" I offer leaving the bathroom after taking a leak.

"That would be great, thanks." She blushes and my dick stirs at the sight. The thought of last night and the blush that covered her chest and body as she came apart beneath me makes me want to jump back into bed with her.

She gives me a small smile, and I realise I am standing here at the end of the bed, naked, just staring at her. "Sorry." I grin. I can't believe she can still be shy around me after last night.

I march over to my chest of drawers, once again feeling her stare on my back, and pull out two pairs of briefs, two T-shirts, and two pairs of tracksuit pants. I pull on my own set and lay Lana's on top of the dresser.

"You can wear those after if you want."

"Thanks." She's sitting up now, the sheet pulled tight around her chest, covering those perfect tits, and I decide to make a run for the kitchen, nodding to her on my way out before I change my mind.

I get to making breakfast, placing the bacon on the skillet as I hear the shower start. I stop what I'm doing and think of Lana. Her slim, naked body. The hot water running down over her tits, down her little waist and through that sexy-as-fuck red hair. *Jesus, Jake, calm down.*

Shaking my head, I readjust myself in my pants and get back to work, cracking and beating eggs for omelettes. I'm not sure what Lana eats so I keep it pretty simple with ham, cheese, and tomato in one, and cheese, tomato, and mushroom in another.

I'm mindlessly whisking when a sweet voice floats though my house. There is a deep and husky tone to it, and even though I'm not down with the top music charts, I'm sure it's an Adele song.

She sings about being someone's one and only, about being worthy, and I want so bad for her to be singing about me.

Her voice is smooth and sultry before she hits a high tone that sends shivers up my spine. It's not lost on me that she sounds like a fucking angel.

It's not long after the beautiful singing stops that feet slap against the kitchen floor and I turn to find Lana standing near the doorway. Something has to be said about a woman wearing her man's clothes. The picture in front of me—Lana dressed head to toe in my clothes—makes my breath catch. Knowing she has my briefs on under there makes my dick stir.

"That was quite the performance." I raise my eyebrows and then chuckle at the blush that appears on Lana's cheeks. "You sing." It's not a question.

"Only in the shower," she says as she walks into the kitchen, brushing me off. But for some reason, I don't believe her.

"Need a hand?" she asks.

"No, I'm good. Just finishing off the toast. Have a seat." I gesture to the kitchen table.

Lana nods and takes a seat at the table, tapping her fingers absentmindedly.

"You okay?" I turn to look at her after throwing the pan in the sink, trying to read her expression.

"Yeah, I'm great," she says, sitting up straight.

I nod but don't say anything and carry both our plates over to the table, which I had set while she was in the shower.

"This looks great. Thank you so much."

"You're welcome. I'm not a bad cook. You should come over for dinner one night. I know Hallie would love that." What I really want to say is come for dinner every night. You could come, eat and then stay.

"I'd love that too." Her eyes shine with excitement and my heart starts beating at double-time. I'm sure she feels the same, feels the connection we have, but I can still see something lingering in the back of her eyes that has her holding back.

Maybe I've just lost it, seeing as I haven't dated in so long. Yeah, that's probably it. I've become desperate, needy, and clingy. I think my biological clock is ticking.

Fuck. I've become a chick.

I pull back on the reins in my head. I don't want to scare her off. I'm going to have to restrain myself from here on in.

Choosing to go with that, I push back the thoughts of trying to have her one more time before I drop her home and decide a cold shower would be best.

Once I've cleared the table from breakfast, told Lana she is not allowed to clean up, and set her up in front of the TV, I head straight for the bathroom and an icy shower. The semi-hard-on I've had all morning is not going to enjoy this, and I cringe at the discomfort I know I'm about to inflict upon myself.

The drive into the city to Lana's brother's apartment is quiet. She fiddles with the material of her dress, which she holds in a folded up pile on her lap, her high heels resting on top.

"Everything okay?" I grab her hand and pull it to rest on my thigh.

"Yeah." Her voice is distracted and her smile weak.

"What's going on, angel?" The weariness and uncertainty is back in her eyes, and I need it gone. I want the Lana from bed this morning. The playful, sweet, and sassy Lana.

"I'm sorry. I'm just thinking about school this week."

"You got a busy week?"

"No." She laughs. "*Us* at school this week."

"Is it against the rules?" Would it matter if it was?

"No, not really. Maybe frowned upon." She shifts in her seat.

"I don't get what's going on here, angel."

"That's kind of my question too," she whispers. My head whips to hers, taking my eyes fully off the road for the first time. A horn blasts and I look to see I am drifting into the next lane.

"Fuck." I drive along a bit further until I find a spot to pull off on the side of the road.

"Are you asking me what this is? *Us?*" I gesture between us.

"Yeah, I guess so." She cringes.

"Angel. Fuck." I shake my head. "I want this. Last night wasn't a one-time thing. I want to date you. To be with you." I try to hide my frustration. Have I not made this obvious? I practically chased her and begged her to go out with me. Then after last night . . . Fuck, women are fickle creatures.

"Oh, okay."

"Oh, okay?" I stare at her expectantly. "Well, is that what you want?" For the first time today, I feel tentative.

She nods. "Yes, it is."

My shoulders relax and a huge smile breaks out on my face. "We're doing this?"

She nods again. There is no hesitation in her eyes. No uncertainty or worry. Pure, unadulterated happiness shines out of those emerald orbs and my heart, loud and proud. I want to fist pump the air. I have caused that smile twice today. And fuck, do I love that.

"We're doing this," I whisper as I lean over the centre console and place my lips on hers. Her surprise only lasts a second before she is wrapping her fingers behind my neck and pulling me to her. Taking my sweet kiss to a whole new level of desire and need.

She sweeps her tongue across my bottom lip, and I immediately open and allow her entrance, our mouths duelling and dancing all at once. I break our kiss and grab her by the waist, pulling her up to straddle my lap.

Nuzzling my face into her neck, I kiss, nibble, and lick every piece of skin, biting her earlobe and then sucking it before pulling back to smile at her.

She holds me tight around my shoulders and smiles down at

me. "We better get going."

I chuckle. Shy Lana is back. I'm going to have to work on that.

Pulling up in front of the café, my stomach turns at having to say good-bye to her. I don't want to let her go, but we discussed taking things slowly. Not only because neither of us has done this for a while and we don't want to rush into anything but also for Hallie's sake. As much as I couldn't stand to hurt Lana, I would die if Hallie got too attached and then we hurt her. No matter what, I have to think of Hallie first, and what is best for her.

Hopping out of my truck, I walk around to the passenger door to open it up for her. I love how I don't even have to tell her to stay in the truck anymore—she just knows. I smile as I pull open her door and she slips out. Before she can pass so I can close the door, I reach around her waist and pull her back to me. Our lips meet and I kiss her hard. I don't know if I'm going to get to see her this week, so I'm going to get my fill.

We kiss until we're forced apart, needing to catching our breath.

"Wow," she exhales.

"Yeah." I try to suck air in.

That kiss is all I think about on the drive to Marley's house to pick Hallie up. How the fuck am I going to go all week without seeing her now that I know she's mine? We need to come up with a better schedule. It's not as if Hallie doesn't know her. And it's not as if I bring random women home. Lana is the first woman in four years, so surely it wouldn't kill Hallie to have her around a bit. In fact, it would probably benefit for her to have a female role model.

Lana said we're doing this. She said she was in. It's balls to the wall.

With my mind made up, I grab my phone from the centre console and make a few phone calls.

When I walk into Marley's place, my head is held high and shoulders relaxed.

"Hey, baby brother." Marley turns from the dishes she is washing.

"Hey." I give her a kiss on the cheek.

"What's that goofy smile for?" She smirks. "Good night, then?"

"Great night."

"Oh my God, look at you. You're practically floating," she teases.

"It fucking feels like it."

"Oh my God." Her face drops. "That's not just *I got laid* happy. You really like her."

"I *really* fucking like her."

"Jake," she screeches.

"Daddy." Hallie comes running into the kitchen, jumping into my arms before I can catch her. She hangs on like a monkey, and I laugh as I settle my arms around her.

"Princess. I missed you."

"I missed you too, Daddy." She kisses my cheek.

"Did you have a good time?"

"Yeah." She sighs. "I beat Thomas in ping pong, and he called me a boy."

"Oh, that's not nice."

"It's okay. I kicked him in the nuts," she says, pride in her voice.

"Hallie."

"What? Brady told me to." I can see Marley watching me, so I sigh as though I'm deeply disappointed. I can't show how proud of her I really am. That's my girl.

117

"I got a surprise for you." I decide to change the subject.

"What is it? What is it?" She bounces up and down in my arms, and my heart warms at her excitement.

"Wanna go get a dog?"

"Oh, my goodness, Daddy, really?"

"Yep." I pop her back down on the floor. "Go pack up your stuff so we can go."

"Yesss!" She runs out of the kitchen. "Thomas, guess what?"

I laugh loudly until I turn back to my sister. Her hands are on her hips and her eyebrows are raised.

"What?"

"You sure you know what you doing?"

"No. As parents do we ever really know what we're doing?"

"No." She laughs. "I suppose not."

I smile wide at her. Fuck. I definitely know I have no idea.

Chapter Fifteen

Lana

"Well, well, well. Look who's home."

I shut the apartment door and turn to see Harper kneeling over the back of the couch, a huge shit-eating grin plastered on her face.

"So last night went well."

I try to act casual, but a warm blush rises up my cheeks. "It was no big deal."

"That outfit begs to differ." She waggles her eyebrows.

Glancing down, I realise I'm still dressed in Jake's tracksuit pants and T-shirt. And his undies, but I won't be telling Harper that. Shit.

"Is Tate home?" My eyes flash around the apartment, waiting for him to pop out.

"Lee called in sick today so he's helping out at the café."

"Thank God," I breathe, relieved.

"Don't want your protective baby brother to see you do the walk of shame?" Harper laughs.

"Shut up," I tell her as I make my way to my bedroom, realising that if Tate was at the café, he probably got a great view of mine and Jake's goodbye.

"Looks good on you," she calls out.

I stop at the threshold of my room. "Jake's clothes?"

"No. That smile. Happiness."

I return her grin before closing my door, throwing my handbag and my folded pile of last night's clothes on the bed and toppling down after them.

I know it makes no difference whether Tate caught me or not—because Harper is going to tell him anyway. God, I can't wait to move back to my own house. I feel like a teenager again living here with those two.

Releasing a deep breath, I roll over and try to close my eyes for a while. Not only did Jake keep me up and active until all hours of the morning, but I was woken early with one of my dreams. Today's has played on my mind longer than the others have. Something didn't feel right about it. I'm not sure why. It was the same dream I've had countless times.

Someone carrying me out, laying me on the front lawn. That blank face. That same blank face that has been torturing me for months. Why can't I see Jake? The only additions I got to this dream were voices. This morning in my dream, I heard two people talking.

Of course, I didn't recognise the voices, and I couldn't make out what they were saying, but something about them bothered me. One of them was angry, frustrated, the other scared and frantic.

My phone rings from my bag, and for a second, I consider

120

letting it ring. Even just thinking about the dream wears me out. But then, who would be calling me on a Sunday?

Jake's name flashes up on my screen, and I try to contain my excitement. It's probably nothing. I most likely just left something in his truck.

"Hello?" I shake my head at myself. He knows his name would've come up on my phone; why do I sound like I don't know who it is?

"Lana."

"Oh, hi." *Jesus Lana, get it together.*

"Hi." Jake chuckles. "I'm coming to pick you up."

"What?"

"I want to take you somewhere. Are you free?" His tone is low with hesitation.

"Yes." I draw out the word.

"Good." I can hear the smile in his voice. "I'll be there in an hour."

He hangs up and I am left staring at my phone, excitement and anticipation flowing through me.

I decide to take another shower since I didn't get a proper one at Jake's. I wash my hair and get to use my favourite Laura Mercier Vanilla Crème Puff Body Wash that Brooke got me for my birthday. It's supposed to lure the men in, she had said. Hmm, maybe she was right. I pour an extra squeeze on the sponge just in case.

When I step out of the bedroom, Harper is still on the couch, watching some bad reality TV.

"I think he might be here," she says, her eyes not leaving the TV. "Quickest date turnaround I've ever seen. You must have really made an impression."

"Shit," I mutter and sprint towards the front door, Harper's laughter following me out of the apartment.

As soon as I step out and slam the door behind me, I see Jake leaning up against the passenger door of his truck as he laughs with Tate. I stop in my tracks and enjoy the view in front of me. Jake's strong arms are folded over his hard chest, his stance casual, and smile relaxed. I love that he's chatting with my brother. That it seems they are getting along. Tate and Craig never got along, although there's no need to wonder why.

I take my time walking down the steps, trying to contain my eagerness at seeing him again.

"Hey," I say when I reach his side.

"Angel." Jake smiles and kisses my cheek. I don't miss my brother's raised eyebrows.

"Lana," a little voice shouts, and I look in the back of the truck to see Hallie strapped in her seat.

"Princess." I smile excitedly as I practically push Jake out of the way to hop in the passenger door. "How was your sleepover? Thomas give you any trouble?"

"Yeah." She sighs.

"You tell him how it makes you feel?"

"Umm, sure." She nods and I laugh, knowing that's not at all how she handled her older cousin.

"You ladies ready?" Jake pops his head inside the cab, and Hallie and I both nod eagerly.

I give Tate a small wave as Jake makes his way around the front of the truck before hopping in. Tate winks and gives me one of his huge grins. Settling back in my seat, I smile. My brother likes my boyfriend.

"What are you smiling at?" Jake asks as he pulls away from the curb.

"Nothing."

"Sure." He smiles.

"So where are we going?"

"Daddy said—"

"Hallie, remember? It's a surprise."

"Oh, yeah." She laughs. "I forgot."

On the way to wherever we are going, we chat about Hallie's night with her cousins. Well, we don't chat so much as Hallie informs us of every little thing that happened, and Jake and I just listen, nodding along.

Jake pulls into the local animal shelter parking lot and parks in front of the building's glass doors.

"What are we doing here?" I ask.

"Getting a dog," Hallie screams from the backseat.

"Really?" I raise my eyebrows at Jake. "Getting a dog from a shelter rather than the pet shop. Always the hero, aren't we?" I laugh but Jake doesn't. His jaw is tight as he just stares at me, his eyes unreadable. "So you gave in, did you?"

"Something like that," he mutters, still not taking his gaze off me.

"Isn't it exciting?" Hallie says, breaking our awkward moment. *What was that about?*

"So what do you need me for?" I ask him.

"We want you to pick it with us. Don't we, princess?" Jake says.

"Yep," She pops the *P.* "Daddy says it's probably going to be your dog one day anyway."

My gaze shoots to Jake, and he winces. When he realises I'm looking at him, he gives me a sheepish smile and a shrug.

"Why will it be yours, Lana? You're not going to steal my new dog, are you?" All the excitement has left Hallie's voice, confusion replacing it.

"No, baby," I say, my eyes not leaving Jake's. He reaches over the console and intertwines our fingers. Squeezing his hand, I give him a warm smile. "Well, let's go then."

"Yeah, let's go then," Hallie shouts, breaking our moment.

Jake and I laugh, and we all get out of the truck and head into the shelter.

Walking through the corridor past all the cages, I realise this probably wasn't a good idea. The sad puppy faces all stare up at me and pull on my heartstrings. I stop at each and every cage, slipping my hand through and giving them a pat.

"Is there something in particular you are looking for?" Brenda, the lady who volunteers at the shelter, narrows her eyes at me.

"Well, we . . ." Jake gestures to himself and Hallie, "are looking for a family-friendly dog, medium to lots of energy, good with other pets. Lana . . ." he points to me, kneeling in front of a cage, "is probably currently planning to stage a breakout."

I glance up to Jake, and he gives me his cheekiest grin. I roll my eyes, laughing, and shake my head.

"Okay." Brenda frowns. "I have a few options down the back in the larger kennels." She moves down the hallway, and Jake and Hallie follow behind. I give Heather, the scruffy Poodle, another pat before I unwillingly straggle behind the group. I wonder if I could get a dog for my place when I move back. Maybe Tate and Harper would like a puppy. Probably not suitable for their apartment. What about Maurice? Don't old single people always want a pet for companionship?

"Angel," Jake calls, and I jog to catch up to them. I'll have to think about my rehoming plan another time.

"Lana, look at this one," Hallie calls from inside a cage.

I crouch down to pop my head in and find Hallie sitting on the cold concrete floor, a huge golden Labrador lying across her lap. Her face is pure elation as she rubs her hand over the dog's back, and he burrows into her.

"Oh Hal, he's perfect."

"His name is Max," she says.

"Awesome name," I tell her, reaching in and petting the beautiful dog's head. He is huge, almost twice the size of Hallie.

"He is a great choice," Brenda says to Jake. "Labradors are known for their great temperament. Great with kids and other animals. They do shed a lot but don't normally drool." Jake nods, his index finger rubbing over his lips as his mind ticks over all the facts. "He is a lovely dog. Only came in a few days ago, and he's only here because his owner passed away and the family had nowhere for him to go. I don't think he'll be with us long."

Jake nods again and then pops his head in the cage. "What do you think?"

"I love him, Daddy," Hallie drones.

I glance at Jake to read his reaction to Hallie's dramatic flare, but his eyes are on me. "What do I think?" I ask, my eyes wide.

"Yeah, angel, what do you think?"

My heart softens, and I worry I'm going to melt into a puddle. He wants to know what I think. How I feel about it.

Even when Craig and I were married, he never asked for my opinion. On anything. He barely mentioned things to me before he just went out and did them. Like the time he emptied out our savings to buy shares in his cousin's new business venture. If he'd asked, I would have told him that outdoor settings made out of old oil drums were never going to be a great seller.

Jake raises his eyebrows in expectation.

"I . . . I . . . I love him. I think he's a great match for you guys, and will love your beautiful big backyard and all the attention Hallie is going to give him."

"For us," Jake says, and his wide smile takes my breath away.

He exits the cage and I hear him talking to Brenda, but I can't make out the words. All I hear running over and over through my head is *for us.*

For us.

"You okay, Lana?" Hallie asks, and when I return to earth, my hand is over my heart and I'm holding my breath.

"Yeah, sweetie." I release the huge breath. "I'm great."

Hallie smiles up at me, and it is so warm and so full of . . . *something*. I can't recognise it. I can't even recognise the emotions flowing through myself.

I'm attached. I know I am. I am picturing a future with these two. Picturing what life could be like. And it scares the absolute shit out of me. Because, deep down, I know what happens to the people I love. I know I never get to keep them.

And just the thought has my heart aching and my feet wanting to run in the other direction.

Chapter Sixteen

Lana

"Well, how much longer?" I snap at Lou, the man in charge of the construction at my house. I'm sitting at the desk in my class while the kids have a lesson with Miss Biels in the music room, and I'm only getting more and more frustrated at the bullshit Lou is spinning.

"Lana, I'm sorry," he sighs. "We've had issues with some of the trades—people not showing up for work, materials not being delivered . . ."

"Lou, I am living in a cramped apartment with my newly engaged younger brother. Give me something." I rub my palm over my forehead, a sudden headache coming on.

"Look, if you don't mind working around us for a little while, I could probably have it good enough for you to move in this weekend."

"Really?" I sit up straight in my chair.

"If that's what you insist." I can hear the displeasure in his tone, and if I could finish off all the work myself, I'd tell Lou to go jump. But I can't, so I'll have to cooperate with him instead.

"Fine. Cancel the guys for the Saturday, and I'll get all moved in. Tradies can start again on Monday."

"They'll arrive early," he warns.

"Yes, fine." I just want to go home.

Hanging up the phone, I chuck it onto my desk, lay my head on my arms, and groan. I can't wait for all of this to be over so I can just go back to my simple life.

"Angel?"

My head shoots up to find Jake standing in the doorway of the classroom.

"Everything okay?" He frowns as he makes his way over to my desk.

"Yeah." I sigh, my shoulders slumped. "I just got off the phone with my construction manager."

"What did he have to say?" Jake moves to stand behind me, and I jump as his hands land on the nape of my neck. "Relax," he whispers.

His hands start moving across my shoulders, caressing in a slow but firm manner, and my body begins to soften. "They're still not finished. I cracked a little tantrum, and he said I can move in this weekend, but they'll need to keep working for a while. There is some plastering, painting, and tiling to do."

"You can move back in. That's great."

"Yeah, I guess so. I'm just not looking forward to living there while I have tradespeople working around the place."

"Hmmm," Jake mutters as he continues his attentions on my shoulders. "Maybe we could work on it?"

"What?" I turn in my seat to face him, his hands falling away.

128

"Didn't you say you were going to finish it off yourself anyway? It's only really adding a few extra jobs."

"Yeah, but I can't do those jobs." I pout, losing the excitement he had built up in me.

"Yeah, but I can. I'll help you. We'll do it together."

"Are you serious?"

"Of course." He grasps my chin, pulling my face up and rubbing his thumb over my bottom lip. "I would do anything for you. We're a team, angel."

"Oh my God," I shout as I jump out of my chair and into his unsuspecting arms, exhilaration running through me at just the thought of telling Lou to go take a hike.

"Well, hello there."

We turn towards the door, Jake's arms still wrapped around me. Georgia stands in the entryway with a shit-eating grin on her face. "You must be Chris." A sweet smile lines her face.

Jake's body stiffens against me.

"Georgia," I scold. "She's just kidding," I say to Jake, who won't look at me.

"Okay, I am. But I just wanted you to know she has other options. She won't be on the market long. She's going to be swept up quick, this one. Just because you rode in during the night and saved her doesn't mean you are a guarantee."

Jake tenses, but when I look up at him, there is not the anger I expect to see. "She's not on the market," he states, his voice cold and unwavering.

Georgia's huge smile reappears on her face. "Perfect," she says, walking over to us. "Georgia." She holds her hand out. "Sorry for being an asshole." She gives him a sheepish smile.

"Jake." He shakes her hand and then leans towards her. "Spread the word around the halls, will you?" He winks at her and she giggles. Giggles. Sounding much like the five-year-olds

I teach.

"Sure will."

I fight. I fight for every sliver of breath I can pull into my lungs. My chest is tight, but I can smell fire, the scent of burning.

I'm swooped up off my bed. Strong arms hold me and I lay against a hard chest, a heart pounding as loud and fast as my own.

I look up into the same face, that same blank face I see each time before I am laid down on the grass.

I wait for it. Wait for the voice I heard last time. Everything is darkness once again but there it is—panicked, fretting, and still having the same one-sided conversation.

I feel myself drift away, away from the voice, the heat of the fire, until there is a second voice to the conversation. Yelling, swearing. I'm picked up and my head lies against something much softer than the ground.

The conversation continues, and I relax in relief.

I know that voice.

My eyes pop open, but my body is relaxed, languid against the soft sheets. My heart isn't beating at double-time as it normally does after one of these dreams. I don't have the yucky taste in my mouth as I usually do.

Not today. Nothing is going to bring me down today.

Today is moving day.

"Moving day!" I fist pump the air.

I haven't been to look at the house for a week or so, and honestly, I don't even care if it's ready—I'm moving in today. If I have to sleep on a mattress on the floor and shower with cold water, I don't care. Today, I get a piece of myself back. My space. My safe haven.

I hop out of bed, an extra spring in my step. "It's moving day," I yell as I swing open my bedroom door.

Harper scowls at me, sitting at the kitchen table with a coffee clutched tight in her hands.

"Come on, don't be like that," I mock her. "It's moving day!" I yell again, smiling so bright my cheeks are starting to hurt.

Harper moans and lays her head on the table.

"Oh, don't worry, Daisy." Tate rubs her head, teasing. "It's moving day. This is the last time your grumpy morning self will have to see her."

"Yeah," she grumbles into the table. "It'll just be your chirpy ass I have to see every morning."

Tate leans into her ear and whispers, "You awoke fine to my chirpy ass this morning."

"And thank God this is the last time I'll have to see any sappy, lovey mush from you two."

"Yes." Tate sighs. "After today, you'll be filling your own place with sappy, lovey mush."

"Yeah right," I deny, trying to hide the smile just the thought of Jake brings.

"I think I just heard Jake's truck pull up."

"Oh." I run to the front door, Tate sniggering behind me. "It's moving day!" I yell when I open the door to see Jake jogging up the stairs.

"It sure is." He chuckles, planting a soft kiss on my lips. "You not ready?" Jake's eyes follow the length of my body covered in blue-checked pyjamas.

"I've just got to grab a quick shower. I thought you and Tate could start loading the heavy stuff." I lead the way back inside the apartment.

"Sure. Hey guys," Jake says, giving Tate and Harper a small wave before closing the door.

"Where's Hallie?" I ask, realising she's not with him.

"I dropped her at Marley's early. I promised her we would both pick her up and we'd go out to eat tonight. Oh, if that's alright?" His eyes are wide with uncertainty.

"Of course, it's okay. I was hoping you were going to bring her today." I smile, trying to reassure him how much I want her around. Even though I thought it would be obvious with how much time the two of us spend together ignoring him.

"I didn't want her getting in the way. Plus, she would probably get bored after half an hour."

"True." I nod. "Okay, I'm going to take a shower."

Jake sits down at the table just as Tate pours him a coffee, and they laugh at something Harper mumbles.

When I step out of the bathroom all clean and dressed in my worn jeans and old Ramones T-shirt, I find Tate and Jake in my bedroom, packing up my bed. I didn't bring many pieces of furniture; my bed was one of the few things not ruined by the fire or smoke. Although I did have to replace the mattress and all the bedding, it still feels like my own piece of home here at Tate's.

I find Harper in the living room; she's in a much better mood now that she has had her coffee and is carrying boxes down to Jake's truck. Picking up a couple of light boxes, I follow her.

"Brooke just called and said her and Sax are meeting us at your place," Harper says over her shoulder as she carefully navigates down the stairs.

"They didn't have to come. It's not like I have that much stuff here."

"I think Jake and Tate just wanted to make sure the house was secure enough. Jake wants their help in case they need to fix a couple of last-minute things." Harper rests her box on the tray of Jake's truck. "Although, I'm not sure why they thought Saxon could help. He's not exactly handyman material."

"Tate probably just wanted him to suffer along with him." I laugh and place my boxes down next to hers.

"Probably." Harper snorts in agreement.

"I'll be happy to see Brooke. It's been a while."

"She wants to make a time for a girls' night out. I told her to check the date with you. I'm always free."

"Me too. It's not like I have a life."

"What about now that you have that fine specimen chasing after you?" Harper's eyes float to the top of the stairs where Jake and Tate carry down my bedframe. "God, he's hot," she whispers.

"Harper." I look at her, my mouth agape.

My eyes go back to the stairs where Jake's strong arms are flexing with the weight of the bed. His top lifts as they hold the bed above the stair railings, showing some of his hard stomach and abs. They reach the bottom of the stairs, and Jake winks at me as they pass to pack the bed into the moving truck Tate rented.

God, Harper's right. He *is* hot.

I wipe the corner of my mouth with my index finger—I'm sure I'm dribbling—as Jake and Tate make their way over to us. Jake smiles at me, and I wrap my arms around his waist and squeeze tight. He rubs my back and looks down at me with a frown.

You okay? he mouths. I nod but don't loosen my hold. Yes, I'm okay; I just want a hug. He's mine, and I can hug him anytime I want.

Mine. Shit, I guess he is.

Chapter Seventeen

Lana

*J*ust as I thought, it didn't take long to pack up my stuff in the small truck Tate had rented and to fill Jake's truck.

We were now heading out of the city to my house; Tate no longer on our tail as we'd lost him, Harper, and the truck a few miles ago when he'd pulled off the highway to get some fuel and snacks.

AC/DC starts flowing through the speakers of Jake's truck, and I release a deep breath full of happiness and contentment.

"You okay?" Jake asks, squeezing my hand that he's holding across the centre console.

"More than okay." I don't remember the last time I felt this content. When was it? In high school, before I lost my grandparents? God, was it when I was a child even, before I lost my mum and dad?

Well, that's how long it's been. So long, I can't even remember. How sad is that?

How did I not realise for so long that I wasn't happy? How have I been living like this? It's as if you don't know you're living without joy until you get a taste of it. A small smidgen of how great things can be.

I know now, as content as I was with my simple life before, I definitely was not happy. How could I ever go back?

"What are you thinking?" Jake's thumb pulls my bottom lip out from my teeth.

"Nothing." I give him a huge smile and lean over the console, resting my head on his shoulder. He lets go of my hand and wraps his arm around my shoulder, pulling me tighter against him. My hand is now resting on his thigh, and his muscles tighten.

Something bold and brash snaps in me, and I rub my thumb discreetly up and down where it rests. Jake releases a small sigh, and it pushes my bravado further, my hand now rubbing up and down his tight muscle.

As I hear his short shallow breaths come faster and faster, I glide my hand farther and farther up his thigh, casually, as if I'm not thinking about every little move my hand makes.

His hand tenses against my shoulder, and I watch as his chest rises with his sharp breaths, my eyes moving to his parted lips then to the pulse in his neck, which now beats wildly.

I want him. I don't think I have ever wanted anything so bad in all my life.

And for once, I'm going to take it.

Reaching out with no thought at all, I palm him in my hand. His semi-hard cock strains against his jeans.

"Fuck, angel."

The truck careens to the right and I'm thrown to the left, the surprise of it causing me to glance up only to see we are turning onto a dirt road. I hadn't even noticed we had gotten off the highway.

I bounce around in the passenger seat as we drive the rough road, my hands fumbling with Jake's belt as I try to get his pants undone. All I see is him and what I want, my attention focused on one thing only.

When I've finally wrestled his pants open, I push down his briefs as much as I can so he falls into my hand, the heavy weight of him in my palm sending anticipation straight between my legs.

Jake releases a breath so I squeeze tighter and begin stoking him. He grunts as he entangles his fingers in my hair and tugs gently. The feel of it only fuels my enthusiasm and need as I thrust my hand faster and faster. Somehow, his pleasure has become my own.

The truck jerks to a stop and throws me forward, my hand still wrapped around him, until he throws his seat belt off and pretty much climbs over the centre console to reach me.

"Lana," he breathes against my mouth as he pushes me back against the passenger door. I bring my legs around so I'm lying underneath him—well, as much as I can in the front seat of a car.

He reaches down with one hand, his other arm resting on the seat, and undoes my jeans, wrestling them down. With only one hand, he doesn't get very far, so I arch off the seat and slide my jeans down my hips. Jake reaches down to my ankle and grabs the hem of my pants, dragging the denim down until one leg is free.

He kisses me fiercely. His tongue demands entrance, and he feasts on my mouth, leaving no room between us. Jake's tongue isn't searching for mine—he doesn't want them in a dance or tangle. He is tasting me. With both hands holding my face, he is taking everything he wants and I can barely keep up. My hands hold his shoulders tight, just hoping I won't melt and slide off the seat beneath me.

Our frantic kissing continues as Jake shifts, trying to move his body up against my own. I arch and try to thrust my hips to meet his. He pulls my leg around his back, grips my ass, and tries to pull me up. We slip away from each other and Jake grunts as he tries again to align our bodies.

He breaks our kiss and our heavy breaths fill the empty and silent cab. Our lust and need cut through the air like a warm knife through butter.

"This isn't really working, is it?" He pants.

"Not really." I laugh.

He sighs deeply and drops his head to my shoulder while I try to catch my breath. We have never made out like that before. It was need, want, and basic human instinct all wrapped up in a breathtaking kiss.

His head pops up and he frowns out the passenger window in front of him. He doesn't say a word as he sits up, getting back in the driver's seat and exiting the truck. I sit up in shock and glance out the windshield. I watch in confusion as he stalks around the front of the truck, flings my door open, and lifts me out of the cab.

"Jake," I squeal as I wrap my legs around his waist and tighten my grip around his neck. I'm sure with his adrenaline alone he would be able to hold all my weight unassisted, but I cling on tight anyway. He is on a mission, euphoria running through every thought on his face. He is a man in desperate need.

I imagine what this must look like. Jake carrying me from the truck with one leg out of my pants, his cock hanging out of his jeans, pointing straight up between us.

Sitting me down on the hood of the truck, he steps back to give me a once-over. His eyes roam from the top of my head down to my feet resting on the bull bar. My body warms under his gaze, and I'm not sure if it's the heat of his stare or the warmth of the engine beneath me. When he nods, seeming satisfied, he steps back between my legs. His hot gaze holds mine and then he rubs the back of his knuckles, slow and teasing, down the centre of my sex.

I close my eyes with the shiver it sends from my core straight up my spine. There's a sharp snap against my skin as material rips and my eyes shoot open to find Jake shoving my now ripped panties into his pocket.

I gasp, my eyes wide and mouth agape, but he just smiles and shrugs. "This isn't the time or place for niceties, angel."

With that thought, I quickly glance around the field Jake has pulled up in. There are miles as far as the eye can see of open space and dry pasture. If I squint, I can see some old country homes behind a row of huge oak trees, but there is not another second to focus on any of that as Jake runs his finger through my folds and then pushes inside me.

"Don't worry, angel, I would never let anyone see us. See you, like this. This is all for me. Mine."

I moan at his possessive words, and the small relief that his touch brings. Jake pulls back before adding another finger, his mouth trailing warm kisses down my throat and over my chest.

Reaching down, I wrap my fingers around his shaft and stroke him from base to tip, giving a small twist as I run my finger over the pre-cum that sits on top. He moans into my neck and drags his fingers out of me. Grabbing his cock from my hand, he lines it up at my entrance and thrusts, fast and hard inside me.

Jake stills when he settles deep inside me, and I wrap my arms around his shoulders, burying my face in his neck.

"Jesus," he groans, slowly pulling out of me, leaving just the tip in before he thrusts back inside.

He continues with the torturous pace, slowly out, hard and fast back in, until I lather small kisses all over his neck and down his throat, and he moans and grunts as his pace quickens.

The more kisses I leave from one side of his neck to the other, the more erratic his pace gets, until any semblance of control leaves him and he is pounding into me as if our lives depend on it.

The pain and pleasure entwine together to torture me in the most satisfying way. My body sits on the edge and my sex pulses and tightens around him as it searches for the gratifying ending. Jake slides his hands under my ass cheeks and tilts them just so, and suddenly every thrust and every movement is a strike of lightning to my core.

One small roll of his hips and the friction on my clit has me coming apart in his arms. My head falls back and I scream into the open air, my overwhelming response too much for me to regulate. Jake leans forward and bites down on my shoulder as he thrusts hard and slow, finding his own release inside me.

We breathe heavy, our chests rising and falling together in unison, our faces tucked into each other's necks. Jake licks and kisses my shoulder, soothing the pain his pleasure caused. I loved it. Once again, pleasure and pain mixed to make the perfect combination.

"Where have you guys been?" Tate asks, leaning against the

porch railing. "You should've been here before us."

"There was an issue with the truck," Jake says, his voice calm. I glance at him, trying to hide my surprise.and his expression is neutral, no tell-tale signs at all. Hmm, Jake Weston can tell a good lie. *Interesting.*

"Your truck?" Saxon asks, pointing to Jake's truck, and I see Tate narrow his eyes toward the offending vehicle.

"Yeah," Jake responds flatly.

"Your truck that is probably less than six months old?"

"Yeah."

"Dude." Saxon laughs. "Did you make a stop on the way to have a quickie with his sister?" He points his thumb towards Tate, who is now flicking his gaze between Jake and I. Saxon laughs again, looking at Brooke. "I'm so glad you made us come, baby."

Chapter Eighteen

Jake

Brooke slaps Saxon's arm and scowls at him. A scowl so fierce I can feel the heat of it from the front lawn. I sense Lana stiffen beside me and when I look down to make sure she's okay, her head is down, her gaze settled on the ground beneath her feet.

"Lana, sorry, hon, can you unlock? I've kind of been waiting for the bathroom." Brooke hops from one foot to the other.

"Again?" Saxon looks at her bouncing on the spot. "You just made me stop at the service station."

"What do you want me to say? I need to go again."

I smile, listening to their banter as Lana makes her way to the front door and unlocks it, turning off the alarm. Brooke runs past Lana and into the house. "To the left," Lana calls out to her as she runs through the house.

Everyone files inside and I'm the last one through the door, giving Lana a smacking kiss as I pass.

Tate stands in the middle of her living room and uneasiness rolls off him in waves. He glances around the room, his eyes taking in everything possible as he avoids looking at Lana. It would almost be comical if I didn't know what it was like to be a brother.

I'll have to deal with that later. Although Lana hasn't told me what her past entails, I know it must be somewhat dark, as she holds those cards so close to her chest. Tate's reaction only confirms my suspicions, as his whole embodiment screams protectiveness, worry, and concern.

"God, that's better," Brooke breathes as she walks back into the entryway.

Saxon's eyes fly to his fiancée, and he is stalking over to her within a second. "Are you okay?" His voice is low, his eyes drawn in concern as he stares at her.

The moment feels too serious, too private, so I turn away and glance around the room.

"Have you got a UTI?" Harper blurts, and Tate shushes her.

"No, I don't have a UTI."

"Well, what's wrong with you?"

Brooke groans. "Nothing, I've just had to pee a lot lately." She storms out the front door, Saxon close on her heels.

"Want to show me around, angel?" I whisper to Lana, while Tate and Harper are distracted, arguing about what's appropriate to ask in social situations and what isn't.

"Don't you remember your way around?" Lana chuckles and my face drops. Fuck. I'm lost for words, completely thrown off by her comment. Lana smiles and playfully hits me. "Come on, I'll remind you which way the bedroom is."

I release a deep breath and she lets me get away with my odd behaviour. Fuck. This lie is going to do me in. What the fuck am

I going to do?

Lana leads me through a hallway on the left, leaving everyone else to his or her own issues. We walk down the short hallway and through a couple of spare rooms. It's hard to imagine Lana in this house. The walls are bare, drywall up and filled but no flushing done, let alone painted. Whatever is left of her furniture is all pushed to the middle of the room and covered with large sheets of plastic.

I imagine the house before the fire—full of character, colour, and Lana's warm personality. I see none of that now but am determined to bring it back to life for her.

She shows me a bathroom, which is modest with white fixtures and has everything but the tiling done. There's also another bathroom, which wasn't effected by the fire, that she shows me on the way to the backyard.

"The porch has been replaced but needs to be varnished," Lana says as we step out the back sliding door, and I take nothing in except the beautiful gardens surrounding the small yard.

"I can see you with a green thumb." I smile over at Lana, who is watching me with anxious eyes. "It's great."

"Really? You like it?"

"I love it. It's beautiful, angel."

Lana gives me a shy smile as she makes her way over to stand beside me, leaning against the railing.

"I do spend a lot of time out here."

"I can tell." I wrap my arm around her waist and pull her tighter against my side, kissing her temple. She snuggles into me, laying her cheek on my shoulder, and I rest my head on top of hers as we look out over her garden.

"Thank you for this," she whispers.

"For what?"

"For being here. For helping me move back in."

"Angel, you don't have to thank me. I'm here for you. This house . . ." I gesture to the home. "We will tackle it together."

Lana looks up at me with nothing but adoration and awe in her eyes, and I want to bang my chest in approval. If that is all it takes to make her look at me this way, then I am going to make sure she looks at me like that every day for the rest of our lives.

I imagine how she'd look at me if she knew the truth; that I've been lying to her all this time. Playing some kind of hero. A white knight in shining armour. What if she knew that my armour was all tarnished. Tarnished with lies and deceit.

"I've already had a few thoughts about the house." I turn and pull her to me, trying to ignore the guilt churning in my stomach. I wrap both my arms around her waist as she links her fingers behind my neck.

"Oh, yeah?"

"Yeah." I nod. "We could go down to the hardware store tomorrow and pick up a few things. I reckon if we spend the weekends here, we could get it finished in no time."

Lana releases a deep breath before stepping up on her tip-toes and placing her warm, soft lips against my own. Her kiss is slow, controlled, and I bask in her emotion. I run my tongue along the seam of her mouth, and she opens up and grants me entry. I enjoy tasting every bit of her.

She pulls me tighter against her and digs her nails in the back of my head. I groan, placing my hand at the back of her neck and pulling her even tighter against me. Our kiss is fierce now, full of lust, need, and want, until a throat clears behind us.

"Umm . . ." Tate stands in the doorway, his eyes travelling the yard at a frantic pace. "Mrs Crimbledon is here. She popped over to see how you were doing. She was rambling about the tradies that have been working here while you've been gone."

"Ughh," she groans, pulling away from my embrace. "It's

my neighbour. She is an eighty-year-old busybody." Lana makes her way to the sliding door and I follow. "I bet she is going to whine about the noise. I'll try and get rid of her quick." She gives me a quick kiss and an apologetic smile over her shoulder.

"You're okay," Tate says to Lana, his eyes solely focused on me. "I'll look after Jake."

His words normally wouldn't bother me. It wouldn't send a nervous tingle up my spine, if, as I said, I wasn't a brother myself. But I know exactly what he's thinking.

Fuck.

I feel a protective *'what are your intentions with my sister'* talk coming my way.

"Okay." Lana draws it out, pausing in the door, indecision on her face.

I give her a warm smile and nod in reassurance, and she nods and steps inside. I don't bother following, knowing Tate is probably about to ask for a chat.

"Can I talk to you for a minute?"

"Sure, buddy."

Tate's face tightens in displeasure. I'm thinking my 'buddy' from this morning is no longer present. Just my girlfriend's currently raging brother. Where is the relaxed Tate? The fun-loving and laidback Tate? This tense and threatening guy in front of me is unrecognisable.

"So, you and Lana seem to be getting serious."

"Yes," I answer simply. Best just to try to placate the beast.

"Is it serious?" His eyes stare so hard into my face. I know he is trying to read me and get his answers from my reactions rather than my words.

I stay straight faced, my voice strong. "Yes, it is."

"I don't know how much Lana has told you—"

"Not much," I interrupt, not thinking it's his place to tell me.

"Well, it's not my story to tell, but she hasn't had it easy."

"I figured."

He narrows his eyes at me. "I just want to make sure your intentions are good."

The laughter I expect doesn't come. This is ridiculous. Lana is not only a thirty-year-old woman, but she is older than he is. His 1960s *'chat'* would be laughable, except I know he is serious. He isn't being a douche. He isn't trying to force some kind of weird power trip. He is honestly concerned about his sister's welfare. Tate's face, unlike my own, shows every emotion he is feeling, and my stomach turns at what I can read there.

He has definitely confirmed it for me. Lana has a dark story. I need to tread even more carefully than I have been with her.

"Tate." I drop my defensive stance. "I care deeply for your sister. This isn't a fling or a for-now thing. I mean, for fuck's sake, I've brought her around my daughter . . . *outside* of school," I emphasise the last bit. "I've never introduced anyone to Hallie. Hell, there hasn't ever been anyone to introduce."

Tate nods, his eyes thoughtful and assessing. "Good. I don't think I have to tell you that if you hurt her I'm going to fucking kill you."

I try to swallow the lump in my throat. I should not be scared. I should laugh at the thought of Tate, a man half my size and built like a twig, threatening me. But I am scared. Because the man in front of me with that psychotic look in his eyes is not threatening me. He is telling me as it is. He is making a promise. A promise I know he will keep good on.

"To . . . to be frank with you . . ." He raises his eyebrows as I stutter. "Your sister holds my fucking balls in the palm of her hand," I blurt out.

Tate nods, understanding washing over his face. "Good luck," he says, slapping me on the shoulder before he turns and goes back inside.

Well. Fair enough then. Good talk.

I know my smile is radiant as I make my way through the house to where everyone is standing in the lounge room. Saxon gives me an approving nod, and I chuckle. Out of all the men I have known over the years, civilians and my fellow brothers, I have never seen any of them as infatuated as these two. They look at their women as if they hung the fucking stars. Lovesick smitten kittens.

Glancing out the front window, I see Lana standing by her mailbox, talking to an older woman, and my feet instantly take me to her. Yep, another enamoured and besotted asshole right here. Who'd have thought? I know I never would have. That I even had it in me to feel this way about a woman astounds me.

I watch Lana flick her long red curls over her shoulder as she laughs at something the older lady says, and I know I had no choice. Had no control over how I feel about her. How could I? She's perfection.

Not wanting to be rude, I slip up beside Lana and place my hand at the small of her back but don't interrupt.

"Well, well, well," the old lady croons. "Who do we have here?"

"Mrs Crimbledon, this is Jake." Lana pauses, her eyes shifting around the space surrounding us.

"Her boyfriend." I help Lana out. "Nice to meet you."

"Ahhh," Mrs Crimbledon says, ignoring my outstretched hand. "Suppose it's a good thing you have a man around now. Next time there's an emergency you won't have to be saved by Callie's dirty late-night visitor."

FUCK.

A car pulling up distracts Lana, and she tilts her head at Mrs Crimbledon. "Sorry?" she says, and I inwardly curse the nosy neighbour. I glance at Lana, then at the old lady. Back at Lana again.

I should just tell her. Get it all out right now. Well, not right now, seeing the very real threat of her brother is just inside.

"Maurice," Lana calls out, jogging across her front lawn to the car that had pulled up. *Saved.* By an old Italian man carrying dishes of food.

I turn back to find Mrs Crimbledon glaring a hole into my head, so I just give her a curt nod and walk off towards Lana.

Fuck. I'm going to have to deal with that soon.

"Jake, have you met Maurice?" Lana bounces on the tips of her toes as I approach them.

"Sir." I hold my hand out.

"Jake." He tests the name on his tongue. "I've seen you around."

I nod and give him a polite smile, and then proceed to take the two big dishes out of Lana's arms that she has stolen out of the front seat of Maurice's car.

We head inside and Maurice follows carrying another two large dishes. *How many people is he planning to feed?*

"Old man," Tate greets Maurice as we step inside the house.

"Don't be a smartass and take these, will you?" Maurice gestures to the dishes in his arms.

Tate laughs but jogs over to relieve him of the dishes.

"Yum, can I smell cannelloni in here?" Tate says, holding the dishes up to his nose.

"Sure can. You got anywhere to store these, pumpkin?" he asks Lana.

"I turned the fridge and freezer on for you," Brooke says. "They should already be cool enough by now."

"Oh, thank you so much," Lana says. "I didn't even think to do that."

"It's okay. I also got Sax to turn your gas back on."

I follow Lana and Maurice into the kitchen and help fill the freezer with all the food Maurice made and brought with him. Once it's full, Maurice turns to me and asks, "Can I have a moment with Lana?"

I inwardly relax as I am saved from having to deal with the lie. I know I am making excuses to push it to the back of my mind, and I also know that time is ticking. No matter how much I don't want to deal with it, I'm going to have to tell Lana sooner or later.

Chapter Nineteen

Lana

Jake's face shows nothing as he nods at Maurice and leaves the kitchen.

"How are you?" Maurice asks me, stepping up to cup my face in his hand.

"I'm wonderful." I smile.

"Ahhh." He nods. "Wonderful to be home or is there something else? *Someone* else, perhaps?"

Heat warms my cheeks and I look down. "Everything." I sigh.

"Good." He smiles and nods, taking a step back from me. "Now tell me how much work we have to do on this house."

"Well, actually . . ." I don't hide my excited smile. "Jake has kind of put himself in charge of the renovations. Maybe you could get him to show you around."

"Well, sounds like a good idea." He winks and heads back to the living room.

When I step out of the kitchen, Jake and Maurice are heading down the hallway, heads together and faces serious as Jake points at the walls and ceiling.

"So . . ." I address the four remaining helpers who are now sitting on the floor in my living room, which Brooke has already vacuumed. "Shall we get started? The quicker we get it done, the quicker it's over."

Everyone except Tate jumps up. He grumbles and staggers to his feet. "I housed you for three months. Is that not enough? I have to help you unpack too?"

"Well, if you don't help me I'll have to stay at your place."

"Daisy, baby, start unloading the truck," Tate calls out, and I laugh and shake my head, following him out the front.

It doesn't take longer than a few hours to move me back in. With everyone chipping in and me only wanting to set up the bare necessities, like my bed, we were done in no time. We decide to leave all the furniture covered in the middle of the rooms, as I want to start painting as soon as possible. Maurice left earlier and promised to bring more food around later in the week. And currently, we are all sprawled around the living room floor, empty beer bottles spread throughout.

"What time you picking up Hallie?" Harper asks, sitting across the room, leaning against the wall.

"Before dinner," I tell her. "We're going out to celebrate."

"Make sure you take those pastries Maurice made for her," Tate says.

"She is going to love them." Jake smiles. "She has a sweet tooth."

"Did Harper mention a girls' night out?" Brooke asks from her spot lying on Saxon's lap.

"Yeah, she did say something. What were you thinking?"

"Low key. Champagne and gossip."

"And wedding plans," Harper adds.

"Oh, yes," I agree eagerly. "Sounds perfect to me."

"If you go to Henry's club on a Friday night, it's more of a lounge bar than the club it is on Saturdays," Saxon adds.

"Really?" Brooke asks, excited. Henry is a client of Saxon's, and we have had girls' nights out dancing at his club a few times now.

"Yeah. Soft music, low lighting, relaxed atmosphere. Everything you girls need for a night of talking about useless topics."

"Useless topics? Like our wedding?" Brooke sits, removing her head from his lap, her hands on her hips.

"No, baby, our wedding is never a useless topic. Unless you are discussing fake tans and waxing for an hour."

"Hey!" Brooke hits his arm. "You caught Harper and I one time at the gallery talking about waxing. Besides . . ." a cool smile overtakes her irritation, "I could just stop doing it, if it bothers you so much."

"Trust me, baby, I have no problem with waxing. I just don't think you need to discuss it for hours."

Brooke glares at Saxon and he holds her gaze, the corners of his mouth tipped up. The tension descends upon the room like a thick cloud of smoke. It's like watching foreplay of the eyes, and after a period of time, I can't help but look away.

When I do, Jake is smirking at me, and I can't help but giggle.

"Time to go." Tate laughs, standing up and pulling on Harper's hand.

Harper wraps her arms tight around me. "I know we joke and mess around, and as much as I'll love living with just Tate, I am going to miss you something fierce."

"I'm going to miss you too. I love you, and I'm so happy my brother found you. You complete our family, and I can't imagine us without you."

"Oh, come on," Tate groans as Harper and I wipe under our eyes. "She's only moving back to her house, not to another country."

"Shut up," Harper says and punches him in the ribs.

"Come on, Daisy, let's go. I want to go home and walk around in my undies all night."

"Awesome. I can't wait," she says, with no humour in her voice and a blank expression on her face.

Tate throws Harper over his shoulder and smacks her ass, and we all laugh and wave them off as they leave, Brooke calling out at the last minute not to forget our girls' night out.

I follow them out to close the front door and Tate deposits Harper on the front lawn, then comes jogging back up the porch steps.

"What did you forget—" Before I can finish my sentence, Tate has wrapped me up in his arms.

"Look after yourself, Lala." My heart melts and a warm smile fills my face as tears build behind my eyes.

"I . . . I will," I stutter over the lump in my throat.

"Don't be a stranger," he whispers before he abruptly lets me go and is off down the steps just as quick as he came. "And bring that princess over to the café so Maurice can spoil her," he calls over his shoulder before he jumps into the rental truck.

I give them a wave as they pull away and wipe an errant tear off my cheek. Two warm, strong arms slide around my waist and pull me back against a firm chest.

"You okay?" Jake whispers.

"Yeah." I force a laugh, trying to clear my throat. "It's stupid. I couldn't wait to get out of there."

"It's okay to admit you're going to miss them." He kisses my neck.

"No, it's not. My brother is an idiot."

Jake's loud laugh brings a smile to my face, and he turns me in his arms until I am staring up at him. "You sure you feel up to dinner? It's been a big day."

"Yes, of course. Seeing Hallie will cheer me up."

He smiles down at me, his eyes warm, and runs the back of his fingers down my cheek. We stand in silence, gazing into each other's eyes, Jake running his fingers all my face. Over my eyes, down my nose, across my lips.

"So, we were going to say our good-byes and head off when you guys came back inside, but we've just been standing there like dickheads for the past ten minutes." Saxon smirks, him and Brooke standing in the doorway.

"Oh shit, sorry." I pull away from Jake.

"I'm not," Jake mumbles.

Saxon laughs as I pull Brooke in for a hug, and he slaps Jake on the shoulder. "Just remember, there are no blinds up." Saxon laughs and takes Brooke's hand to lead her to the car.

We wave good-bye and head inside. "I'll just lock up, and we can go get Hallie if you like."

"Is there much point in locking up? Your back door is still a plastic tarp." Jake raises an eyebrow at me.

"Hardy har har." I poke my tongue out at him. "I'll set the alarm."

Chapter Twenty

Lana

"Lana!" Hallie screams as she runs towards the front entry.

"Hello." I laugh, picking her up in my arms. "How was your day?"

"Long." She sighs, wrapping her small arms around my neck. "It went *so* slow."

"She has been asking when you were picking her up for dinner since just after breakfast." Marley hands Jake her bag.

"Oh, what? No invite for coffee?" Jake teases.

"There is no way she is letting you stay for five minutes, let alone a coffee."

"Alright then." He chuckles. "How was she?"

"No worries. Her and Thomas were at each other all day. Just the norm."

"He called me stupid," Hallie protests.

"And what did you do?" Marley raises her eyebrows at Hallie.

"Kicked him in the nuts," she whispers.

"What?" Jake asks, leaning closer to Hallie, who is now gripping onto my neck for dear life.

"I kicked him in the nuts," she repeats in a loud voice. No remorse in her tone.

"Right." Jake nods. "We'll need to talk about that in the car."

"She needs a sibling," Marley states.

My eyes go wide, and I glance at Jake who looks, surprisingly, not at all affected.

"Say thank you to Aunt Marley."

"Thank you, Aunt Marley."

"You're welcome, darling." She places a kiss on Hallie's cheek. "I'll see you on Monday."

The stern talking-to starts as soon as we are on our way. Even though Jake doesn't talk about being in the Army much, there are moments when, even if you didn't know him, you would know he's served.

This is one of those moments.

His firm words and unyielding tone leave no room for argument, which Hallie normally does. It's as if he has flipped a switch and she knows that when that switch flips, she's not to push him. She's all 'yes sir'.

"So because of this, you won't be having dessert tonight after dinner."

"Jake," I blurt, before I have time to sensor myself and cover my mouth with my hand.

"Yes?" he asks with caution in his tone.

"Nothing." I take a deep breath and place my hand back in my lap.

"No, it's not nothing. What is it?"

"Well . . ." I glance out of the window, trying to think of something to say.

"Well, what?"

"I . . . I just . . ."

"You just what?"

Oh, fuck it. "I just think it's a little harsh that you are punishing her for something that happened today at your sister's. For something that you didn't see and something that could've happened more than eight hours ago. I'm sure your sister dealt with it as it happened, and it doesn't seem fair to punish her twice."

"Right," he says, his jaw tense.

"I mean . . ." I try to placate him. "If you give her to your sister to look after, you have to trust her to discipline her. I'm sure Marley sorted it. It's not good to harp on about something when the moment has passed."

Jake's face is rigid as he pulls his hand from mine, laying it on the gear stick and not saying a word the whole way back to his house.

He unlocks the front door and Hallie runs straight through the house to let Max in. Jake stands aside for me to enter but doesn't meet my eyes as I go to pass.

Reaching around him, I pull the front door closed, leaving us on the front stoop, and Jake's attention is brought to me.

"I'm sorry," I plead. "I should mind my business. I didn't mean to tell you how to raise your daughter."

Jake sighs, his shoulders dropping. "I'm sorry for being such a prick. It's just . . . I'm doing the best I can. The best I know how."

"I know." I place my hand on his forearm.

"I don't have a fancy degree in education to help me along the way."

I pull my arm away, stepping back, my eyes wide. "I'm going in there to shower and change." I raise my bag of clean clothes as if to solidify my threat. "Hopefully, you have a better attitude when I come out."

"I'm sorry. I'm being a prick again." He wraps his arms around me and pulls me tight.

"Yes, quite frankly, you are."

He chuckles and presses his lips to the top of my head. "I'm sorry," he whispers.

"That's okay." I relax in his arms. "Just cut it out."

He laughs as he grabs my hand and drags me inside.

I feel a million times better once I've washed all the dust and dirt off me from the day of packing and unpacking. I'm standing in Jake's bathroom, wrapped up in his huge towel, doing my hair and makeup when Hallie strolls in with Max, casual as anything as she sits herself on the closed toilet and smiles up at me.

"What's up, babe?" I ask, smiling down at her and Max lying by her dangling legs.

"You take a long time to get ready." She sighs.

I laugh. "Do I?"

"Yep."

"Well, it takes girls a long time to get ready."

"I don't." She scrunches up her face in disgust.

"Not now. But probably when you're older, you will."

"What's that you're putting on?" She sits up straighter to see me in the mirror.

"Eye shadow."

"Oh."

"Have you ever had any before?" I ask, turning to look at her.

"No." She shakes her head.

"Wanna try some?"

"Could I?" Her eyes light up.

"Sure." I chuckle, kneeling down in front of her on the cold tiles. "Close your eyes."

Hallie closes her eyes, a huge smile still plastered on her face. I brush the eye shadow over one lid and blow the excess off, before repeating the same on the other lid.

"Okay, open," I tell her.

She blinks her eyes open and I smile warmly at her. "Perfect."

"Can I see?"

I reach behind me to grab my makeup mirror off the bench and hold it in front of her face.

"Oh, I love it," she squeals. "Is that glitter?"

"It sure is. But I don't think the look is complete."

"No?"

"No. How about . . ." I stand and rifle through my makeup bag, "lipstick." I turn and hold it up to her.

"Oh, yes."

Kneeling down again, I open the lipstick. "Okay, go like this." I part my lips.

Hallie copies without hesitation, and I glide the pale pink colour over her petite lips.

"Okay. Now like this." I smack my lips together. Hallie copies again, and my heart melts. I didn't have these special moments with my mum. Well, not any I can remember. It occurs to me this is probably a first for Hallie too.

"Can I see?" she asks again.

"Of . . . of course," I stutter. I hold the mirror up for her, and seeing her eyes sparkle with happiness draws tears to my eyes.

"Beautiful, princess." Jake's soft murmur flows from the doorway.

"Do you like it, Daddy?" Hallie jumps off the toilet seat and

159

runs to hug Jake's legs as he stands leaning against the door-frame, his arms crossed over his chest.

"Sure do." He picks her up. "Why don't you go and feed Max before we go."

"Okay." She wiggles out of his arms and runs off down the hallway.

Jake's eyes immediately find mine and I stand, stock-still in the middle of the bathroom. His eyes are fierce, but his signature blank face is on, which means I can't read the emotion rolling through them. Shit. Have I overstepped my boundaries again?

"I'm sorry," I blurt out as Jake steps towards me. "I should've asked if you were okay with that before I just did it—"

His lips meet mine, cutting off my words. His hands grip my head and I'm being pushed back into the glass shower screen. So much is happening in such a short space of time, I am lost and confused for a second.

"What the?" I breathe out when Jake finally takes his lips off my mine.

"Angel," he whispers, before his lips are on mine again.

This time I am ready for him, my tongue reaching out to meet his with enthusiasm. I grab onto his strong shoulders, my nails digging in with the overwhelming yearning from his kiss. It's hard, it's raw, and there is almost a vulnerability to it. It speaks a thousand words, and I just hope he can hear what I'm saying back.

Jake pulls back, our breathing shallow and erratic, our chests pumping fast, our eyes wide. That kiss was too much. It said too many things that neither one of us had planned.

"Angel," he sighs, resting his forehead against mine. I don't say a word. I'm not sure if I'm even breathing anymore as I continue my tight hold on him.

"Are we going yet?" Hallie runs in and skids to a stop when

she sees us.

"Let's give Lana a minute to finish up, okay?" He kisses me lightly on the head and takes Hallie's hand as they leave.

Holy. Shit.

I lean back into the shower-screen, hoping it will hold my weight as my hands cover my out-of-control heart. What the hell?

Elation flows through me as happiness eats me up. I'm ruined. He has ruined me.

Dread fills me as I realise how sunk I really am. How will I cope if this doesn't end well? Hell, even if it does end well. I won't survive if it ends at all.

Worry floods me, yet somehow, I can't find it in me to care. I'll have to deal with that if and when it happens. I can't think about that now.

Chapter Twenty-One

Lana

Jake's hand doesn't stop touching me the whole way back to his house—gripping my own hand, resting on my leg, rubbing up and down my thigh. He was the same during dinner. So attentive and loving. As if he's enamoured with me.

The emotions and feelings his actions stir in me are addictive. I've never felt so special. So worthy. As if I'm someone's whole world, the only thing they can see. And he somehow did this without alienating Hallie or ignoring her presence. He still made her the centre of everything we do. How does he do that?

We pull up in the driveway, Jake cuts the engine, and we both glance to the backseat. Hallie is fast asleep, her head falling forward onto her chest. "I'm just going to put Hallie to bed. And then, I want you."

I nod, eager for what has been building all night.

Jake hands me the keys so he can lift Hallie out of the truck, and I lock it after him and run ahead to unlock the front door.

Pushing the door open, he moves past me and I'm left standing in the foyer, alone, with nervous excitement running through my veins. It's so different starting a relationship as an adult. When you're in college, it's all sex, sex, sex, every day, all day. When you're an adult, it's full-time jobs, responsibilities, and sometimes children. I've not seen Jake this week, and it feels as though it's our first time all over again.

I throw his keys on the small stand by the door and head straight to his bedroom. Once I'm inside and the door is closed, my top is up, over my head, and thrown to the floor before I fumble with my jeans button and zipper.

I'm bouncing around on one foot, trying to slide down my extra-skinny skinny jeans, when I realise Jake wasn't specific about wanting me. I'm finally able to kick off my pants and I'm taking off my underwear mindlessly as I think about Jake maybe not being comfortable having sex while Hallie is in the house. God, maybe he didn't even want me to stay? Maybe he does want to have sex but then have me leave afterwards?

Oh, my goodness. Isn't being an adult discussing these things before you get into an awkward situation? You know, a situation like me standing butt-naked in the middle of his bedroom?

"Lana?" he calls out from the hall.

Shit.

I am reaching down to snatch up my undies when the door opens and Jake is standing in the arch.

"Well, hello."

Heat warms me from the tips of my toes, and I feel it climb the length of my body until it covers my chest and face. Then I notice even though his eyes are wide with surprise, they are full of lust and appreciation.

My arms, which had automatically gone to fold over my stomach, fall away to my sides, and I release a soft breath of air. Only a second passes before Jake is stalking towards me, stripping off his T-shirt as he goes.

When he stands in front of me, I reach out and run my hands over his warm chest and hard stomach, letting my fingers fall in all the curves and divots. Jake runs his hands from my shoulders over my breasts and down my sides and then pushes, forcing me to fall back onto the bed.

I yelp in surprise, but Jake shedding his briefs and jeans at the same time has me clamping my mouth shut. In only seconds, he is standing over me, perfect and astounding in his naked form.

My eyes roam his body, head to toe and everything between, trying to take in as much as I can while he is so open in front of me. My eyes stare so hard I'm sure I can feel him, feel that smooth, tanned skin underneath my touch.

Jake closes his eyes for a beat, mumbling a 'fuck', and when he opens them again, something has snapped. A switch has let loose and he crawls over me, his hands everywhere, running up my legs, over my stomach, grabbing my breasts.

His touches are hard and rough, and even though they instil twinges of pain mixed with the pleasure, it's an exhilarating combination. I moan and Jake swears as our movements become needy, desperate. I'm grabbing at his body, not able to pull him close enough, writhing and whimpering beneath him. He is kneading, biting, and sucking any bit of skin he can find, groaning and cursing as he goes.

Without warning or any preamble, he thrusts a finger inside me. I moan as he glides into me easy with all my tension and anticipation. "Oh, fuck," he groans, closing his eyes for a beat before he loses all control.

Jake flips me over, straddles my thighs and pulls my arms behind my back, securing my wrists in one hand. I feel him grab his cock with his other hand and position himself at my entrance. In one quick, hard thrust, he is inside me, buried to the hilt. He stills before pulling out slowly and pushing back in a few times, almost testing my readiness. I don't need to feel my slick pussy squeezing him tight to know I am more than ready.

He apparently agrees as he pushes my thighs together, lies over me and begins thrusting relentlessly. He holds me down with the weight of his body, and all his hard and unforgiving muscles trap me underneath him.

He slides his hand under me and begins to caress my sex. Up, down, and all around himself pushing inside me, before his touch drags up and focuses on my clit. He circles it and rubs over it, and I feel it building. The euphoric sensation he causes as his deep thrusts tickles my core and moves my body into another realm.

I scream as his ministrations cause me to come, and my body shakes, grinding against his fingers as he continues thrusting into me, his pace only picking up with my ecstasy.

The pressure of him lying on top of me, not allowing me to move an inch to ease the overwhelming sensation, has my orgasm carrying on and on until my screams sound like a plea for help. But Jake doesn't help, doesn't even send for it, as he continues torturing my body until I lie limp beneath him.

He kisses, licks, and sucks on my shoulder blade, and his heavy breaths are all I can hear. I focus on them, using them to centre me as the feeling of him becomes too much. He brings me back to earth as he bites my shoulder, and stills deep within me, and I scream out as he finds his own release.

Holy. Shit.

Jake slides off me and onto his stomach beside me, our bodies still entangled

"Are . . . you . . . okay?" He gets out between his heavy and fast breathing.

I nod until I realise his eyes are closed. "Yes."

Shifting, I lie over him, my head resting on his shoulder blade with my arm and leg thrown over him.

We lie quietly as our bodies shake with our heavy breathing and my legs quake with the remaining sensations of my orgasm.

As we begin to settle, I run my fingers lightly over his back. Tracing the curve of his muscles, I press soft kisses to my favourite tattoo.

Jake rolls over onto his back, taking me with him, my legs straddling him as I now lie on his chest.

"You okay?" he asks again, looking into my eyes this time.

"Perfect," I breathe.

We go back into our comfortable silent bubble, and I lay my cheek against his pec.

"Oh my God." I lean up. "I forgot to ask you if it was okay. You know, with Hallie in the house."

"Did I fight it?"

"No, but how could you when I just let myself into your bedroom and stripped down naked?"

"Angel." He chuckles. "Letting yourself into my bedroom and stripping down naked is something you don't ever have to apologise for."

I lay my head back down on his chest, a frown on my face as silence envelops the room again. What now?

"Well, should I get going?" I ask, staring at his bedroom door. I don't want to go; I want to stay here wrapped around this gorgeous man.

"Why would you leave?" All humour has disappeared from his voice.

"Hallie," I say simply. I don't have children, but I know how important their emotional development is after working with them for so long. How big a decision it is to introduce them to their parent's new partners or people they are seeing. Some parents don't even introduce their kids to their new partner for months, let alone have them stay over.

"Angel." Jake grasps my chin to lift my head, my eyes meeting his serious ones. "I want you here. Hallie wants you here. And after what I saw in the bathroom tonight, I know we need you here." My shoulders drop and my face softens, along with my heart as I feel it melt away. "I never realised there was so much I couldn't give her. I mean, I thought I would be good enough for her. I never thought about all the little things. Make-up, hair. Fuck, what am I going to do when it's time for bras, periods, and boyfriends?"

I rub my hand over his cheek, cupping his face. "Hopefully, you won't have to deal with it alone."

I don't say me. But that is sure as hell what I'm thinking. *Please, please let it be me. I want to be there for both of you.*

"And that's why I want you to stay."

God, I hope he means forever.

Jake leans forward and takes my mouth with his. His kiss is soft, gentle, and coaxing. It goes on and on, and even though it's the complete opposite of the needy, desperate kisses from before, it speaks a thousand times more to me. Our two souls conversing from the simple touch of our lips.

He doesn't break the kiss as he rolls us over. Once he's settled himself over me, he slides inside in one smooth motion. He moves slowly. Taking his time, appreciating. Making love.

In all my years, I've never had anyone be intimate with me like this. Every move is gentle. Every touch is reverent.

And I'm going to cherish it for as long as I'm allowed.

Chapter Twenty-Two

Lana

I'm on my bed, the heat of the fire surrounding me, but it's as though I can't get up. I can't move, can't run. I try to scream but nothing comes out. There is no sound except for the crackle of fire burning the house around me.

As I'm reaching the edge of panic and moving into hysteria, I am swooped up off my bed and my heart begins to relax as I'm carried out of the house.

I smile in reverence and force my eyes open, wanting to see Jake holding me. Except, it's not Jake. Dark, frantic eyes are laced with long lashes. Black thick hair hangs over his forehead as he glances around in horror.

As always, my eyes shoot open and I'm gasping for breath. Who was that guy?

Before I can overanalyse my dream, the intense stabbing pain between my eyes has me clenching them shut. I try to swallow, and it's like razor blades sliding down my throat and my nose wheezes as I breathe in and out.

Great, I'm sick.

"Ughh," I groan into my pillow as I roll over.

"Jeez, I didn't think waking up next to me was that bad."

My head whips up toward the voice. *What the hell?* Jake's warm brown eyes smile at me, and I groan again. Oh my God, I stayed at Jake's last night.

"Could you have moved any farther away from me?" He chuckles.

Lifting the sheet and glancing around, I see I'm lying right on the edge of the large king-size bed. I give him a sheepish smile and scoot across the bed to lie beside him, my head resting on his shoulder with his arm underneath me.

"No wonder I moved so far away." I sniffle. "You are so hot."

"No, angel. I think that's you." Jake leans down and presses his lips to my forehead. His normally warm lips are cool on my hot skin. "I think you have a temperature."

I sigh. "I'm actually not feeling very well this morning."

Jake pulls away and frowns at me. "Are you okay?"

"Yeah. I just have a stuffy nose and sore throat. Probably a cold."

He leans forward and places a soft kiss on my lips. "Gah, don't kiss me. I'm full of germs. You'll get sick."

"I don't care." He kisses me again. "I'll take care of you today." Another kiss.

"Take care of who?" Hallie asks as she approaches the bed.

Jake pulls away from me, his arm, which was once underneath me, throws me across the bed. I pull the sheets up and ensure everything is covered. I didn't even hear her come in.

She must have tiptoed or something. Why can't the kids be that quiet at school?

"I'm going to take care of Lana today. She isn't feeling well," Jake tells her.

"Oh no, do you need to poop? Whenever I have a sore tummy, Aunt Marley tells me I probably need to poop."

"No." I laugh, pulling the sheet tighter against me as she crawls onto the end of the bed.

"Lana has a cold," Jake tells her.

"Oh, okay. Well, can I help look after her?"

"Sure you can help. Why don't you go pick some movies she might want to watch?"

"Okay." She jumps off the bed. "Can I watch them too?"

"If it's okay with Lana."

"Of course. I would love that," I say.

Hallie skips out of the room and Jake turns to me. "Is that okay? If you want to rest, I can take her out for a while."

"Jake, firstly, this is your home. You are not taking Hallie out so I can rest. I can go back to my own place—"

"Well, that won't be happening," he snorts.

"And secondly . . ." I mock glare at him, "I would love Hallie's company. Yours too, if you're up for it."

The huge smile that lights his face brings instant happiness, and I can't help but imitate it.

"Are you hungry?" he asks. "I can make you something."

"No. I'm actually feeling a little nauseated."

"Okay, stay here. I'm going to get you set up." He kisses my nose and hops out of bed, picking up last night's clothes off the floor.

I watch in crude and lustful wonder as he throws them in the hamper and grabs a fresh pair of jeans and a T-shirt out of his drawer. Jake dressing himself is like a show put on just for me, and I wonder if he even knows how sexy he looks doing it.

"By the way . . ." I say, reality crashing down on me, "maybe next time we should dress before falling asleep. This morning could have been a lot worse."

"Oh yeah." He rifles around in his drawer. "Here." He hands me a huge college football T-shirt and a pair of his briefs. "You can wear that, if you like."

He goes back to getting dressed, and I go back to watching unabashedly. "We're lucky," he says. "Sometimes she crawls into bed with me in the middle of the night."

"That would've been awkward."

"Yes, it would've been." He laughs as he heads toward the door. "I'll be back."

I make a mad dash to his bathroom, holding the T-shirt and briefs up against my naked body in case Hallie returns with the movies. Once I've done my morning business and freshened up, which included blowing my nose about a hundred times, I head back to the bedroom.

I straighten up the sheets and quilt, and then arrange the pillows for all of us to lean on before I hop back into bed.

Laying my head back, I close my eyes. I hate being sick. I doubt I'm going to be much better tomorrow, so I go to grab my phone off the bedside table to text the school, but it's not there. Shit, of course it's not. It's still in my purse, which could be anywhere. God knows where I dropped it in the haze of lust I was in last night.

Jake and Hallie step through the bedroom door, both of them with arms full of goodies and Max trailing behind.

"What have we here?" I ask, smiling at the three of them.

"I've got some DVDs and tissues," Hallie says, throwing them onto the end of the bed. *Thank God.* I reach over, pull a couple of tissues out, and then proceed to blow my nose for the one hundred and first time.

"And I've got a hot honey and lemon drink and some pain relief," Jake says as he places the mug and tablets down on my bedside table. *My* bedside table. Yes, I want it to be mine. I want to fill it with all my useless stuff from my own drawers at home. Except my B.O.B. He doesn't need to come.

"Lana?"

"Sorry?" I shake my head, clearing my thoughts. Great, my head is so stuffed with snot I'm losing it. Losing it and thinking all crazy thoughts. Like how much I want to become a permanent fixture here. You know, like the bedside table. Except one that's bolted down and can't be moved.

"Lana?"

Oh God. "I'm sorry."

"Are you okay?" Jake chuckles.

"I think I just need to lie down for a minute. My head is spinning a little." To say the least.

"Okay, we'll leave you to rest—"

"No!" I shout and wince at the sharp pain in my head. "Please stay. Put on the movie and watch it with me."

"Okay." Jake smiles warmly at me as he pulls my quilt up and tucks me in.

I shuffle down the bed and burrow into my pillow. If I could breathe through my nose, I'm sure the pillowcase would smell like a blend of Jake and me. My sweet scent mixed with his manly cologne.

I try to shut off my rampant thoughts while I listen to Jake and Hallie talk and work in perfect harmony as I drift off to sleep.

They make a good team. I hope they let me join because I think I'd make a great player.

Chapter Twenty-Three

Jake

This is what dreams are made of. Lana in bed sick, and Hallie and I taking care of her. Well, not Lana sick, but this is the dream. The three of us living in the real world, dealing with real-life situations. It's not all romantic dates, hot sex, and forgetting your responsibilities. This is real. It's snotty colds and flus, it's bad kid's movies, it's being with the ones you love, even when there's nothing you can do for them but be there. *Love? I thought . . . love?*

Lana sleeps on the pillow next to me, Hallie squeezed between us. She's snoring on account of her blocked nose, every now and then gurgling the phlegm in her throat, and even still, I think she is the most beautiful thing I have ever seen. Yeah, this is definitely love.

She passed out first thing this morning, not taking her pain relief or even a sip of the honey lemon tea I had made her. She snorts, and I can't help but laugh. Even with the restless sleep she's having, she looks peaceful. Totally at ease and comfortable.

She looks so good in my bed. In my bed, in my life—in Hallie's life. I haven't stopped staring at both of them all morning, hence why Hallie has long since fallen asleep and I'm still watching *Cinderella*. Lana belongs here with us. Of that, I have no doubt.

She stirs and her eyes pop open to directly meet mine. At first, she is shocked, her eyes wide, as they take stock of the room.

"Hey, sleepyhead," I whisper. "Feeling okay?" She nods and gives me a warm smile but doesn't speak. "I'll go make you a fresh honey lemon drink if you like. You should take some pain relief, and I'll make some soup for lunch. You shouldn't take it on an empty stomach." She nods and smiles again, and I lean over Hallie to place a soft kiss on the tip of her nose, leaving one on the top of Hallie's head as well before I hop off the bed.

I set to work in the kitchen making the hot drink and warming up the soup. Marley had made me a few batches of chicken noodle soup a few weeks ago when the weather had cooled down, and luckily, I still have some in the freezer.

While the kettle boils and the soup heats on the stove, I make some ham and cheese sandwiches for Hallie and I, and Lana if she's up to it.

Once I'm all ready, I pile everything onto a tray and tread carefully down the hallway. As I'm balancing the food and drinks, I hear murmuring coming from the bedroom. I poke my head through the door before I step inside and my hearts stops.

Lana and Hallie lie facing each other on the bed and Hallie rubs her fingers down the side of Lana's face as she caresses her cheek. My heart kicks back into gear and pounds at double its normal speed. I don't think it can take finding these two in any more of these intimate moments.

I never realised how much Hallie could benefit from a woman in our lives. I'm not an idiot; I know there are things that, as a male, I can't provide, but she has Marley and Jamie's mum. I thought we would be enough, and that between us we could give her everything she needs. But taking in the sight in front of me, I can see how much we can't give her. How much she would love to have a mother figure of her own.

"My other sleepyhead is awake," I say as I enter the bedroom, my heart still playing to its own beat.

"I didn't sleep, Daddy. I was just closing my eyes for a little while."

"Really?" I laugh. "Is that why *Cinderella* is playing for the second time?"

She laughs, removing her hand from Lana's face, and sits up to see what I have on the tray. Lana follows her and I place the tray on her lap, grabbing Hallie's sandwich and setting it in front of her. "That's for you." I tell Lana, "I have a drink, some water for that pain relief, and some soup for you."

"Thank you," she croaks out.

"I also made extra sandwiches in case you wanted one."

She smiles up at me and I grab my sandwich, walking around to the other side of the bed, rubbing a sleeping Max's head on the way. I sit down next to Hallie and we all eat in comfortable silence as we watch *Cinderella* from the start, the third time for me.

The rest of the day goes on much like this. Lana in and out of sleep as we watch more princess movies. Hallie and I doing anything we can think of to make her more comfortable. In between washing uniforms, making tomorrow's lunches, and packing our bags, I help Lana take a cool bath and get Hallie ready for bed.

By the end of the night, I am wrecked and slip into bed beside a sleeping Lana. I give her a light kiss on the mouth, careful not to wake her. I want to wrap myself around her, but I worry about what the heat of my body will do to her temperature. So, when gentle, petite arms wrap around my waist and a soft kiss lands on my shoulder, I can't contain my elation.

Lana's snoring starts up not long after. I drift off to sleep with a huge smile on my face and a sick Lana wrapped around me.

Chapter Twenty-Four

Lana

I wake with a jolt as I feel someone tugging at me. I am wrapped around Jake, my face pressed to his back. My arm is pulled off him, and I squint my eyes in the dark to see Hallie kneeling over us.

"Are you okay, sweetie?"

"Yeah." She nods. Is she sleepwalking?

She continues tugging at my arms and legs until she has pried me from her father's body. She then lies on top of Jake and squeezes herself down between the two of us. I chuckle and move over to make room for her.

"You could've just asked." I laugh. "I would've moved for you to sleep next to your dad."

Hallie smiles at me as she positions her body to face mine. Her hand runs over my face just as she did earlier today. It's soothing, calm, and gentle, and tears build in my eyes.

I have worked with kids for a long time, but you are always their teacher. There is always that intimacy that they have with their parents that you don't get from them. I always knew I wanted children. Maybe not Craig's, but I wanted them.

I never, in all my wildest dreams, thought it could be like this, though. An emotion so strong you feel as though your heart is beating on the outside of your body. Hallie stares into my eyes, a content expression as she continues her soft caresses on my face.

After a long while, she closes her eyes and I follow, a huge smile lining my face as I go back to sleep.

The smile doesn't last long though, as I'm brutally abused in my sleep. An elbow to the ribs—a slap to the face. At one point, Hallie ends up sideways between us and I cop a foot to the gut.

After a restless sleep, commotion from the kitchen startles me awake. It doesn't take as long this morning to remember where I am. I smell Jake's lingering scent on the pillow and re- alise my nose has somewhat unblocked. Nuzzling my head into the pillow, I pull in a long sniff.

"Are you right there?" I peek out from the pillow, and Jake stands by the end of the bed, a towel wrapped around his trim waist as water beads run down his chest.

"I . . . I was . . ." He chuckles and I burrow my embarrass- ment in the pillow. The bed dips and Jake's warm lips are on me. On my shoulder, my jaw, my cheek, my head. I smile and turn to face him. A loud clatter comes from the kitchen and I remember what woke me.

"What's going on in there?"

"Hallie." Jake smiles and rolls off the bed. "I better get in there before she has an accident."

I watch every sinewy muscle contract in his back as he

walks. They all move in perfect sync with his footsteps. Who knew a back could be so built?

Sighing, I roll over to face the ceiling. I feel a little better than yesterday, but still not the greatest. Thankfully, I thought ahead and called in sick to school last night.

Hallie comes running in and bounces onto the bed. "I'm going to miss you at school today."

"I'm going to miss you too." I smile. "You're going to be good for the substitute, aren't you?"

"Yes, she is," Jake says, as he enters carrying a plate of toast and a glass of orange juice. He sets the plate on Hallie's lap and hands me the glass. "I'm getting dressed and we're going, Hal, so eat quick."

"Oh my God, I'm sorry." I throw the blankets back. "I'll get ready."

"For what?"

"To go." Jake raises his eyebrows expectantly, still not understanding my meaning. "Can you drop me home on the way to school?"

"You want to go home?"

"Well, I can't stay here while you guys are at work and school."

"Why not?" Hallie and Jake respond together.

"Well . . . because . . . umm—"

"Good, it's settled. Stay in bed and rest." Jake begins to get dressed, not looking at me, making a point that the decision has been made. "Once I've finished work, I'll pick up Hallie from Marley's and come home and get dinner."

"Well . . . if you like . . . you can get Marley to drop Hallie off here so you don't have to go pick her up."

Jake's head snaps up to me, only his arms through his Army T-shirt. "Really?"

"Of course. Why not?"

"I don't know. You're sick." He pauses a moment. "She's not yours," he says, his voice quiet.

My heart thuds, and my pulse races. I remain calm, cool, and collected. "Hallie, sweetie, can you go get your bag ready?" I smile down at her, sidled up next to me.

"Sure."

Expectant silence fills the room as Jake watches me, and I watch Hallie skip out into the hallway.

"Angel—"

"Don't ever say that in front of her again," I seethe. "As a matter of fact, don't ever say it again at all."

"I'm sorry." He tries to interrupt, but I'm on a rampant rage.

"I know I'm not her mother. She knows I'm not her mother. I'm not trying to replace her. I just want a piece of Hallie. I want her to feel like she can belong. Belong to me."

"I'm so sorry, angel." Jake crawls onto the bed and over to me. "That was a fucking stupid thing to say. It just came out totally wrong." He grabs my hand and entwines our fingers, bringing it up to his mouth and laving light kisses on it. "I just meant that most mums enjoy getting rid of their kids if they can, so why would you want her if you didn't have to?"

I frown at him. "No, Jake. Most mums don't want to '*get rid of their* kids'." He frowns back at me, as if he doesn't understand that concept at all. "I love Hallie. She is an awesome kid, and I enjoy her company. I don't just want her around because she is yours or because I have to or because I feel like I should. I want her."

Jake stares at me with a blank expression on his face.

"I'm ready." Hallie runs back in the room, struggling with the backpack that is almost as big as her. I leave Jake to his own thoughts and focus on her.

"Awesome. Have you got your lunch?" I ask her.

"Yep."

"Your reader bag?"

"Yep."

"Your drink bottle?"

"Yep."

"Your jacket?"

"Yep."

"Well . . ." I smile widely. "You've got me. You're just way too organised."

I turn back to Jake and his look of shock has turned into wonder and awe. He doesn't take his fierce eyes off me and even as I glance back at Hallie for some reprieve, I still feel them burning into me.

"I wish we could stay home and look after Lana." Hallie pouts.

"Me too, princess. Me too."

I spend the day much as I did the day before. Sleeping on and off between boring daytime TV. Eating soup and drinking honey lemon drinks, although I'm having much more of them than yesterday. The pile of tissues around me also isn't as big as yesterday, and I enjoy the day of recovery.

The day drags on with only my own company so when I'm watching some mind-numbing afternoon talk show and I hear the front door open, excited doesn't even cover how I feel.

"Lana." Hallie comes bolting onto the bed, laying her little arms around my neck.

"Hey, princess." I squeeze her tight.

"Slow down, monster." Marley steps into the bedroom, panting for breath. "Are you sure you want this tornado around for the afternoon?"

"Definitely." I give Hallie a cheeky smile.

"Okay then." Marley's arms are full, and in one swift motion, she drops it all to the floor. Hallie's backpack, her lunch bag, her reader, and some paintings. "Be good, squirt." She comes and kisses Hallie on the forehead. "I'll pick you up tomorrow."

"I will."

"Oh, before I go, is there anything you need?" She turns back to me.

"No, I think I'm good," I reply surprised by her question.

"You sure? I was given strict instructions to make sure you were okay. Make sure you had everything you needed."

I laugh, understanding dawning. "No, honestly, we are fine."

"Don't laugh. I wish John cared about me that much when I was sick."

"I'm sure he does."

She grunts noncommittally. "Okay, well I have three other ratbags to get home." She turns and heads to the door, waving over her shoulder. "I'll see you both tomorrow."

"See ya," Hallie and I call out in unison.

"So." I snuggle down with Hallie sidled up next to me. "How was your day?"

"Good." She sighs.

"Uh-oh. What happened?"

"Nothing."

"Nothing?"

"I didn't like the teacher," she blurts out.

"Oh?"

"She was old. And fat. And she had a huge mole on her face."

"Halllie," I scold her. "That's not very nice. Do we talk about

182

what other people look like?"

"No," she mutters. "But she was mean," she says as if it justifies her actions.

"And we can talk about that, but we don't need to talk about how she looks, do we?"

"No."

"Okay. So tell me, why is she mean?"

"Some of the kids were laughing at me."

"Okay . . ." I draw out the word, realising I'm going to have to push her for further information. "What were they laughing at you for?"

"We were giving ideas for what kinds of things we could do at the Mother's Race Day." Oh. I had forgotten about the Mother's Race Day. I also didn't really think about how it could affect each different child. "When it was my turn to say something, Ben yelled out that I don't get to pick something to do seeing as I didn't have a mum to take to Race Day."

What. The. Fuck?

I knew kids could be cruel. Hell, I'd dealt with my own fair share during my own schooling years, but shit, this young?

"Okay," I murmur, not able to concentrate on finding any other words. Warmth fills my body, but I know it's not the good kind. Not the kind I get when Hallie strokes my face. No, this is rage. The kind of rage a mamma bear gets when someone messes with her cub. Someone like a little punk named Ben.

"All the kids started laughing at me," Hallie continues, oblivious to my emotional breakdown.

"What did the teacher do?"

"She told them off."

"Okay." I think about all the facts she has given me so far. "So why is *she* mean?"

"When I told Ben that I would be taking you to the Mother's

Race Day, she told me I wasn't allowed to."

"What?" I snap.

"She said you were not my mum, and I had to come alone or not go."

"What the . . . fudge?" I finish as Hallie's eyes go wide.

That bitch is on my list. When I find out who the hell she is, I am going to come down on her so hard she is not going to know her head from her—

"Why can't you come with me?" Hallie's small voice interrupts me, and my heart shatters into a million pieces. I've been through heartbreak—losing my parents and then my grandparents, living in and then escaping an abusive relationship—but none of it compares to this. To the wretched pain I feel at her trembling lower lip.

"Of course, I can come with you." I pull her close and wrap my arms around her.

"Really?" Her head pops up from my overly tight embrace.

"Of course. I'm not sure what she was talking about. Maybe she was just confused." Yeah, about as confused as she's going to be when my fist hits her face.

"I didn't like her."

I weigh up the teacher and the friend. The responsible adult and the father's girlfriend. The role model and the 'what could be'.

"I don't like her either." Hallie graces me with the biggest grin, and it totally makes crossing the moral line worth it.

Not being able to let it go, I sneak into the other room a few minutes later while the TV distracts Hallie.

"Hey, babe." Georgia answers on the third ring. "How are you feeling?"

"Better," I whisper.

"Have you lost your voice?"

"No. I'm just talking quietly because Hallie's in the next room and I don't want her to hear me."

"What? What's going on?"

"Who had my class today?"

"Some old lady called Mrs Burnheart. Why's that?"

"Did you hear about any drama in there?"

"No. Why? What's going on?"

I sigh and quickly look around the corner to make sure Hallie is not coming before I lay all the details out for Georgia. Well, what I know at least.

"That bitch," Georgia snaps.

"Right?"

"Is Hallie okay?"

"Yeah. I told her I'm going with her."

"Good. What a cow."

"I know."

"You should put in a report to Julia." Julia is our principal. She is an older lady who is firm but fair. "They had called her in from the temp agency because all our regulars were busy. Julia should know so we don't use her again."

"Yeah." I sigh. "I'll talk to her about it when I discuss the Mother's Race Day."

"Do you think she'll have a problem with it?"

"I hope not. I don't want to have to cause a scene at work."

Georgia laughs, the sheer volume making me to pull the phone away from my ear. "Look at you. You date a soldier for a few weeks and suddenly you're Rambo."

"Shut up." I laugh.

"You at his house now?"

"Yeah, I've been here for the past couple of days."

"Is he looking after you?"

"Yes, he's taking very good care of me, as a matter of fact."

185

"Oh, I bet he is."

"Oh my God." I laugh. "I'm going now. Talk to you tomorrow."

"Bye." She gets out around her hysterical laughter.

I don't stop smiling for the next two hours. Hallie and I watch some kid's TV for an hour and then go throw the Frisbee to Max for a while before we decide to make Jake dinner so he doesn't have to come home from work and cook. Finding some steaks, we put them in the oven while we start preparing the vegetables.

Being like this with her sets some maternal hormone off in me, and I feel protective and possessive. As though she is mine. As though I can shield her from all the wrong there is in the world. As though we could spend every afternoon together like this for the rest of our lives.

I want that. I want this little girl. And not as my boyfriend's daughter. I want her for my own. When there's a mother's only event, I want there to be no doubt that I'll be there because that's what I am to her.

I sigh as I look over at Hallie, who is now setting the table. Have we rushed this? Have we involved her too soon? What if Jake doesn't feel the same as I do about it? What if we are on completely different wavelengths when it comes to our relationship and Hallie? I don't want her hurt. I also don't want *me* hurt.

The front door clicks, and Hallie and I make eye contact, a second passing before we both grin and race towards the entry.

Jake is stepping inside as we reach him and his face lights up. "Hey. My girls."

Hallie jumps into his arms and he barely catches her as he laughs and pulls her tight against him. A man can do many things to get the hormones in a woman flowing—wearing a suit, opening a door, riding a motorcycle. But there is something insanely hot about a man with his child.

With what I'm sure is a goofy grin, I step up to them and place my hand on Hallie's back. "Welcome home."

"Hi." He smiles. "You look much better."

"I'm feeling much better."

"Good." He leans forward and places a light kiss on my lips. "Hi."

"Hi."

"We made you dinner," Hallie exclaims, wiggling out of his arms.

"I thought something smelt good."

Jake kicks off his boots and follows us to the kitchen. He sits at the table and we all chat about our day as Hallie finishes setting up, and I serve the steak, pumpkin, potato, peas, and corn.

As I'm pouring the gravy over the meat, I feel his heat before I actually feel him. He steps up behind me and wraps his arms around my waist.

"Please tell me you'll stay," he whispers into my ear, and my whole body shivers.

"Tonight?" I croak.

"Forever."

I turn around in his arms to search his face. There is no humour there, no amusement. He is dead serious. I try to swallow the lump in my throat as I wrap my arms around his neck and pull him down tight against me.

He just voiced every thought I'd had today in one word. I want to stay. I want this to be permanent.

I nuzzle into his chest, and his smell overtakes me. Diesel and grease fill my nose and even though it sounds incredibly unappealing, it's not. There's something manly about it. Something so comforting. I take a huge sniff.

"Are you alright?" Jake laughs. "Did you just smell me?"

"Yeah, I totally just did." Why try to hide it?

"Umm, okay. I probably stink. I was working on an engine all day."

"You smell awesome." I take another huge sniff. This could become addictive.

"Now that's one I've never heard before." Jake laughs again. "Kind of turns me on."

"Does it?" I lean back to look at him.

Jake grabs my hand and slyly squeezes it between us and down to his semi-hard cock. *Wow, he's not kidding.*

"I love these hands too." I bring our joined hands back up and lay them on his chest as my fingers run over his.

"Okay, now you are fucking with me. They're dirty and rough."

"I know. I love it."

"Okay." He laughs and slaps my ass. "Time to eat. You are lightheaded."

I frown at the disappearance of his heat before I finish serving the food and Jake helps me carry the plates to the table.

"So how was your day, princess?" Jake smiles at Hallie as she shoves another piece of potato in.

Hallie tells Jake all about Mrs Burnheart, including her mole, and everything that happened at school today. He frowns and nods as he listens, letting Hallie get everything off her chest before he comments.

"Hallie," he starts, his voice serious.

"Don't worry about it, Dad. Lana already said she'd come with me."

Jake's head snaps to me, and I give him an awkward smile. "Really?" he asks, but he doesn't turn to Hallie.

"Yeah. She doesn't like Mrs Burnheart, either."

I cringe. I physically cringe.

Jake stares at me with hard eyes for a moment before turning to smile at Hallie. "Well, we can talk about that another time, okay?"

Oh, shit.

We eat in silence, and it's not the comfortable kind. It's full of animosity, confusion, and questions. I fear I've stepped over the line here, and I don't know how to pull it all back.

Once we've eaten, Jake takes Hallie to take a bath while I clean up and do the dishes. I was happy for the distraction at first, but apparently, washing a sink full of dirty dishes doesn't take enough brain space to clear all the stuff running through my head.

The thoughts overtake me and I consider grabbing my handbag and getting the hell out of here.

"Hallie, say good night to Lana." Jake's voice is cold and a huge knot forms in the pit of my stomach.

"I want Lana to put me to bed."

"Hallie."

"Please?" she begs.

"I can put her to bed."

"Okay, give me a kiss." He picks Hallie up, and she wraps her tiny arms around his neck and kisses his cheek. A faint smile lifts Jake's lips, and I'm not surprised. I know how it feels to have her affection.

When he places her on her feet, I take her hand and we head down the hallway. I hold my head high as Jake narrows his eyes on me, trying to pretend I am a lot stronger than I really am.

Hallie picks a book from her shelf, and we read it three times before her eyes are drooping shut. I close the book and sit next to her as she dozes off to sleep. I watch her, enjoying the peacefulness of it. I start picking up her room, books and toys that lay on the floor.

In truth, I am biding my time. It's obvious that Jake is not happy, and it's obvious it's because I agreed to go to the Moth-er's Race Day. It's also obvious that I am a complete coward, and am, in all honesty, shitting myself.

"How's it going?" Jake pops his head in and I freeze.

"Good, she's asleep. I'm just tidying up."

"Can I talk to you when you're done?"

Fuck. "Sure."

I pick the last doll up off the floor and put it in the doll's crib. Standing in the middle of the room, I glance around, just in case I've missed anything. No. So I just stand there, tapping my leg as I continue looking around. For what, I'm not sure. An escape route?

Once I stand there for as long as I think I possibly can, I shuffle out to the living room.

Jake is sitting on the couch, flipping through the channels. I don't bother sitting down; I'd rather get this over with so I stand in the entryway. Standing here dressed in Jake's tracksuit pants and T-shirt only makes me feel more vulnerable. I wish I were in my own jeans and T-shirt. That way I would feel more like myself. More able to cope with the argument I know we are about to have. Because if he thinks he can scold me about the Mother's Race Day, he has another thing coming.

Jake sighs and shuts off the TV, chucking the remote on the coffee table, before shifting to look at me. "What were you thinking?" He doesn't explain what he's talking about, and we both know he doesn't need to.

"I was thinking there was a very upset little girl and I could make her feel better. Make things right."

"At what cost?"

"What does that mean?" I frown.

"You can't make decisions for my family, Lana." My stom-ach turns. *His* family. I'm no idiot. Of course, they aren't my family, but the way he says it makes it seem like it's a done deal. Like there is no possibility of *us* ever becoming a family.

All my thoughts from today, of us being something, fall from my mind. "I didn't think it was that big of a deal. She didn't want to go alone."

"Well, she could've skipped it."

I see red as rage overtakes all the hurt and rejection, and I hold my tongue no more. "Give me a break, Jake. You can't hide this from her. She's not silly. You can't pretend her mother never existed. How is that fair to Hallie? Or to Jamie?"

Jake's face contorts in anger, and my eyes go wide. I have seen that face many times. I know it well. I know what comes next. I just never imagined I would see it on Jake.

Chapter Twenty-Five

Jake

"Do you think I don't know how to raise my own kid?" I scream, and Lana flinches. Her eyes are wild, and her face is pale. She flinched. It was barely noticeable, but I saw it. She flinched. Because of me. I scared her.

I release a deep breath, calming myself down, and step towards her. "Angel."

She immediately takes a step back, holding her hands up in surrender. "Don't."

I take another small step. "Fuck, angel, I'm sorry." She retreats again, and my heart stills. "Are you afraid of me?"

She takes another step back and doesn't answer me as she turns and runs out of the living room.

"Fuck."

Rushing down the hallway, I hear the bathroom door slam. By the time I reach it and try to push it open, it's locked. She's locked herself in the bathroom? Fuck, this is bad.

"Lana," I call through the door. "Please open the door. I'm sorry." There is no response but I hear muffled crying coming from the other side. What the fuck? I rest my forehead on the door. "What did he do to you?"

The crying turns to sobbing, and I can't take it anymore. "Lana, open the door or I'm breaking it down."

The weeping continues and I hope to God it's muffled because she's on the other side of the room. I step back from the door and use all my force as I bring my foot up against the hard wood. Thankfully, the door is not solid, and my foot goes straight through the plywood. I fiddle around inside and see if I can unlatch the lock. When I can't, I step back and give the door one more solid kick.

It flies open and smashes against the back wall. Lana sits on the floor between the shower and the toilet, holding her knees against her chest as she rocks back and forth, bawling her eyes out.

My heart shatters, but I don't have time to focus on it as I rush over, pulling her into my arms and holding her tight as I rock side to side.

"It's okay, angel, I'm here. I'm sorry." Lana has a death grip on my shirt, and she uses it to pull me closer. The relief that flows through me when she doesn't pull away from my touch is indescribable. I don't want her to be afraid of me. But I know she is afraid of something, and right now, she is clinging to me like I am her lifeline. Her saviour. The hero who dragged her from her burning house. And that's exactly how it should be. Except it's all a lie.

"What did he do to you?" I whisper against her head as I rest my cheek on it. I don't need to tell her who *he* is.

She starts to stutter between sobs as she tries to talk. "Shh, It's okay," I tell her. I'll sit here for as long as she needs before she can speak.

It's a while before her breathing begins to slow and her crying begins to ease. "He was abusive," she hiccups.

I tense. My body is tight with all the anger that is forming just under the surface. As she continues, the rage boils and weaves itself so intricately through me, it's as though I'm being strangled.

"He was . . . just horrid, to be honest."

"Did he . . .?" I can't finish my question. Just the thought of someone putting their hands on Lana has my head spinning in a frenzy of wrath.

"Yes," she whispers.

I pull in a sharp breath and tighten my hold on her. My hands shake and my breathing becomes erratic. I don't know if I can sit here and listen to this. Closing my eyes, I focus on drawing air into my lungs at a controlled pace. I have to be strong for her.

"He was controlling. Wouldn't let me go out with my friends. Barely let me visit Tate or Maurice. He wanted power over every aspect of my life. What I wore, down to where I worked."

I kiss her head, letting her know I'm listening.

"He wasn't violent to begin with. Just more emotional abuse." She pauses to pull in a breath. "Until one day when he found my birth-control pill."

"What?" I ask confused.

She stares out into the bathroom now. Going right back to that moment. "We were trying to have a baby. Or at least, he thought we were."

I close my eyes in understanding.

"I couldn't bring a baby into that. I don't know what I was

thinking. I knew I wanted kids, but I knew I didn't want kids with him. But then I couldn't leave him, either. I don't know how I thought that cycle was going to play out."

I rub my hand over her head in a soothing motion. "How did it play out?"

"He found me in the kitchen getting dinner ready. He confronted me about the pills and I had nothing to say. He attacked me. Pushed me to the ground and kicked me in the stomach."

"Oh, angel."

"I don't actually remember it. I must have hit my head when he pushed me. All I remember is his screaming, but the doctors told me what they suspected had happened."

Lana's hand naturally drifts down to her stomach and I cover it with my own, offering comfort in the only way that feels right in this moment.

"As soon as the hospital released me, I went to Tate." My mind flashes to Tate and the '*brotherly chat*' we had. The anger and fury that flashed in his eyes definitely makes sense now. "He sorted everything. Got me out of there, filed for the restraining order when Craig returned a few months later. He saved me."

"He shouldn't have had to save you."

"I know. I was stupid—"

"No. Don't even go there, Lana. You were scared."

"Yes," she whispers against my neck.

"Angel, you were scared of me before." It's not a question, but she answers anyway, her voice breathy.

"Yes."

"I would never hurt you, angel. You have to know that." I pull back to meet her gaze, to make sure my message gets across. Her eyes are red and raw, and I would give anything in this moment to take all the pain away from her.

"I do know that. I am so sorry for freaking out on you."

195

"No. God no, angel, you don't ever have to apologise for that. Ever. I will never speak to you like that again. I swear."

She nuzzles my neck, and her body shakes with wracking sobs. I close my eyes and tears drip down my cheeks. I wipe them away and glance at my hands. I'm crying. I'm fucking crying. I don't think I've shed a tear since I was seven years old and I fell asleep on my bike, crashing it into the riverbank.

And this is not just one tear. I feel them, uncontrolled, running rampant down my cheeks. There's no break as they just flow and flow together.

We sit here together well into the late hours of the night before we both finally settle, and I pick her up and carry her to the bed, wrapping her in my arms so tight that nothing can touch her. Not even her memories.

Tonight, we cried together. Cried for each other. Both our individual pain, demons, and fears melding together in our tears before they were washed away.

Lana shifts in my arms and I peel my eyes open to find us in the exact same position we were in when we went to sleep. My head throbs, and my eyes feel dry and irritated. The sun is only just peeking through the side of the curtains so I know it's still early.

"How are you feeling?" I ask when I feel her move again.

"Terrible," she says flatly, making me chuckle.

"I'm so sorry about last night," I say, remorse lining my voice.

"No, Jake, it was my fault. I have no experience with kids besides being a teacher and that doesn't even come close to being a parent. I have no idea what I'm talking about."

"Neither do parents." I force a laugh. "We just play it day by day, hoping for the best. I should've listened to you. Discussed it with you."

"No, I shouldn't have said anything to Hallie without talking to you first. Besides, it's none of my business," she states defiantly.

"No, angel, it is your business. I want it to be your business." I whisper the last part, and her eyes flash up to mine, wide and shocked.

"What?"

"I want it to be your business. I want us to be a partnership, working together in all aspects of our lives. I want you to be there for us and for us to be there for you. You, me, and Hallie. That's what I want."

Lana's eyes soften and she jumps on top of me, wrapping her arms around my neck and knocking me onto my back. "I want that too," she says into my neck. "I want that too."

We lie in silence, letting the moment of decision settle in. I rock her from side to side as she holds on for dear life, as if she never wants to let me go.

"I scared you," I whisper, finally bringing up the sore point that has been on my mind since last night.

"Hmm?" Lana leans back to look at me.

"You flinched when I yelled. I scared you. You were scared."

Lana's eyes drop as her body relaxes. There's no denying it.

"Why did you marry him?" My voice is soft. There is no disgust in my tone, just wonder.

"After my grandparents died, I felt more alone than ever. Then with his constant manipulation, telling me no one else would want me, I figured where would I go? I lost a lot of the woman I once was."

My whole body stiffens and the same spirals of unadulterated rage from last night move through me once more. I pull Lana tighter against me, holding her close, more for me than her.

"Where did he end up? You never saw him again?"

Lana's face says it all. *As if he would let her leave that easy.* "He came after me a few months later, drunk as hell, looking for money. Looking for revenge, I think."

My teeth grind, literally grind, as I hold onto my fury at the man who hurt this woman. My woman. "How did that end?"

"I have no idea, really. Tate sorted everything. A restraining order, a lawyer to take care of my divorce and settlement. He organised my inheritance money, bought my house with it, and invested the rest for me." I narrow my eyes at Lana. "I never really asked for the details. I know that's probably stupid, but I didn't want to know. And I don't think Tate really wanted to tell me."

"That's understandable." I pull Lana's head back to rest in my neck where she had it before. I can't listen to any more; my heart is breaking.

Chapter Twenty-Six

Jake

I laugh as I watch Lana and Hallie doing the three-legged race down the one hundred-meter line. They are unstable and slow, and they laugh so hard that Lana is wiping tears away.

We spent the week walking on eggshells after our fight, neither one of us wanting to bring it up until we realised that we both wanted Lana to take Hallie to the Mother's Race Day. And not only did we both agree, but Hallie wanted it too. Hallie wanted it so much that I don't think she stopped smiling for days.

And now here we are, on a beautiful Saturday morning down at the school oval, watching children's races. Lana and Hallie are laughing so uncontrollably now that just as they reach the finish line, in last place mind you, they go crashing down in a pile of limbs and giggles.

As I make my way over to them, Georgia says, "Well, you guys did . . . you tried really hard." She's looking down at Hallie and Lana on the grass, both still in fits of laughter.

"Come on." I reach down and Lana takes my hand, letting me pull her up. She does the same for Hallie, and the laughter begins to settle.

"That was tough." Lana tries to catch her breath.

"It was a bit silly," Hallie agrees.

"Sillier than the egg and spoon, and the Frisbee throw?" I ask.

"I guess not," Lana says, and they laugh again.

"Come on, you two," Georgia says in mock frustration as she leads us over to the water relay. "I'm going to set Hallie up at the other end."

"Okay." Lana smiles. "Kick ass," she calls to Hallie, who turns back and gives her a thumbs-up.

When Lana turns that huge smile to me, I raise my eyebrows. "Whoops." She giggles and covers her mouth. "I forget I'm here as a teacher as well as a mum—oh . . . a guardian . . . well . . . you know."

I grin as I grab her hand and pull her against me. "I have not seen Hallie have so much fun in a long time. And I don't think I have heard that cute little giggle of yours before."

A blush covers her cheeks, and it sends warmth running through my chest. I kiss her nose before nuzzling my face in the crook of her neck.

"Thank you for doing this," I whisper into the soft skin just under her ear.

"Thank you for letting me."

"Hey," Georgia yells across the oval, interrupting our moment. "The race is about to start. Get into position, Miss Washington."

Lana laughs and gives me a peck on the lips before she lines up at the starting point.

I don't think I have felt so happy in a long time. Maybe ever. Watching them together, so happy and having so much fun, makes me feel things I never thought I would. Also, watching Lana in a pair of skin-tight yoga pants is no hard feat, either.

Once they have tried and utterly failed at the water relay race, dodgeball, and the obstacle course, we make our way over to the ceremony tents for announcements and awards. Not expecting a mention, we stand at the back of the crowd.

"We going for pizza after this?" I ask Lana.

"Yeah, I just have to help pack up all the equipment."

"No worries. We can help, can't we, princess?"

Hallie scrunches up her nose as if she can't think of anything worse, and Lana and I chuckle.

"Oh, by the way, I invited Georgia to dinner. I hope that's okay."

"Of course." I have come to learn that Georgia is Lana's closest friend outside of her family. Lana has expressed some worry for her during the last couple of weeks, so of course I would never say no. Apparently, she is down on her love life at the moment. Having a 'mid-life crisis', as Lana put it.

Hallie and I sit on the oval reading together while we wait for Lana and Georgia to finish packing up and conclude their teacherly duties. Families have long since left and the oval is quiet as the sun sets behind the large trees lining the area.

"Ready?" Lana asks, as her and Georgia make their way over to us.

Hallie and I stand to greet them. "I'm starving," Hallie groans.

"Ready." I give Lana a chaste kiss. I have been warned not

to flaunt our relationship in front of Georgia. When I'd laughed, Lana had glared and sternly reminded me no public displays of affection. We aren't really an overly affectionate kind of couple, so I wasn't sure if I was going to be reprimanded for that kiss later tonight or not.

"So, how did today go? You taking Hallie," Georgia asks Lana as we slide into the booth at the pizza place, with Lana and I sitting across from Hallie and Georgia.

"Good." Lana nods. "The school was okay with the idea, and the parents didn't say anything."

"I caught a few sidelong glances," I tell her.

"I did notice that," Lana agrees. "But that group of mothers are always looking for something to gossip about. I wouldn't take it to heart." She places her hand on top of mine, which is resting on the table. "I thought the kids were great with Hallie," she says, her voice low as she watches Hallie colouring in her kid's menu.

"Good."

"Kids can be cruel," Georgia adds. "Real assholes, actually. You can't let it get you down. Or . . ." She gestures to Hallie.

That's the last thing I want—for this to affect Hallie in any negative way. So far, it has been positive, and all I can see is the wonderful things Lana has brought to our family since she became a part of it.

"I'm pretty sure she is so happy nothing could bring her down." I squeeze Lana's hand and smile at Hallie, who is still studiously colouring, completely oblivious to the conversation going on around her.

"My God, you guys are too much," Georgia groans, and Lana pulls her hand off mine, making me glare at the spot where her warmth once was.

The waitress interrupts our awkward silence. "Good evening, my name is Marcy, and I'll be your host tonight. Did you want to start with any drinks?"

We order some Cokes and a couple of different large pizzas to share. The waitress returns with our drinks in no time and promises our pizza won't be long.

"So, Jake." Georgia leans forward on the table. "Got any single friends?"

"Georgia." Lana spits out her Coke.

"What? He's obviously a good catch, and let's face it—he's in the Army! He must know heaps of eligible bachelors."

Lana's cheeks flood red and my eyes shift around the room, wanting to look anywhere else. But Georgia remains straight-faced, her eyes on me.

"Most the guys I know are married . . . or old . . . or perpetually single."

"That's okay." Her voice is serious. "I don't need a man, just his sperm."

"Georgia, enough," Lana snaps. "Hallie's here."

"Huh?" Hallie looks up from her colouring.

"Nothing, princess," I reassure her.

"Don't look at me like that, Lana. I'm getting desperate. I don't need a daddy for my baby, just a donor."

"Go to a sperm bank," Lana mumbles.

"Too expensive."

"So what? You're just going to go out and trick some guy into knocking you up?"

"I would never trick him." She balks. "I'm going to ask."

Lana and I erupt into loud laughter, which halts abruptly when we realise Georgia is not laughing. My eyes go wide as I take in her stoic expression. *She's not kidding.*

"What the hell?" Lana squeaks.

"What? If I can find a guy who agrees to get me pregnant

with no strings attached, then what's wrong with that? Two consenting adults, making a joint decision."

Before Lana can protest, the waitress delivering our pizzas interrupts us, but I see the words on the tip of her tongue.

I'm sure this is a conversation for another day, and one that should be between just the two of them, so I hastily change the subject. "Are we working on your place next weekend?"

Lana turns to me, her eyes still wide and her mouth still hanging open, as she processes what I'm asking her.

"Yeah," she drags the word out. "I'm hoping to get a lot of the painting done."

"Cool. I'll call Marley tomorrow to see if she can have Hallie."

"Good idea. I don't want her around all those paint fumes."

My face lifts into a grin. I love when she gets all motherly and protective over Hallie. She is going to be an awesome mother, whether it be to Hallie or to her own kids as well. Hopefully *our* own kids.

Thankfully, my tactic works, and the subject of Georgia's reproductive plans doesn't come up again as we eat our pizza in silence. Each one of us scoffs down enough so that there is nothing but a few crusts left when we're finished.

"God, I'm stuffed." Georgia rubs her hand over her stomach.

"That was awesome," Lana agrees, nodding.

"I could go for some ice cream," Hallie says, before she slurps down the last of her lemonade.

"How about we grab some on the way home?" I look at Lana for confirmation, rubbing her thigh underneath the table.

"Sounds good to me."

"Oh, you guys are killing me." Georgia stands from the booth. "Please don't ever let me be the fourth wheel again."

We laugh as she ruffles Hallie's hair and waves on her way

out of the restaurant.

We follow her lead and decide to get going. I pay the bill while Lana takes Hallie to the toilet. Another small blessing that I don't have to stress about anymore—male and female toilet trips. When we're all done, we put Hallie in the truck and head to the ice cream parlour.

"She wasn't serious, was she?" I ask.

"Who?"

"Georgia. About having a baby?"

"Oh God only knows," Lana says. "She is so fixated on getting old and missing out on having a baby."

"She's not that old."

"I know!" Lana protests, her voice high.

I laugh at her outrage. "It's none of our business."

"Like hell it isn't," she mutters under her breath.

As I said, a conversation for the two of them for another day.

Chapter Twenty-Seven

Jake

"Does that look even to you?" Lana asks, throwing her paintbrush onto the plastic-covered floor.

My eyes roam over the wall she has been painting all morning. "Looks good to me."

We've spent most of the day here, arriving early to get some painting done. I don't know why we're bothering, though—Lana hasn't left my house for weeks. We have somewhat just settled into this domestic bliss—Lana taking Hallie to school, them spending the afternoons together before I get home from work, and then us cooking and eating together. Lana and I share the duties of dishes, bathing, and putting Hallie to bed.

Nothing has been said or decided; we have just fallen into this seamless living arrangement.

I like it. No, I fucking love it. It would make me the happiest guy on earth to live out the rest of my days in this simple manner.

"God, my body is sore." My thoughts clear as my vision zeros in on Lana stretching her arms to the ceiling as she stands on her tiptoes. Her tight singlet riding up her body reveals her flat stomach, and her stance causes her tits to push together.

I admire the view unabashedly with my eyes wide and mouth hanging open. Lana then bends over, keeping her legs straight, as she grabs onto her ankles. Her ass in those skin-tight yoga pants has my dick standing at attention.

"God." She groans. "That feels good."

I can't hold back any longer and stalk across the room until I am standing behind her. My hands are tight on her hips, pulling her ass against the erection that's already stretching my old torn jeans.

"Fuck, that *does* feel good," I groan.

"Jake," Lana squeals, but I don't let go. I reach down and grasp the back of her knees, giving them a squeeze before I graze my palms up the back of her thighs and over her ass. Her yoga pants are so tight, she may as well be naked, and when her whole body shivers at my touch, I know she must be thinking the same.

She stays bent over as I caress her ass, rubbing my hands over every inch. Without warning, I grip the waist of her pants and strip them down to her ankles, taking her panties with them. Trailing light kisses up her calves and thighs, my hands follow until I bury my face into her ass.

Lana groans and pushes back into me, but I lean back to take my fill of her. It's the hottest fucking thing I have ever seen. She's still bent over, gripping her ankles, and her pussy is now on display, glistening with her own arousal.

Burying my face back between her legs, I lap at her, kissing, licking and nibbling at every piece of flesh I can find. She groans in frustration but only gets more and more aroused with my teasing, as her moans get louder.

When I finally run my tongue from her ass through her folds to her clit, she releases a long, deep groan that has my dick jumping in excitement and my control snapping.

Pulling her to a standing position, I turn her around so I'm on my knees in front of her, my face buried back in her pussy within seconds. Lana moans and whimpers as I grab at her hips, trying to get some leverage, but I can't get a good grip.

Releasing her for just a second, I push her back against the wall and am able to lift her leg over my shoulder to gain better access to the taste that sends me wild.

I hear a muffled, "Jake, the wet paint," while I'm between her legs, but I just couldn't give a fuck.

"I'll deal with it later," I say against her skin.

Lana moans and must lose all care as she relaxes onto me, and I grip her harder to hold her up against the wall. I taste every bit of her as I run my tongue all over her pussy and thrust it inside before I finally give her the attention she craves and focus in on her clit.

She screams out my name as she rolls her hips over my mouth, and her body shakes in my arms. I don't relax my attention until she stands limply in front of me, resting the majority of her body weight against the freshly painted wall.

"That's it, angel, that's it." I kiss up her body, stand, and pull her tank top over her head before thoroughly devouring her mouth. Lana wraps her arms around my shoulders and pulls me tight against her as she wraps a leg around my waist.

Rolling my hips, I ground my hard cock into her, revelling in the sounds she makes. "What do you want, angel?"

Lana's patience must snap as she reaches down and fumbles with my jeans until she is pushing them down my legs.

When my pants are around my ankles, she practically jumps into my arms, and I help her by grabbing her thighs and hoisting her up against the wall, getting a good grip of her ass once she's secure.

"Fuck, angel, you are so wet," I tell her as I rub my cock through her silken lips.

"Jake, oh God, Jake."

I tease her for a little longer, extracting all types of moans and whimpers from her, before I settle my cock against her entrance. She sighs in relief just before I thrust deep inside her, and her sigh turns into a gasp.

I don't give her time to get used to me before I thrust hard and fast. Her pussy clenches around me and it only spurs me on more, my cock out of control now.

She holds on so tight it's almost painful, but I feel nothing else as my dick searches for its own release. And it's not long before it finds it, and I'm biting down hard on Lana's bare shoulder as I jerk inside of her, that familiar ecstasy flowing through me.

"What . . . the . . . hell . . . was . . . that?" Lana breathes, her chest rising and falling with harsh breaths.

"I'm sorry, angel. Are you okay? Did I hurt you?"

"No."

I don't know what came over me. Well, I do. *Lana.* I can't fucking control myself when I'm around her. The guilt of not getting her off a second time assaults me so while I'm buried deep inside her, I lay light kisses down her collarbone and across her chest.

She sighs in contentment as I trail my lips up the other side of her neck and nibble on her earlobe. Making my way back down her chest, I lick across the tops of her breasts before I take her nipple into my mouth and suck it hard.

I give the same attention to her other breast before I graze the back of my knuckles down her stomach and pull my now semi-hard cock out of her. Lana lifts her hips as if to meet my fingers halfway. Chuckling, I give her what she wants and slide two of my fingers into her warm heat. She is soaking wet now as both our arousals fill her, and I use it to rub all through her folds and over her clit before my fingers enter her again.

I thrust them deep, searching for that magical spot that makes her purr, and as if on cue, she does. Her whimpers of pleasure only make me hard again, and I impatiently pull my fingers from her, turn her to face the wall, and push her against it. I grip my cock and stroke it before I thrust into her again.

Lana moans as she tries to grip the wall and I place my hands next to hers on either side of her head, never breaking my rhythm. I push my body harder against her until there is no space between her and the wall, and between her and me. I hold on with one hand as I grab her breast with the other, kneading, pinching, and caressing.

Sliding my hand down her stomach, I find her swollen clit and tickle it as my hard thrusts continue. Lana's pussy tightens around me and I will myself to hold off, which should be a lot easier seeing as I only found release a matter of minutes ago.

I continue my more controlled pace until Lana's body shakes against me and she calls out my name once more. Letting go, I rest my head against her shoulder as the state of euphoria takes me over.

Lana's chuckle pulls me from my relaxed stupor. "Oh my God, how much mess have we made?"

Lifting my head off her shoulder, I take a look around. White paint covers her whole back, there's paint all over my hands and a tin of paint spilt on the floor. I can't imagine what she looks like from the front.

"Just a little bit," I lie, and then kiss her shoulder blade before I stand back and give her room to turn.

"How bad is it?" she asks as she turns to face me.

I can't help it; I laugh. I laugh my fucking my ass off. "I'm not going to lie, angel, it's not fucking good."

Lana groans, and I pull her into my arms. "It could be worse. I bet you're glad you let me spend more on the water-based paint."

Lana laughs and I kiss the tip of her nose. One of the very few places on her body that isn't covered in paint. "Come on, let me get you cleaned up."

I pull my jeans back up, and we leave the living room in a state of disarray as I lead her to the bathroom to wash up.

Lana laughs at herself in the mirror as I get the shower started. "Oh my God, I hope this all comes off. I can't go to work looking like this."

I laugh when I really look at her. Paint covers the left side of her face, her breasts, all down her thighs, as well as her back and the top of her perky ass.

"I'll get it off. Come on." Holding the shower door open, I smirk and gesture for her to get in.

She stands under the hot water, which starts to thin the paint as I load up her puff with body wash. Inhaling big, I appreciate the smell that is Lana, the vanilla aroma filling the shower.

Pulling her out of the stream of water, I start the long process of removing the paint, rubbing small but firm circles all over her skin.

Her soft and pale flesh becomes red and angry from all the scrubbing, so I lean down and lay soft kisses over every piece of it I can find.

211

"I'm sorry." I kiss across the top of her back. "Does it hurt?"

"No," she whispers. "Actually, it feels great."

I smile against her skin as I trail my mouth down her back, over the top of her ass and back up again. "There's even paint in your hair." I flick her ponytail.

"Well, what do you expect? You practically attacked me." Lana laughs, but I growl as I turn her around to face me and lift her up against the shower wall, all in one swift move.

"No—this is me attacking you." And I do. I attack with everything I'm feeling. All the passion, all the lust, and all the love. Yeah, that's what this fucking is. Love.

Chapter Twenty-Eight

Jake

"Hello." I walk into Marley's kitchen to pick up Hallie after school and find Marley and Hallie sitting together at the kitchen table with a plate of cookies in front of them. "Hot chocolates?" I gesture to their mugs as I take a seat.

"Yeah, you want one?" Marley asks.

"I'd love one."

She hops up to grab a mug out of the cupboard.

"How was your day?" I ask Hallie, who is happily munching on a chocolate chip cookie.

"Good."

"Just good?"

"Yeah." She pouts. "I just miss going home with Lana. It's boring here."

"It's boring here?" I laugh. "You have three cousins to play with. At home you're all by yourself."

"I have Lana. We do stuff together."

"I know, but she has a life too." I grab a cookie off the plate. "She can't be with us twenty-four/seven."

"What's twenty-four/seven?" Her little nose scrunches up in confusion.

"It means all day, every day."

"Oh. Well, I know that."

"Hallie, why don't you go and pack up your homework and get ready for Dad to take you home?" Marley says as she places my mug down on the table.

"Okay." She hops off the chair, her shoulders slumped and her head down.

"Here," Marley calls to her. "Take the plate of cookies out to the boys."

I quickly grab another cookie off the plate as Hallie mumbles her response and takes the plate.

"So," Marley says, after she waits for Hallie to leave the kitchen, "what was Lana up to today?"

I take a huge bite of my cookie. "She's going on a girls' night out tonight. She spent the afternoon with a friend."

"Oh, right."

"Oh, right what?"

"Nothing. I just wonder how you'll cope without her for the evening." She laughs.

"I'm not going without her for the night," I snap. "She's coming home afterwards."

"Home?" Marley sputters.

"You know what I mean."

"Are you picking her up?"

"No." I take another bite of the cookie to bide myself some

time. "I offered to, but she wouldn't let me drag Hallie out of bed at that hour. So I gave her a spare key."

"You gave her a key?" Her mouth drops open.

"Is that a problem?"

Her eyes shine with indecision. "No."

"It's not a big deal. I want her coming home to me."

"Oh my God, Jake," she practically shouts. "It's a huge deal. She's really gotten under your skin."

"She isn't just under my skin. It's more than that. She's the blood running through my veins."

Marley's eyes are wide and her mouth is open enough to catch flies. "Jake," she says, her tone warning. "Be careful—"

"Marley, don't."

"I'm just saying—"

"I don't want to hear it." I huff in frustration, frustration at myself for even saying something.

"Jake, listen to me." She places her hand over mine. "I love Lana. I think she is the best thing that has happened to you guys—"

"She is—"

"I know," she snaps. "I'm just saying I want you to be careful. Things are moving so fast, and I'm worried that you and Hallie could get hurt."

"We'll be fine."

"I'm sure *you* will be. But what about Hallie? What about Lana? I don't think she's as strong as she seems."

I nod in thought. I can't tell Marley how on the mark she is. They are not my secrets to tell, and as new as this thing is between Lana and me, I know she's not the type to want her dirty laundry aired all over town. Even though it's only been a couple of months, I feel like I know everything about her.

Thinking about her secrets and the fact that I know them all sends a rip-roaring pain through my gut at the secret I still hold from her. The stupid insignificant secret that has now built into such a fiasco it's all I can think about most days.

Do I tell her, even though I've had countless opportunities to do so and haven't, thus risking further wrath, or do I just take it to my grave, hoping that it will fall away as something small and inconsequential the bigger and stronger we become?

"Listen." I pull my hand away from Marley's to pat her shoulder. "I know what I'm doing. Please don't worry about me. Or Hallie, or Lana. I know Lana's issues, and I'm watching out for her. I love her, Marley." She smiles at me, all warm and soft. Her eyes mist over as she nods. "I love her."

"Have you told *her* that?"

"I'm ready to go, Daddy." Hallie clatters back into the kitchen dragging her schoolbag behind her.

"Okay, princess."

"Hey." Marley smiles at Hallie. "How about you stay here tonight? We have the boys' football in the morning but we're going to get ice cream after. You can keep me company."

"Can I, Dad?"

I raise my eyebrows at her. "I thought it was boring here?"

"Well . . ." She stalls. "Not all the time."

Chapter Twenty-Nine

Lana

"You know Harper. Have you met Brooke before?" I ask Georgia as we greet the girls at the couches they nabbed in Henry's club. Saxon was right; it is a lot different when it's set up as a lounge bar rather than the club.

"Yes. We met when I picked you up from Tate and Harper's once."

"Oh, that's right; great to see you again." Brooke smiles. "And this is my friend, Rachel."

Georgia smiles and nods a hello to Rachel. "Thanks for letting me tag along. Although I'm sure it's more to appease Lana's worry about me."

"It is not," I defend myself. But it is. I *am* worried about her. This talk of her going out and finding herself a baby daddy has me all riled up and unsure of what to do.

"It's girls' night; the more the merrier." Harper waves to the waitress as Georgia and I take our seats.

"And I'll take any help I can with the wedding plans," Brooke adds.

"Wedding plans." Georgia's smile is forced, and suddenly I think maybe I shouldn't have brought her. I thought it would be good for her to see women who thought they would never find someone and then did. Women who thought it would never happen for them, only to be swept off their feet when they least expected it, myself included. But maybe it's just rubbing salt into her already sore wound. I'm the worst friend ever.

"Drinks, ladies?" the waitress asks.

"Planning a wedding," Georgia whispers to me. "I'll need booze." Then she says to the waitress, "A house white."

"I'll take the same." I smile.

"Me too," Harper and Rachel say at the same time.

"I'll just take a sparkling water please," Brooke adds.

"Water?" Harper scrunches her face in disgust. "It's girls' night out."

"I know, but water is fine." Brooke smiles awkwardly, looking anywhere but at Harper, and Rachel has a grin from ear to ear.

"Oh my God," I breathe.

"What?" Harper frowns at me, while Brooke smiles sweetly and Rachel is full on laughing now.

"You're pregnant?"

"What?" Harper screeches, looking at Brooke, whose huge smile tells her everything. "Oh my God, you're pregnant!"

"Shhhh." Brooke laughs. "Yes, I'm pregnant. It's still early days."

Georgia reaches over and grabs the waitress's arm before she turns to leave. "I'll take a scotch on the rocks," she tells her.

"And make it a double."

Rachel and I laugh, and I shake my head. Georgia just winks at me and shrugs.

"It's okay. I'll take the same for the single ladies." Rachel smiles at Georgia.

"I can't believe you're pregnant. What the hell happened?" Harper's eyes are still wide in disbelief.

"I'll explain it to you later." Rachel smirks.

Brooke laughs. "It just happened a lot faster than we thought it would."

"I work with you every day; how did I not notice?"

"You've been too wrapped up in a hot tattooed biker." Rachel laughs.

"I bet Saxon is pleased," I say with a smile.

"Ecstatic. He's been dying to tell everyone."

"Oh, that's what that stupid grin he's been wearing for the past week has been about."

"Yes." Brooke laughs at Harper's sour face.

"And that's why you've been peeing like a race horse these last few weeks."

"Yes." Brooke laughs again. "Speaking of . . ." She stands and heads towards the bathroom.

"She just went when we got here." Rachel shakes her head in disbelief.

We chat amongst ourselves as the waitress delivers our drinks.

"How's work going?" Harper asks me.

"Good."

"Just good?"

"Lana is way too invested in a certain soldier to care what's going on at work. I doubt she even remembers she has a job."

"Shut up." I laugh at Georgia. "She's just a little sour," I tell

219

Harper.

"Who's sour?" Brooke asks as she returns to the table.

"Georgia. She just wishes it was her wedding we were planning," I tease.

Brooke and Harper both frown at her in sympathy, and Georgia laughs. "It's okay. I'm coming to terms with the fact I might be single forever. In fact, make sure you get me home before dark. I don't want to miss the *Jeopardy* reruns."

I laugh and shake my head. Georgia is a classic beauty. With her blonde curls and flawless face, she is the poster child for sweet and innocent natural looks.

"I'm just kidding," she says. "Not about *Jeopardy*; I really like that show. But let's plan your wedding. I'll actually probably be really good at it. I'm an organisational freak."

"Oh my God, stay single," Rachel groans. "Why would you want the drama of a man?"

"You are so cynical." Brooke shakes her head. "How are we even friends?"

"I keep you grounded."

"Sure," she snickers.

"How are the in-laws coping with the news?" Harper asks.

Brooke's smile fades instantly. "Mark was over-the-moon excited. I don't know if he's even told Jeanie yet."

"I doubt he'll tell you." Harper rubs Brookes arm. "He wouldn't want to upset you if her response is less than happy."

"Which it will be," Rachel mutters. "I don't know why you care anymore."

Harper nods her agreement, but I meet Brooke's gaze with a sad smile.

I know why she bothers. I know why she hangs on, hoping things will change. When you lose someone you love, you realise how important it is to have people around. To keep the rest of the people you care about close.

Harper doesn't see her parents much, and I know they have a strained relationship, but she has them. They are there if she needs them or just wants to see them.

I know what it's like to feel lonely. To have almost everyone you love somehow taken away from you. If I were Brooke, I would be hanging onto any family I could find as well.

"Speaking of family." Harper looks at me. "Your brother wants me to ask you when you are going to come sing at the café."

"Umm, never," I snort.

"You sing?" Georgia asks, her eyes wide and mouth hanging open.

"No."

"Yes, she does. I hear she has a beautiful voice, but she refuses to sing for us." Brooke pouts.

"Come on, Lana. I am dying to hear you sing. We could make a night of it at the café. We'll get everyone there." Harper gives me her best puppy-dog eyes.

"Oh great," I say sarcastically. "You're going to invite everyone we know to watch me sing for the first time in years. Awesome, can't wait."

"Don't be like that." Rachel laughs. "Help your brother out."

"Speaking of my brother, shouldn't we have another wedding to plan?" I quirk an eyebrow at Harper, and she sighs.

"Good change of subject." She glares at me. "Tate and I aren't sure what we are going to do yet."

"What do you mean?" Brooke asks.

"We want to elope."

A round of *'hell no'*, *'I don't think so'* and *'no way'* echoes around the table.

"It's our wedding, and we'll do it how we want."

Brooke glares at Harper before turning to me. "What about you?"

"What about me?" My eyes are wide.

"Will we be hearing wedding bells for you soon?"

"Oh my God, no," I state firmly. "Jake and I have only been dating a couple of months."

"So?" Brooke frowns.

"Well, from what I hear, you have practically moved in together already," Harper says haughtily, as though she knows a secret I don't. I know she's just trying to get revenge on me for bringing up her non-wedding plans.

Brooke and Rachel's eyes rest on me, waiting expectantly for my response. Georgia's wide eyes are full of excitement as she glances from Harper to Brooke and back to me again.

"Where did you hear that?"

"Well, when Tate went to check on your place the other day and see how things were coming along, Mrs Crimbledon stopped him to chat and happened to mention she hadn't seen you stay at the house for weeks."

"Hasn't seen me for weeks? Well that's a bit exaggerated," I huff.

"Is it?" Harper's face breaks into a knowing smile.

"A little bit." I can't help but smile. "We've just fallen into this easy relationship. I know it sounds cliché, but it's as though it's . . . just meant to be."

"Awwww," all the girls gush.

"Shut up." I smile. "Everything about us is perfect."

"Like how he came in and saved your life that first night." Harper smiles.

"Yes." I smile. "Especially how he saved me. Even that was perfect. I've just never been in a relationship like that before."

All four of the girls frown at me. All four of them know what

222

I have been through in the past.

"I'm worried I'm falling too hard, too fast. What if I lose him? I don't know if I could go on without him and Hallie."

"Why would you lose him?" asks Brooke.

There is no way I'm going to explain to them how every single person I have ever loved has been taken from me. So instead, I just shake my head, avoiding her question.

"So . . ." Georgia winks at me, saving me from the awkwardness, "let's talk about this wedding."

After a couple of hours and two bottles of wine, talk of the wedding is long forgotten and Harper is regaling us with stories about her many years spent dating.

Rachel chokes on her wine as Harper tells us of a man who arrived to their date wearing high heels.

"No way did that happen," Georgia argues.

"I'm not kidding. Ask Tate; he saw it himself."

I laugh now, almost uncontrollably. "Could anyone else have such bad luck?"

"Clearly not you." Harper smirks. "First date in years and you nab a winner."

"I did, didn't I?" I smile widely, which can't be helped when I'm thinking about Jake. Especially when I've had countless glasses of wine and my mind goes to painting my house last weekend.

"So tell us, how is Jake in the pants area?" Rachel asks.

"Excuse me?" I laugh.

"In the pants area. How is his piece, his tool, his schlong, bone, Johnson." Laughter rings out around the table, which only encourages her to go on. "You know, his pecker, his disco stick, his love muscle."

"Oh my God, you can't be serious."

"How come there are so many cool names for a penis and

none for a vagina?" Georgia slurs.

"Vagina has some," Harper responds. "Pussy, twat, cunt," she whispers the last one.

"Yeah, that's like two. Penis has hundreds. Cock, dong, wang—"

"Beaver basher, one-eyed trouser snake, tan banana," Rachel yells.

Georgia laughs. "Tallywacker, cum gun, heat-seeking moisture missile—"

"Yuck," I screech. "That's friggin' disgusting."

"Yeah, a little overboard on that one." Brooke takes a sip of her water.

Georgia pouts. "Well, it's true. There are no good words for a vagina."

"Beaver," Brooke says.

"Oh, that's a good one." Rachel laughs. "Lady garden."

"Oh, yeah? What about love tunnel?"

We are all in fits of laughter now. Tears run down my face, and I hold my stomach as my laughter becomes more hysterical.

"Panty hamster," Harper offers.

"Bearded clam . . . furry taco." Rachel gets out between breaths.

"Oh my God, you guys are so gross," I tell them. Thankfully, the lounge has filled up and the music is louder than it was when we arrived, so we aren't drawing too much attention. Except from the table of guys next to us, who are now staring with smirks on their faces. My laughter stops, and I give them an awkward wave as I turn back to the girls and crack up laughing again.

"Hot box, front butt," Georgia calls out excitedly, completely oblivious to the attention we have garnered. "Penis sheath," she yells.

The laughter ceases and all eyes are on her.

Brooke shakes her head. "Too far, Georgia. Too far."

"What?" She frowns.

We all shake our heads at her until we can't control our laughter anymore and break into another fit of hysterical giggles.

The rest of the night continues in much the same silly fashion. There is something special about girl-only time. Something that sends us a little crazy. Where we can be totally immature and ridiculous and not worry about what anyone would think if they saw us carrying on like teenage girls. We could never act so shameless if all the guys were here.

When we decide to call it a night and organise our way home, it's well after midnight and the bar has filled right up.

Rachel, Harper, and Brooke share a cab for all the city drop-offs, and Georgia and I share one out to the suburbs.

Jake had offered to come and pick us up as the cab fare would be quite substantial and Hallie was staying with Marley anyway, but I didn't want him to have to wait up for me and then drive into the city that late.

The excitement of Jake giving me a key this morning has nothing on the giddiness I feel at actually using it to let myself into his place. I told Jake I could just go back to my house, but he insisted he wanted me to climb into bed with him, no matter what time of the morning it was.

And so I do. I sneak inside, tiptoe down the hallway, and strip my clothes off, leaving just my panties and a small singlet. I crawl into the bed, wrapping my arms around Jake, my chest pushed up against his back.

His sleepy voice catches me off-guard. "You're home. Have a good night, angel?"

"Yeah," I mumble into his back. With Jake being so much bigger than me, I'm almost smothered trying to spoon him.

Thankfully, he rolls over and takes me into his arms. "I'm glad, but I missed you."

"I missed you too," I whisper and fall asleep with a content grin on my face.

Chapter Thirty

Lana

The grass is soft beneath me. I'm cold and my body is shaking. Although the grass is wet, it feels like a source of heat, as though I am so cold that even the frosty grass is warmer.

I see his pacing. Feel his distress. His voice is panicked and frenzied. He is worried, anxious about something.

I force my eyes open into slits and squint at the figure in front of me. His thick black hair is long and wavy, and I focus all my attention on the back of his head as he paces.

He turns, and my heart stops as his face becomes clear. Every detail is in perfect clarity, from the darkness of his eyes to the stubble on his jaw. His eyes shoot to mine for the first time, wide and panicked, and I gasp for air.

I take long deep breaths as I try to slow my breathing. That face. Who is it? And why does it creep me out so much?

I lie still for a minute or two, trying to gather my bearings and get my breathing back on track. I don't need to look beside me to know the bed is empty. I feel him missing. I miss his presence as though it's vital for me to breathe.

After lying without him for a moment, I get antsy and decide to go in search.

Throwing on one of his T-shirts, I rush through freshening up in the bathroom before I make my way down the hall.

As I step into the living room, I freeze when I see Jake standing there with another man. I didn't hear two voices when I was coming down the hallway.

Jake turns to look at me, his face pale and eyes wide. "Sorry." I pull the hem of his T-shirt down. "I didn't realise you had company."

As soon as the thick black head of hair turns to face me, I stop breathing.

It's him.

"Lana." Jake steps towards me.

"It's you," I breathe, not taking my eyes off the stranger. "It was you."

"Lana," Jake says, his voice full of panic now.

I hold my hand up to stop him, my gaze unwavering.

"Lana," the guy says. He's so casual, as if he's known me for years.

"Who the fuck are you?" I screech.

He jumps back, his eyes wide before they skirt to Jake. My eyes follow and Jake stands there defeated, his shoulders caved in, his eyes sad.

My phone rings from my handbag, which is still on the entry stand from last night, but I ignore it as I just stare at Jake. He doesn't take his eyes off me, but he doesn't attempt to say a thing. I guess he doesn't need to. We both know what's going on here.

My phone rings again and again, and I ignore it.

My voice is shaky as I try to swallow the lump in my throat. "I don't understand. Why? Why would you lie?"

"Lana."

"You knew how much it took for me to let you in, and you've been lying to me all along."

"I didn't want to. I didn't know how to tell you."

"Is this some kind of joke to you? A fucking sick joke?"

"No! Fuck no. This is the best thing that has ever happened to me. You saved me, angel."

"Well, you sure as shit didn't save me."

"Angel."

"Don't," I scream as he takes another step towards me. "Don't call me that. Don't ever call me that again."

My phone rings again, and Jake and I both curse. Shaking my head, I go over to grab it. Harper. Fuck, not now. I consider calling her back later until I realise she has been calling nonstop for five minutes.

"Hello." My frustration is clear in my voice.

"Lana." Instantly, I hear it. The fear. The panic.

"What's going on?"

"It's Tate." Her voice is laced with tears, and hearing them alongside my brother's name twists something in my stomach.

"Harper. What is it?"

"There's . . . been . . . an . . . accident."

"Is he okay?" Warm hands grab my shoulders and I realise I'm screaming and tears are pouring down my face.

"He's at the hospital."

"Are you there?"

"They've shoved me in a room. No one can tell me anything." She is crying earnestly.

"I'm coming. Text me where to go. I'll be there soon." I hang up, not waiting for her response, and drop the phone into my bag. Sprinting back to the bedroom, I'm in a haze of fog as I search for any of my clothes. Clean, dirty, creased, I don't care.

I run back down the hallway, still pulling a T-shirt over my head.

"Lana," Jake shouts.

"What?" I slip on my other shoe and pick up my handbag off the floor.

"What are you doing?"

"It's Tate. I need to get to the hospital." I fling open the front door and head out.

Once I step out onto the porch and grab my phone from my bag, I realise I have no idea what I'm doing. My car isn't here. I don't have the number for a cab company, and I really can't wait twenty minutes for one to arrive.

I'm pacing the sidewalk mumbling to myself when Jake rushes out the front door, jumping around on one foot, trying to get his other boot on. "Lana, wait."

I watch him, still in a daze, as he runs to me, grabs me by the shoulders, and leads me to his truck.

"I'll take you."

Luckily, Hallie is still with Marley so I let him place me in his truck, blindly doing everything he says as I stare off into space.

Tate. Nothing can happen to him. He is all I have left.

"What's going on?" Jake's low tone draws my attention.

"I don't know. Harper just said there had been an accident. They're at the hospital."

"I'm sure it's nothing—"

"It must be something," I snap. "He's been taken away, and

they haven't told Harper a thing."

Jake reaches over and tries to grab my hand, but I pull it away. He doesn't say anything about it and doesn't bring up this morning's whole fiasco, and for that, I am thankful. I don't even want to think about that right now. We ride to the hospital in silence, but the tension surrounding us is nowhere near comfortable. Our emotions are running high, and it feels like a pressure cooker about to boil over.

It's a long, excruciating drive into the city. My body is tight the whole way, until I am running through the emergency room following the directions Harper texted me with, Jake hot on my heels.

"Tate Washington," I say to the nurse behind the main desk in the emergency room.

She glances over the paperwork in front of her and then looks up at me with sad eyes. The change in her demeanour has my knees buckling and my body wanting to drop to the floor.

"Are you family?" Her voice is soft and gentle. A warm hug on a cold winter's day.

"I'm his sister."

She nods in understanding and comes around the desk, taking my elbow and swiping the card that's hanging around her neck on the huge doors next to reception. She leads me down a hallway, and finally, after what feels like the walk of doom, opens a door.

As soon as I see Harper folded over into herself on a couch, I run to her, dropping down to the seat and pulling her into my arms. Harper is petite, but seeing her like this, holding onto herself like that? She looks like a small child, a wounded animal. Tate would freak out if he were here to see this.

She breaks into wracking sobs so strong her whole body shakes with emotion. I give her a minute to release everything she's probably been holding in for the past hour or so before I speak.

"What happened?"

"He was on his bike," she cries. "He was going to play golf with Saxon."

"Okay, shhh." I try to placate her as her sobbing starts up again.

"The police knocked on the door. There was an accident."

"What happened?"

"I don't know. I don't know anything. No one will tell me anything." She slams her hands down onto the couch, and I catch them up in my own and squeeze them tight.

"Harper." I try to draw her focus. "Is Tate okay?"

"I don't know. He's in surgery right now, but they have told me nothing. Absolutely nothing," she screams.

"I'll be back in a second," Jake whispers to me, but I don't acknowledge him.

I'm too busy trying to stay in the here and now and not fall inside myself. My chest is tight and my stomach is roiling. When I think of losing Tate, my body goes into a panic. My heart rate skyrockets, and my head goes dizzy. I can't lose him.

Tears run down my face as I hold Harper again, rocking her from side to side. Neither one of us speaks. What could we say? Neither one of us wants to voice the real fears going through our heads.

I don't know how long we sit like that before the door opens and Jake steps through with an older man dressed in scrubs. The doctor, with his white-as-snow hair, has sympathy pouring out of his eyes, and Harper tenses against me at the same time as my heart stops.

"Doctor Saracen, this is Harper, Tate's fiancée, and Lana, his sister." Jake gestures to us and then takes a seat on the other couch.

"Ladies." The doctor pulls off his cap. "I'm Doctor Saracen. I'm sorry no one has come by to update you, but it was a little touch-and-go back there, and the best thing we could have done for you was to look after Tate. So that's what we've been doing."

Harper and I nod along as the doctor tells us about Tate's condition. After letting us know he is still in surgery and it may be a little while before we can see him, the doctor rushes back through the doors as quickly as he came.

No one speaks a word after he has left. We all just sit in a state of shock.

"He's going to be fine." Harper finally breaks the silence.

Glancing over, she is wringing her hands in her lap. I don't respond. Her statement doesn't fill me with confidence. I think it's great she's trying to be positive and hoping for the best. But dread fills me and doom blackens my mind, and unfortunately, I can't do the same.

"I'm going to get you guys some coffee, as shit as the hospital stuff is. If I get some food, will you eat?" I gaze up at Jake without really looking at him. Just the thought of eating makes me wants to vomit.

"No thanks," I mutter. He nods, leaving Harper and me alone once again. We sit in silence but both of us settle back into the couch, almost admitting we are going to be here for a while.

The day passes in much the same way. Sad silence surrounds us while Jake runs errands and looks after us, constantly making sure we have everything we could possible need. He makes the few phone calls needed to Maurice and Saxon and keeps them updated on what's going on, telling them there's no point coming in yet as we still don't really know what's happening.

It's nearly dinnertime when we are updated again, this time by the attending surgeon, and we're told they have placed Tate in a medically induced coma to protect his brain.

"Besides his head trauma, he actually got away with just bruising and scratches. Of course, the brain is so fragile so it hasn't been an easy ten hours, and the days ahead will be crucial," the surgeon tells us. "I really wish I could give you more information or a more accurate prognosis, but unfortunately, it's just a waiting game from here."

"Thank you, Doctor," Jake says, once again taking care of things. "When can the girls see him?"

"They are moving him to the ICU now. A nurse will come and get you when he's settled. It's normally only two people at a time but with a little persuading, I'm sure Nurse Jenny will cave."

"Thank you, sir." Jake extends his hand and the doctor shakes it before giving Harper and me a sad nod.

"I need to see him." Harper flops down onto the couch.

"Not long now." I sit next to her and grab her hand.

"It sounded like positive news," Jake says. "But maybe prepare yourselves. I'm sure he's pretty banged up, and it could be a shock."

The knowing tone in Jake's voice brings my gaze to him. His eyes are sad but accepting. I wonder how many people he's seen in such a position or even a lot worse. How many times has he waited for hours on end waiting for good news, or sometimes, just news at all?

The three of us are back to sitting on the edge of our seats, knowing it won't be long until we can go in. I can't wait to see him, but I also dread it.

I don't have time to focus on that thought as a nurse comes to gather us. The woman smiles consolingly at us and something about the older, tubby woman speaks comfort. We follow her down hallway after hallway until I see a sign for the ICU.

"Judy, this is Tate Washington's family. He's in three fifteen."

Judy nods sympathetically, which, now being the third person, doesn't feel as good as it once did. In fact, if someone else smiles at us like that, I might punch something. "Bea will show you through, but I'm here all night if you need anything."

"Thanks," we all mumble before Bea shows us to room three fifteen.

My heart races as I step over the threshold. I pull in a sharp breath as my eyes land on him.

"I know," Jake whispers in my ear as he puts a hand on my lower back, ushering me in. The touch feels unfamiliar, and I realise it's the first time today he's put his hands on me.

I thought he was just on edge because of Tate, not wanting to upset me or Harper, and being as helpful as he could, but now I think it has more to do with this morning's revelations.

My thoughts are instantly still as I glance back at my baby brother.

Tears fill my eyes and my legs go weak as I take in his swollen and bruised face. He is barely recognisable, and my heart breaks to see him like this.

Harper's loud shriek pulls me back to the now as she throws herself over him, and her body shakes with sobs. I go over to her, placing my hand on her back as I rub gently to console her.

The room becomes suffocating as I think of the many times I have been in the hospital with my loved ones over the years. I'm all too familiar with the process. All too familiar with the different emotions one experiences. Harper has no idea what is in store, and all I can do is be here for her.

More hours pass after Harper and I have settled in to sit on either side of Tate, each of us holding one of his hands. Jake watches on from a chair in the back corner of the room.

Harper cries every now and then as the time passes, but I sit still as shock, anger, fear, and realisation all run through me.

I can't lose him. He's all I have left. I don't think I can go through this again. Losing another person I love. How many will I have to give up? How many will be enough?

I'm cursing God, tears running down my face, when I feel two strong arms wrap around me.

"Shh, it's okay. It's going to be okay," Jake whispers into my ear, holding me tight. "I'm here; I'm always going to be here. I'm not going anywhere."

I look up into the concerned eyes of the man I love. Someone I have brought into my life and become attached to. Someone else for me to lose. And how would I live through that?

Anger and frustration build inside of me as the unfairness of it all hits me. I shove him away, and he falls back onto his ass. "How can you say that?" I scream. "You can't promise that. Look at him." I gesture to Tate. "He promised me we'd always have each other. Now look at him."

"Lana—"

"No. You need to go."

"Angel."

"I need you to go," I shout.

"Why?"

"I just do."

"Is it because of the fire?" he whispers.

"Yes." *No.* It's because I can't stand to lose anyone else in my life. And loving you only means I'll eventually have to let you go.

"Lana, I—"

"Please, just go. I need you to go."

He stands slowly, his eyes full of sadness and hurt, and I quickly look away.

I sense him lingering in the doorway and I close my eyes,

praying he will just leave. If he pushes me, I will tell him it has nothing to do with the fire. That I don't care he lied to me or why. That my love for him has so outgrown any petty details that I don't even care. But I can't have him become just another person I'll eventually lose.

I always thought Tate and I were jinxed. That it was destined to be just the two of us. Now here I sit, clinging to his hand like a lifeline, hoping and praying I'm not going to be left here alone.

Maybe I'm the one who's jinxed.

I know the second Jake has gone, and I feel his loss like a knife in the gut.

"What the hell, Lana?" Harper stands, her eyes wide and confused.

"I can't lose him too. I can't keep going through this. Loving all these people just to have them taken from me."

"We're not losing Tate, Lana," she says with a harsh tone. "That's not fucking happening."

"I can't do it. I can't lose him too."

"You just did." Harper gives me a sad shake of her head and leaves the room.

Tears fall down my cheeks as I lay my head down on Tate's bed. Despair flows through me. How am I going to do this?

Chapter Thirty-One

Jake

Sitting in the emergency waiting room, I wait. Waiting for what, I don't know. Bent over myself with my head in hands, I pull at what short hair I have. What the fuck am I going to do? How am I going to fix this fucking mess I've made? Well, the mess fucking Brad made.

God knows what he'll say after I told him to fuck off and practically kicked him out of my house this morning. He fucking deserved it, though. I know he felt bad for me, but if only he'd kept his fucking dick in his pants, then I wouldn't be dealing with this now.

Where do I go from here? I don't want to leave Lana alone to go through this, but she clearly doesn't want me here, and I don't want to upset her any more than she already is. I growl in frustration and tug harder at my hair. If I could pull it all out from the roots I think I would have by now.

A warm hand taps my shoulder and I jump up, ready to fight for us. Harper jumps back at my over-the-top reaction, and my fight disappears.

"Is she okay?" I blurt out. I feel like a right prick. Her fiancé is in a fucking coma and I'm worried about my girlfriend dumping me. "I'm sorry. Is everything okay?" I say, more calm now.

"She's just scared, Jake."

"I'm sorry. You have so much more to worry about today than this."

She sits down on the seat next to me and I join her, deflating like a balloon. "To be honest, I think I am handling this better than Lana. Actually, I *know* I'm dealing with it better than her. Tate is going to be fine; I know that with everything in me. It's not being hopeful or wishful thinking—I just know." She pauses and glances around the waiting room before looking back to me with sad eyes. "I don't know if Lana is going to be though."

I nod solemnly. "I fucked up so bad."

I explain all about the fire; how I came to be there in the first place. I tell her about how it all came to a head this morning right before she called.

"It has nothing to do with that, Jake. I'm sure of it." She rests her hand on my forearm.

"She was so fucking angry at me."

"I'm sure she was. But that's not why she kicked you out to-night. She's scared. She's scared she is going to lose her brother. Lose you as well. Those two have been through a lot, suffered through so much loss—first their parents and then their grand-parents. They only have each other, and today has shaken that up for her and she isn't thinking clearly. Although, I'm sure she thinks the opposite," she mumbles.

I nod, hoping to God she's right. Praying that once Lana

knows Tate is okay and everything goes back to normal, she will forgive me. Forgive me for being such a selfish fucking idiot.

"Go home, Jake. Lana will be fine."

I release a deep breath as Harper squeezes my shoulder again before standing and heading back towards Tate's room.

Still feeling unsettled, I sit for a while longer before I pull my phone out of my pocket and search for the number I need.

The phone rings and I pray it's not too late and that I haven't missed him.

"Hello." I recognise the accented voice instantly.

"Maurice . . . It's Jake again. The girls . . . they need you."

"I'm on my way."

The phone beeps in my ear as he hangs up and I lean back in my seat, preparing for the wait for him to arrive. It's only when I see him storm through the emergency waiting room on his way to the ICU that I stand to go.

Now that I know the girls have him, and that someone is here is to watch over them, I can leave.

Still delaying the inevitable, I slowly make my way out of the hospital and to my truck.

When I called Marley earlier today and told her what was going on with Tate, she told me to leave Hallie with her to sleep over, and that she would get her to school tomorrow. But as soon as I sit in my truck at the hospital, I know I can't go back home alone. Not without Lana *and* Hallie.

I'm in a state of denial the whole way back to Marley's place. Things aren't as bad as they seem. This morning wasn't the colossal fuck-up I think it was. Tate is going to be fine. And Lana didn't just end things with us.

She's scared. She just had a moment and freaked out, is all. I'm sure when I call tomorrow, things are going to be fine. She'll apologise, tell me Tate is awake and will be coming home soon, and I'll finally tell her how I really feel.

That I love her.

That I am so in love with her I feel fucking lost without her. That leaving her at the hospital tonight has broken something so strong in me that I can't breathe.

When I finally pull up into Marley's driveway, I shut off the engine but can't bring myself to get out. I don't think about anything as I stare vacantly out the windshield at the grey garage door. Studying every inch of it easier than facing the truth.

A knock on my truck window has me cursing as I jump in my seat. The greying hair and worried blue eyes of John pop into my vision. He nods at me, and I release a breath as I open the door and step out of the car.

"What'd you tell Marley you were doing?" I gesture to the cigarette in his hand.

He smiles ruefully. "I'm taking the garbage out."

"Right."

John assesses my face with scrutiny and frowns. I see his eyes ticking over in thought as he wants to ask me if everything is okay, but let's face it—we're men. We're not going to talk about it.

"Your daughter is inside beating up on my boys again." He pulls a drag from his cigarette.

"Good. Someone needs to toughen your princesses up," I tease.

"I'm an accountant, Jake, not a tough soldier. I did four years of college, not boot camp."

"Don't worry." I laugh. "Hallie will take care of them."

"No doubt."

"I'll see you inside." I head towards the front of the house as John starts wheeling the bins out to the street. "Spray some cologne or something," I call over my shoulder, and he lifts his cigarette in acknowledgement.

When I head inside, I find Marley curled up on the couch, holding a coffee and watching *The Voice*.

"He smoking?"

"Yeah." I laugh. "You know?"

"Of course, I know. He thinks he hides it, but he comes in here smelling of smoke, and he brushes his teeth like a hundred times a day."

I flop down onto the recliner and stare at the TV. "Why don't you say anything?"

She shrugs. "I enjoy the five minutes of peace."

"Fair enough." I chuckle and shake my head.

"I thought Hallie was staying tonight?"

"Nah. Thought I may as well come get her."

"Oh okay. They are all just getting ready for bed. I went to your place earlier and grabbed her some pyjamas and her school stuff."

"Cool, thanks."

"Is everything okay?" I don't miss the caution in her tone, and I think I must look as bad as I feel.

My chest clenches tight and my eyes burn. Leaning forward, I rest my elbows on my knees and rub my thumbs into my eyes.

"Jake, oh my God. What happened? Is Tate okay?"

"Still as stable as when I called earlier," I assure her, trying to calm her panic. "It's Lana."

"Lana?"

"I didn't get to tell you when I called but she found out about the fire."

"When?"

"This morning. Right before she got the phone call about Tate."

"Oh, Jake." Marley hops off the couch and makes her way to

sit on the arm of the recliner.

"Brad came over this morning. Lana must have remembered him."

"Oh, fuck."

The severity of what happened hits me hard. I know it takes something big to get my sister to curse. For the first time, I let myself think properly about this morning. How angry Lana was. How betrayed she'd looked. She'd looked at with me derision, and just picturing her face makes my heart shatter into a million tiny pieces.

"She kicked me out of the hospital tonight." Marley rubs my back but doesn't say anything. "She was fine today. Well, not fine, but she let me look after her, comfort her—help her. Tonight, she just lost it and told me to go."

"Are you sure it was about the fire then? It seems like a delayed reaction."

"I don't know." I sigh. "She said it was, but afterwards, Harper found me in the waiting room and told me Lana was just scared."

"Scared?" She frowns.

I wave my hand in dismissal, not wanting to talk about Lana's issues.

"I'm sure she'll come around."

"That's what Harper said." I rub my hands over my face. "But what if she doesn't? What if she doesn't forgive me for lying about the fire? What if I lose her?"

The front door shuts and John clears his throat. "Umm . . . everything okay?"

"Yeah," we respond in unison.

"Okay . . . cool. I'm . . . just . . . I'll . . . I'll just go brush my teeth."

Marley raises her eyebrows at me, and I can't help but laugh.

"Want to stay here tonight?" she asks. "I can get Hallie ready in the morning and take her to school for you."

"Sure." I nod, not having the energy to go home.

By the time I've helped Marley get all the kids breakfast and ready for school, I'm knackered. It's like a fucking mad house here. How my sister does it daily is beyond me, and it makes me reconsider my thoughts about having more children.

Instantly, my mind goes to Lana. Well, if I'm having more kids, then it's going to be with her. I wonder if they've had any news this morning. I didn't sleep at all last night just thinking about her and wondering how she was coping.

I stare out the kitchen window as I take a sip of my coffee, enjoying the peace and quiet of the house now that Marley has taken the kids to school. Pulling my phone out my pocket, I stare at it for a minute as I debate calling Lana. It doesn't feel enough to just call her and have some superficial conversation over the phone, so I empty my coffee into the sink, shove my phone back in my pocket, and head out to my truck.

The whole way to the hospital I go over and over the different possible conversations we could have. I have officially lost my balls as I sit in my truck and overanalyse everything.

When I'm finally at the hospital, I stride inside with nothing but determination. It fades quickly though after I request to see Lana at the nurses' station and the older lady calls up to Tate's room.

"I'm sorry, hon, but they're only letting family in to see him."

My mouth drops open, and I stare blankly at the nurse. Out of all the conversations I thought we could have, Lana refusing to see me never even entered my mind. I feel my grip on her loosening, and Harper's supportive words from last night no longer hold any value.

She's done with me.

Thanking the nurse, I move into a seat in the waiting room, pull out my phone, and dial her number. It rings three times before she cancels on me. She fucking cancels the call on me. If Tate wasn't still in the ICU, guarded by locked doors and a nurses' station, I'd walk right into his room and demand she talk to me.

I sit in the waiting room for God knows how long. Waiting for God knows what.

Fuck. She really is done with me.

Chapter Thirty-Two

Lana

"Well, at least you don't stink anymore," Harper says as we wait for the doctors to do another check on Tate.

We've been here all week, both of us by his side, waiting for any news. The doctors were pleased with his progress, and on day three, finally started to wean him off the drugs keeping him in a coma.

Once Tate had been taken off the ventilator and finally opened his eyes two days later, Harper and I both decided it was time for us to get our shit sorted. First order of business being both of us going home to shower and change.

Tate has been awake on and off for a couple of days now, becoming more lucid and staying awake for longer periods each time. He has been up this morning so far for the longest period and seems to finally be more like his normal self. He's looking more like himself too as his bruises are starting to fade and his scratches are starting to heal.

"Didn't they say breakfast was coming?" Tate asks.

"You need to see the doctor first," Harper tells him as she straightens his sheets. She hasn't stopped fussing with him at all since he first woke.

Just as though she wished on a lamp, the doctor enters Tate's room. "Good morning, guys," he greets us. "Tate, how are you feeling today?"

"Good. Hungry."

Doctor Saracen laughs. "You are looking well. You were okay after those sandwiches last night?"

"All good."

"Excellent. Well, I'll tell them to bring you a light breakfast."

Tate's face falls at the word *light,* and I can't help but giggle. Of course, that's all he would be thinking of.

Once the doctor has completed his checks and leaves the room, Tate frowns at Harper. "Light?"

"Oh come on, you need to take it easy."

"Fine, I'll just have you to eat after." He pulls her hand until she falls on top of him. I should've known that would be the second thing on his mind.

My phone buzzes in my pocket, and I pull it out and glance at the screen. Georgia. I can't deal with her right now. I have been avoiding everyone since Tate's accident, only sending Georgia a text every so often to keep her updated on what's going on. I'll text her tonight when I go home.

Shoving the phone back in my pocket, I look up to find Tate and Harper looking at me. I know what they are thinking, and Tate confirms it.

"Where's Jake?"

Harper and I share a look, and Tate looks back and forth between us before frowning at me.

"Lana . . ." His voice is firm. "Where is he?"

"I'm not seeing him anymore," I say as I jut my chin out in defiance. I know how this is going to go down, and I'm prepared for battle.

"What happened?"

"I'm going to grab some coffee and see if I can wrangle any snacks out of the vending machines." Harper crawls off Tate and gives him a light kiss before leaving us alone. *Subtle, Harper, subtle.*

I stare out of the hospital window as if something enthralling is happening on the grass below. *I wonder if I jump to escape if I would survive.*

"What happened, Lana?" Tate's tone tells me that even if I were to jump, we would still be having this conversation.

"It didn't work out." I sit up straight and cross my arms.

"Don't even bother. You know we are going to talk about this."

Sighing deeply, my eyes meet his and I decide to go with the official party line. "I've been having dreams about the fire."

"Nightmares?"

"No, not really. Just weird dreams. Each dream would show me more and more of what happened until I had remembered the whole thing."

"You remember it?" His eyes are wide with worry.

"Yes."

Silence falls between us and I let it until I figure out what to say next. "In the dream, it wasn't Jake who pulled me out of the house."

"What?"

"Some other guy carried me out. Jake was there, and the other guy must have fled or something because he wasn't there when I woke up on the lawn, but Jake lied about being alone. He lied about finding the fire and being the one to carry me out."

Mrs Cribledon's words hit me hard and fast. *"Suppose it's a good thing you have a man around now. Next time there's an emergency you won't have to be saved by Callie's dirty late-night visitor."* Holy shit. How many other clues were there that I missed?

Tate frowns but he doesn't look nearly as pissed as I think he should. "What did Jake say about it?"

"Nothing. I woke up on Sunday morning and found the other guy in his house. I freaked out and that's when I got the phone call about you."

Tate's eyes travel around the room and I can tell he is thinking it over. Knowing my brother so well, I could probably pinpoint exactly what he's thinking.

"So what happened after?"

"Nothing. He brought me to the hospital and from then, all I could think about was you. I told him to leave."

Tate purses his lips and narrows his eyes at me, and I shift in my seat under his scrutiny. "Harper mentioned yesterday how great Jake was that day. Getting you girls drinks, food. Getting the doctors in to see you and keeping you updated."

"Yeah, he was great." I look out the window again.

"So, when did you tell him to leave?"

"Sorry, what?"

"When did you kick Jake out of the hospital, Lana?" The harsh tone of his voice rings throughout the sterile room and my defences drop.

"When you were moved into this room after surgery." My voice is weak and holds none of the defiance it did earlier. I can't look at him. Can't let him see the truth that I'm sure fills my eyes.

"Right." He draws the word out. "So once I was moved in here and you were able to see me for the first time after the accident you freaked out and told Jake to leave."

"I didn't freak out—"

"So, when you finally saw me after waiting all day and found me like this . . ." he gestures down to himself, "you kicked him out."

I squirm in my seat. "Something like that."

"So, when you came in here and saw me, your only family left in the entire world, you asked Jake to leave and decided you didn't want to see him anymore?"

"Tate." My voice is pleading.

"Lala." The use of his childhood name for me, and the tone he carries with it, causes tears to well behind my eyes.

Grabbing his hand, I finally meet his gaze. "I thought I'd lost you."

"And you thought pushing away the people you would need the most if that happened was a good idea?"

"I didn't push him away. He lied to me, Tate. And not just a little lie."

"Are you seriously going to stick with that story?"

"It's not a story. Shouldn't you be more pissed? Threatening that when you get out of this hospital bed you are going to go kick his ass?"

"No."

"No? I'm your sister."

"Yes, you are. And I want you to be happy. I want what's best for you. And Jake is what's best for you. He makes you happy."

"He's a liar."

"You're a scaredy cat."

"Did you just call me a *scaredy cat*? What are we, ten?" I

say, my eyes bugging out.

"Yes, I did because you are. You aren't angry about the fire. You know as much as I do that he probably has a good reason. Jake is a good man. He loves you."

I can't focus on all he said. It's too much. Jake loves me? "It is about the fire."

"Lana," he says, frustration in his tone. "We're not jinxed."

My eyes shoot up to his and I stare at him. Is he a mind reader now too?

"I know that's what you think. I thought it for a long time too. Hell, I don't know if I still think that. But I'm not missing out on life just in case. I'm not giving up Harper on the off chance I might lose her one day."

The tears are back, and this time, I let them fall. "I can't do this anymore, Tate. Seeing you like that, feeling that way again . . . I don't have it in me."

"Lana, call Jake and explain. Tell him how you feel. He'll understand."

"No," I snap.

"Lana." His eyes are wide.

"How are things going in here?" Harper steps inside the room, her arms full of goodies.

"Not the best," Tate answers, as I say, "Good."

"Do you need another minute?" She fidgets from foot to foot.

"No, Lana knows what I think." Tate frowns at me then looks away and gives Harper a huge smile. My heart drops. I don't want him to be upset with me. He just doesn't understand.

My throat constricts and I stand from the chair, pushing it back away from Tate's hospital bed.

"I'll be back," I mutter as I pretty much run from the room and out of the ICU into the waiting room. The glass emergency doors slide open as frantic people enter and I bolt out of them, desperate for a breath of fresh air.

Jake's face when I told him to leave enters my mind, and I bend over and vomit into the garden. My stomach turns with pain, and I retch until my body physically can't anymore.

I make my way on shaky legs over to the drinking fountain in front of the hospital and rinse my mouth out before finding a bench to fall on.

Jake. Letting him go is high up on the list of the most painful things I have ever been through. But I know if I stay with him, love him, and make a family with him, that losing him years from now will well outdo any of the pain I have previously suffered.

I won't survive that. I won't have the strength to go on. I can't do it.

Hours have passed when a warm arm goes around my shoulder as someone sits down next to me on the bench.

"Tate says you've lost it. That you've finally cracked? Is that true, pumpkin?"

I smile at the man who is the closest thing to a father Tate and I have.

I lean my head on Maurice's shoulder and enjoy the comfort of his embrace. "No. Tate's sticking his nose into things he doesn't understand."

"You don't think he understands?"

I frown at his thoughtful question. Maurice, always the mediator. "He doesn't understand my way of thinking or feeling."

"Well, that's true. We all handle things differently. But sometimes we get so caught up in our own way of thinking that someone else's clarity on the situation can be very helpful."

"Mmm." I nod to appease him, not wanting to talk about this anymore.

Maurice squeezes my shoulder and lays a light kiss on my

head. "You are such a special girl, Lana. You have always felt things more than others, held onto things harder. I hope you're not mistaking your sweet, loving heart to be weak and fragile. Because you are strong, pumpkin—one of the strongest women I have ever known, besides your nonna."

Smiling sadly, I snuggle closer to him. My nonna was one of the most wonderful women I have ever known. I wish I had even half of her strength, courage, goodness, and kindness.

"I won't say any more about it, but your nonna would want to see you happy. I hope you're not making a big mistake."

Chapter Thirty-Three

Lana

I only returned to Tate's hospital room to say good-bye to him and Harper and let them know to call me if they needed anything. Now that the nosy, interfering brother of mine is on the mend, I'm happy to get the hell out of that hospital room and go back home. Back to *my* reality and *my* life.

Not just my life, but also my life before Jake.

I spend Saturday night at home with pizza and a good book, and Sunday working in the garden and around the house.

And today I am back at school facing the music.

Over the weekend, I went over and over how I could possibly avoid seeing Jake at drop-off, and, God forbid, pickup. There were no excuses I could use, and nothing I could do to get out of being in the classroom. Besides calling in sick all week, of course, but I think I've already pushed my luck having last week off.

No, I have to pull my big girl panties up and face this mess head-on.

Now *this* is why teachers are not meant to fraternise with parents. This right here is what the school is trying to avoid. I totally get it now. New rule for me, in the future—no more dating parents.

Not that I think it's ever going to be an issue as I don't plan on ever dating again, but making the rule somehow makes me feel better.

Pottering around the staff room, I try to put off going to class. I have thought about this scenario a million times. No matter what crazy ideas I come up with, nothing can prepare me.

I don't know how Jake is going to react to seeing me. He must know we are going to come face to face, and I assume that's why his calls have slowed down the last few days—he figured he'd be seeing me on Monday anyway. Before that, he had been blowing up my phone ever since I kicked him out of the hospital, and my life, for that matter.

Phone calls, voicemails, text messages—I haven't listened to, read, or responded to any of them. Thankfully, he hasn't shown up to my house; although, I have a feeling if he didn't have Hallie with him, he probably would have.

Hallie. What will this do to her? What will losing her do to me?

I know I can't stay with Jake just for Hallie, and I know she is just another person for me to love and lose, but it's a concept I can't fathom. A pain that stings my heart more than I'd imagine.

We had built a special relationship during the past couple of months, and I'm not sure just seeing her in class every day as my student will be enough.

"You'll have to go to class eventually. You may as well get it over and done with." Georgia gives me a sad smile as she steps up to the photocopier I am currently occupying.

"I know. I just need to finish this."

Georgia's brow furrows. "You *need* to finish copying those Christmas activity sheets?"

"Yes."

"It's September, Lana."

There's an awkward silence as I stare at the copier while it flings pages and pages through. It stops and I grab my stack of paper as I huff and head to the classroom, Georgia's laughter following me all the way out of the staff room.

As soon as I reach my classroom, I see Jake is waiting out front. Luckily, due to my being late, so are several other parents. I avoid eye contact with any of them as I unlock the door. The heat of his stare burns into my back, and I know I'm not going to be able to avoid him.

Once I've turned on the lights, I head straight to my desk and start busying myself. It's only a matter of seconds until he's standing behind me. I don't need to see him; I don't have to smell him. I can feel him. I can sense his strong and powerful presence towering over me.

"Lana." His voice is tight. It must be hard for him to stay somewhat composed in here with ten other parents present.

Pulling together all my strength, I turn and face him. My heart soars at the same time as my stomach drops. Even with his tired eyes and defeated body stance, he is still the most handsome man I have ever seen.

My hands ache to reach out and touch him. To slide my palm over his cheek and let him nuzzle into it in that way he does.

I can see he wants my comfort. Needs it as much as I need his. And I want nothing more than to give it to him, but I am weak. I'm a coward.

"Good morning, Miss Washington." Hallie winks—well, she tries to, at her use of my school name. I smile widely at her, unable to speak through the lump in my throat, and tears well up behind my eyes.

I turn back to my table, willing the emotions to go away.

"Lana," Jake says again, his voiced pained.

"Now is not the time, Jake. I'm sorry."

"When is the time? Not when I've been calling and texting you all week. Should I schedule a parent-teacher conference?"

"Please," I beg. "Not at school. I told you in the beginning that parents and teachers should not date, and this is exactly why."

His face falls at my words and a bad taste sits in my mouth at using that against him just to get myself out of the situation I created.

"You're right. I'm sorry." Once he says good-bye to Hallie, he turns and walks out of the classroom, his head down and his shoulders slumped.

The bell sounds and my shoulders drop in relief that I won't have to deal with any other parents this morning. Turning to face the class, I take in a deep breath. "Okay guys, let's get started."

The parents slowly dwindle out and we start our day off with show and tell. I use this time to find my bearings and remember that I am at work. The children are who matter, and I need to pull my head out of my ass and do my job.

The day drags, and I dread seeing if Jake is going to be the one to pick up Hallie. So when Marley strolls in the classroom in the afternoon, I'm surprised when my body relaxes not only in relief, but also in disappointment.

Did I want him to pick Hallie up? I definitely don't want a repeat of this morning's awkward performance, but another

257

chance to be able to see him? Yeah, I would take that selfish opportunity.

Marley gives me a sad smile, but thankfully, doesn't approach me. I really don't feel like talking about my decision with another *caring* family member.

Family. Is that what I think of her already? That we are family?

Jesus, Lana, get it together. This sulking and overthinking period has gone way too far.

I don't relent in my sulking all week. It's Friday afternoon, and I had the kids doing activity time for the last lesson of the day. In other words, I opened up the art cupboard and let them go wild with the materials and glue.

I'm sitting at my desk now that all the children have left, resting my chin in my hand as I stare into space when Georgia enters the classroom carrying a huge vase of mixed flowers.

"These arrived for you before school finished, but I only just got to the staff room. One of my parents were late picking up." I stare at the beautiful bouquet as she places them on the corner of my table. "I wonder who they're from?" she teases in a singsong voice.

Grabbing the card from the flowers, I shove it into the top drawer of my desk.

"Still ignoring him?" She frowns.

"It's best for both of us." And easier for me.

Georgia releases a deep sigh as she sits in one of the children's chairs in front of me. "What are you doing, Lana?"

"Georgia," I warn her. I am sick of everyone being concerned about this Jake thing. I made my decision based on what I think is the right thing. For all of us. I'm tired of hearing all the *'well meaning'* opinions from those who *'just love me and want to see me happy'*.

"Hey, I'm not judging." She holds her hands up in surrender. "I know. I've got a whole load of crazy up here." She gestures to her head. "Hell, I'm currently in search of a baby daddy." I stare at her, unamused. "But at least I'm looking for happiness, Lana. Opening myself up and putting my heart on the line instead of running away in fear."

I don't know if I should admire her level of crazy or not. She's definitely out there; that's for sure. "Look, Georgia, I know you mean well, and trust me, you aren't telling me something I haven't already heard from everyone else, but I'm doing the right thing. For all of us."

"Ugh." She groans as she stands from the small table. "At least text him and thank him for the flowers."

She leaves with a wave, and I'm once again left sitting and staring into space.

I know I'm weak, a sad excuse for a human, but I'm doing the right thing. I'm protecting us both from major pain in the future. My forehead hits the table. God, my nonna would be so ashamed.

The need to feel close to Jake overpowers me, and I pull the card from my desk drawer.

'How long do we have to feel like this?'

I stare at his manly script on the card and think of him sitting down to write it.

'How long do we have to feel like this?'

I don't want to feel like this. I don't want to go to bed every night and wake up every morning with an ache in my chest because he is the last and the first thing I think of. I don't want to spend my lonely nights thinking about how great things were and how wonderful they could've been. I don't want my gut to churn every time something happens and I want to tell him about it. I don't want to cry every morning after he's dropped Hallie off and I can't wrap my arms around him and kiss him.

But feeling all of this is much better than the alternative.

Having to go through the pain of losing someone else I love? I know I couldn't handle it. The feelings you go through after that are indescribable. I don't have the words to explain it, but it makes the split between Jake and I look like a walk in a field of fricking daisies.

I'm just sick, Harper tells me. *Thanatophobia* it's called. The fear of death and losing someone you love.

I laugh out loud when I think of her face when she informed me of my *'disease'*. She was dead serious. Apparently, I'm not an idiot or a masochist; I just have a mental disorder. All I need is Jake, Hallie, an open mind, and a kickass therapist, and I'll be fixed.

Except I'm not a broken toy, looking to be fixed. I'm someone who has lived to see and experienced enough that I now know my capabilities. I know what I can handle and what I can't. What I refuse to.

My phone buzzes from my drawer and I pull it out to see Tate's name on the screen. For the first time since the accident, my heart doesn't skip a beat when I see him or Harper calling. Since Tate was released a couple of days ago, I have been able to relax a little more. Only worrying over him the normal amount an older sister should.

"Hey, what's up?" I answer.

"Hey, Lala."

I'm instantly on guard with Tate's use of my nickname. "What do you want?"

"Can't a guy just call his big sister to see how she's going and invite her over tonight?"

"Sure, if that's all he really wants."

"It is."

I smile. "Good."

"So you'll come to the café?"

"You're going to open mic night?" My voice is laced with concern. "Are you up to that?"

"Yes." He groans. "I'm feeling great. And it's not like it's a tough job to introduce the acts."

"Fair enough."

"So you wanna come watch? Harper says you shouldn't be alone at this time."

I roll my eyes at the dramatics of the two of them. "I'm sure I'll survive, but I'd love to come. Got any new talent tonight?"

"Yeah." He drags out the word. "Some old talent too who'll hopefully be performing for the first time in a long time."

"Cool, alright, well, I'm still at school so I'll just pack up, go home, and get ready, and I'll be over."

"Cool. Come early. Maurice has dinner for you."

"Okay, see ya."

"Bye." There's a smile in his voice, but I ignore it as I quickly tidy the classroom before grabbing my things and locking up.

When I start my sprint down the hall, I run into Georgia locking up her own classroom.

"You look much happier than you did earlier. Those flowers must have done the trick." She gestures to the bouquet in my arms. "Did you text a certain someone?"

I choose to ignore all her not-so-subtle comments. "I'm going to the café for open mic night."

"Oh, awesome, can I come? I love Friday nights at the café."

"Sure. I'm heading in early though."

"Will you feed me?"

"Yes." I laugh. "I'm sure I can share whatever Maurice has for me."

"Good. I'll drive then."

We walk out of the school together discussing pickup times, and then go our separate ways.

Chapter Thirty-Four

Jake

I'm in a foul mood and not even a couple of beers and the game on TV can help soothe my wounds. If I didn't have Hallie I would try something a lot stronger, but I don't drink like that when she's here. *I could try working out again.*

Over the past couple of weeks since Lana kicked me out of the hospital, I've been working out like a motherfucker. Twice, sometimes three times a day. I don't know why I bother; it hasn't done shit to keep my mind off her or to help me get some kind of sleep at night.

I throw the bottle cap I've been bending in my fingers across the table. "Fucking hell."

I wasn't under any deranged idea that those flowers would fix everything, but fuck, I thought I'd at least get a call or text to say thanks. Something to start communication again. Something to give me hope that there might still be a chance for us, but there's been nothing but radio silence since I got confirmation from the florist that the flowers had been delivered this afternoon.

Harper said to give her time, but I'm just sitting around twiddling my fucking thumbs. It's exactly what Lana wants and the complete opposite of what she needs.

She wants me to leave her alone, to let her go on her merry way without having to face the decision she made. She wants us to go away easily and without a fight.

What she needs is us shoved in her face as a constant reminder of why we are so good together and how much we need each other.

A decision needs to be made. Something needs to be done.

Without a second thought, I am up off the couch and storming down the hallway. Scooping Hallie up into my arms, I grab a blanket from the hall cupboard as I pass it and head out to the car. Waking her in the middle of the night and dragging her around town is becoming a bad habit. One I hope I can break after tonight.

When I've settled Hallie into the truck with the blanket over her legs, I get the heater going and we head off.

Lana has another thing coming if she thinks I am just going to roll over and take this. Walk away without another word.

I've been in the Army since I was eighteen years old. It's all I know. It's all I have done since the day I became an adult. Well, I'd thought turning eighteen made me an adult. Little did I know it would take months of hard combat training. The Army didn't just turn me into a soldier—it turned me into a man. They didn't just teach me to shoot, to communicate, and all that good stuff; they taught me life lessons. The Army was where I learned to fight for what I believed in. It was drilled into me to never give up, to never accept defeat, to never quit, and to never leave a fallen comrade.

She's fucking delusional if she thinks I am leaving her behind.

Pulling to a sharp stop in the driveway, I take Hallie in my arms again and make my way to the front door, banging on it in such an urgent fashion you would think there was a fire.

"Jake," Marley huffs out, her hair mussed. She looks behind me. "I thought there was a fire."

"I need you to take Hallie tonight."

She pulls her robe tighter around herself. "What the hell is going on? It's . . ." she looks down at her watch, which isn't there, and then glances at the clock on the wall behind her, "ten o'clock." I raise my eyebrows at her. "Screw you. You try having three boys. I'm lucky if I last until eight thirty."

"Can Hallie stay or not?"

"Of course, she can. Calm down." She steps back to let me pass. "Go to Thomas's room."

I head down the hallway and Marley closes the front door before pushing past me to step into the bedroom first, pulling the trundle from underneath Thomas's single car bed.

Pulling back the sheets, I lay Hallie down before tucking her in and giving her forehead a light kiss.

"Alright, I'm out of here," I say as we make it back to the living room.

"Hold on. You need to tell me what the hell is going on. The last time you were driving around with Hallie in the middle of the night, you got yourself into a bit of a situation."

I roll my eyes. "Thanks for the reminder."

"I'm just saying." She holds her hands up in surrender.

"Well, don't. I'm on my way to go fix it."

"Now?"

"Yes, now."

"Is that a good idea? It's late."

"We don't all have three boys," I tell her as I open the front door and step out.

"You wouldn't cope," she grumbles just as I shut the door.

I'm laughing all the way to my truck until I'm seated in the driver's seat and remember what the fuck I'm supposed to be doing.

Right. Battle face on. It's go time.

Chapter Thirty-Five

Lana

Taking another sip of my wine, I glance around the café. I don't know why Tate invited me. He and Harper have been busy running around trying to organise everything, and I've pretty much spent the night by myself since Maurice left earlier. He was kind enough to sit with me while I ate dinner at least.

Georgia had disappeared pretty much as soon as we walked in, finding some guy to entertain her. I guess she thought he might be daddy material?

Either way, four hours sitting alone is a long time to over-think everything, and I can't help that my mind turns to Jake. I miss him. Every day that goes by gets harder and harder to hold my resolve. I feel myself letting go and wanting to throw caution to the wind; say to hell with it and deal with whatever comes our way.

Just as I grab my purse off the floor and stand to leave, Tate slips into the seat next to me.

"How's everything going?" he asks as his eyes shift around the room.

"Fine," I respond wearily, sitting back in my chair. "What are you looking for?"

"Nothing, nothing." He brings his full attention back to me. "How are things going, Lana?"

"Okay." I frown. What does he want? I know my little brother, and his fidgeting posture and weird attitude means he is definitely up to something.

"Did you think about what I said?"

"Tate, not now." How do I tell him that it's all I've thought about? All night every night, in fact. I want to talk about it. Talk about how much I miss Jake and Hallie, and how much I want them back. How I think I made one of the worst decisions of my life. But I want to talk to Jake about it. Jake and nobody else. *Whoa. I want to talk to Jake.*

"I worry about you." Tate looks at me with sad eyes.

"A little too much."

"Well, I didn't worry enough last time," he mutters, but I hear it loud and clear and freeze on the spot.

The guilt that drips from his voice has my chest tightening. After everything that happened with Craig, I never once considered how that had affected Tate. How him having to watch me go through that, and then pulling me out of it, may have had a lasting impact on him.

We both sit in silence as our gazes go to the young girl on the stage. She is singing a rendition of Paloma Faith's "Only Love Can Hurt Like This".

Yes, Paloma, so true. Only love *can* hurt like this.

I could fix this. I could take away all of my pain. All mine, Jake's, and Hallie's. I'm the one who caused it all.

"Lana, are you ready?" Harper's voice interrupts my depressing thoughts.

"Ready for what?" I look back and forth between Tate and Harper as they share an awkward glance. "What's going on?"

"I thought you said you already asked her?" Harper snaps at Tate.

"Daisy, I was working on it."

"Working on what?" I demand.

"Well, you have about ten minutes to work on it." Harper's eyes flash in annoyance at her fiancé.

"Guys, what the hell?" I put a stop to their domestic. "What do you want?"

"Tate needs you to sing tonight."

"What?" I screech and Tate winces.

"I couldn't find anyone else to fill the final few spots. You know I would do it myself if I could."

"Why can't Harper do it?" I sulk.

Tate's eyes go wide. "Have you ever heard the sound of a bag of cats being thrown against a brick wall?"

"Hey," Harper protests.

"Please, Lala, do this for me?" Tate bats his long eyelashes at me, and I curse the day my mum gave me a baby brother.

"Fine," I growl. "One song."

"Two?" My eyes shoot daggers at him. "One. One is awesome."

Tate and Harper scurry away from the table. Probably off to suck blood from someone else before the night is through.

I take a deep breath and metaphorically grab my lady balls and head to the side of the stage to speak to the band manager.

He doesn't have much of a range in their songbook so I make

a request for "The Story" by Brandi Carlile, and he assures me they can make it work.

Standing about for ten minutes before I go up has my stomach in my knots. I haven't sung in a long time. It's been even longer since I did it in public. The nerves start to rise, and I try to shove them down.

What makes a good performance is feeling the song. Singing the lyrics as if they're your story, as if you wrote the words specifically to heal you.

I may as well have.

Singing a song that speaks of exactly how I feel about Jake may have been the best or worst idea I have ever had. I might regret it later but when I thought about doing this for Tate, this song is the only one that popped into my head, regardless of the fact I've never performed it outside the shower before.

Tate takes to the stage to introduce me and my heart beats so wildly that I'm worried I won't be able to hear the band.

"Hi everyone." I wave awkwardly at the small audience in the café. Seeing as I'm the last to go on, I'm kind of hoping they are too drunk to notice my unpractised voice. "Tonight I am singing a song that's very special to me and close to my heart."

The audience cheers and I'm not sure at what exactly, so my hopes of their alcohol levels being high are looking good.

The first verse is awkward and shaky. The lights are dim and I can't see more than a meter or so in front of me, yet my nerves are still sky-high.

I barely get through the chorus. *Come on, Lana, snap out of it.* I close my eyes and imagine Jake sitting on a stool in front of me, smiling encouragingly. I think of his warm chocolate eyes, his mesmerising gaze.

My voice picks up as I go into the second verse. I sing about hiding the mess in my head and the words I want to say behind a fake smile. I really find my tune and belt out the chorus. Singing about the scars of my past and letting only him see the real me. Him being the only one I can talk to. Me being made for him.

I sing through the last chords and before I've even finished the last note, the audience is screaming, cheering, and clapping. My eyes pop open but everything is blurry, and that's when I realise I have been crying.

Wiping away the tears flowing down my cheeks, I say a quick thank you and dart off the stage, looking for some repose.

Tate hands me a glass of water wearing a huge smile. "That was beautiful, Lala. Fucking beautiful."

I laugh through my tears as I throw back some water and try to catch my breath and gain some composure.

"You can't leave them with just that one."

"Tate."

"Go on. You've broken your nerves. Give them one more."

The crowd is still cheering and the adrenaline helps me step back on stage without thinking twice about it.

After chatting with the guitarist, who was pretty much no help, I approach the keyboard player.

"May I?" I gesture to his instrument.

"Of course." He steps away from the keyboard. "As long as we get to hear that voice again."

I give him a shy smile and stretch my fingers above the keys. I don't say anything to the crowd before I begin playing the notes.

I close my eyes and sing the first lines of Beyoncé's "Halo", not taking any time at all to get into it. The crowd goes wild— well, as wild as a small audience in a café can go. This is no Madison Square Garden.

With only the notes of the keyboard and my voice booming throughout the café, this song is a lot softer but packs a lot more emotion and heartbreak.

This time, I'm aware of the tears as I sing about how I let my walls down and let him in. How I've broken all my rules and taken a huge risk to trust him. How he's awakened me, my saving grace.

All I think about and focus on is Jake. This song speaks so close to home there's a weight on my chest the whole time I'm singing. I think about his face when he left the classroom earlier this week. How hurt and upset he looked.

More tears fall, and all I can think about is going to find him. Begging him to forgive me, and promising never to hurt him again. Telling him that being with him and Hallie is worth the risk.

When I sing about never shutting him out, I put everything I have into it. I mean it. If Jake could ever forgive me, I would never push him away again. I will work through my stupid fears with him and not live everyday worried about what might be.

This time, when I finish the last notes, I don't stop to smile or say thank you as I run off the stage, wiping the tears from my face. I have to go. I have to find—

My heart skips a beat as my feet come to a screeching halt.

"Jake."

Chapter Thirty-Six

Jake

I had no fucking doubt in my mind that those songs were about me. For me.

The nerves that I walked in here with dissipated completely when I listened to the words she was singing. Her angelic voice filled the room and left me feeling nothing but peace.

She loves me. She fucking loves me.

She wants this as much as I do. She wants to try to make it work.

I'm full of confidence as I make my way to the side of the stage during her last few notes. You can't hide the kind of emotion she is showing. Those songs were Lana, raw and uncut, and I couldn't be more fucking pleased.

No more playing games, saying she's feeling one way when

it's obviously another. No more hiding behind her strong façade or stupid excuses.

"Jake."

Her eyes are wide. She's a deer in the headlights as I corner her against the wall.

I don't speak a word; I just place my lips on hers, kissing her with all the emotion she had in those songs. The kiss is hard, strong, and unforgiving.

"I love you too," I say against her swollen lips.

Her head hits the wall as she pulls back to narrow her eyes at me. "I never said I love you."

"Uh, yeah, you just fucking did." I point towards the stage.

Lana mock glares at me and my heart soars. "Well, I do."

"You do what?" My heart races and warmth radiates through me. I can't believe this is finally fucking happening.

"You know what."

"Say it." I move my lips back towards her. I want to feel it when she says it.

"I do love you."

My face stretches into a huge grin I couldn't contain even if I wanted to. "Fuck yeah, you do."

Lana laughs, but I cut it short as my lips smash down on hers. Our kiss, even though full of love, is rough, raw, and un-restrained. It's all teeth smashing, tongues duelling, and lips seeking.

After who knows how long, I pull back, breathing hard, but needing to clear up a few things.

"I want you, angel. Forever. No more pushing me away."

"I'm sorry, I want you too. I was just scared—"

"I know. It's a disease. A problem we can fix. Something we can work on together. You can go speak to someone and—"

Lana tries to hold in her laughter but is unsuccessful. "Have you been talking to Harper?"

"She may have reiterated something like that over the phone."

"Is that how you knew I was here?"

Both our gazes travel to the bar, to Tate, Harper, and Georgia all watching on with huge goofy smiles on their faces.

"They care for you." I look back at her. "They want you to be happy. I can make you happy, angel."

"You do make me happy. You're my hero."

We smile as our foreheads meet and I hold her tightly as I breathe her in.

Everything feels right. This is right. *She* is right. And I'll do whatever it takes to keep her.

Lana and I don't hang around the café for long after getting the congratulations and backslaps. We drive home in my truck, and I'm out of the truck and dragging her inside at record speed.

"What about Hallie?" she asks as I shut the front door and push her up against it, kissing her ferociously.

"She's at Marley's," I explain between kisses.

It must set Lana's mind at ease as she places her arms around my neck and climbs up my body, wrapping her legs around my waist.

In this new position, our bodies align perfectly for me to thrust and roll my hips into her, rubbing my hard cock in the most satisfying way to elicit the most beautiful sounds from her. Her little whimpers and moans only stir my libido more and I storm to the bedroom, her ass squeezed in my strong hands.

I throw Lana on the bed, and she laughs as I crawl over her, kissing along her body as I go.

I stare straight into her eyes, my gaze burning with everything I'm feeling. "Welcome home, angel."

"Tell me what happened that night." Lana's soft voice echoes in the silence of the room.

As much as I want to enjoy this moment, the two of us wrapped up in the sheets after some thorough and apologetic lovemaking, I know we need to talk about this.

"The guy in my house that day, the guy who pulled you out of the fire." Lana tenses against me, her mindless touching paused. "He is my friend Brad. I've known him for years—met him the day I left for boot camp."

"Okay." Her light touch starts again as she rubs her fingertips over my chest and lays her head on my shoulder.

"Well, that night I got a call from him, saying that he needed me. I didn't think twice. Packed up Hallie in the truck and went to meet him."

Lana leans up on her elbow now, those piercing green eyes watching me acutely.

"When I got there, your house was already on fire and you were lying on the neighbour's lawn. Brad panicked and I couldn't get much sense out of him. He wanted me to say I had been driving past, saw the flames, and pulled you out."

Lana scrunches her face up in confusion, and I hold back from leaning forward to place a kiss on the end of her nose. "I don't get it."

"He saw the flames from your neighbour's place. That blonde?"

"Callie?"

"I guess."

"So what?" she asks, her voice laced with frustration.

"Brad is married, Lana. And not to Callie."

276

"Oh my God," she breathes, her face relaxing in understanding.

"Lana, I have known Brad for over ten years. We've worked alongside each other ever since we met, and we deployed together four times. He was with me through Jamie's death and taking on Hallie by myself. As pissed as I was with him that night, I never second-guessed my loyalty to him. That's how I am wired."

"What about your loyalty to me?" Her voice is strong with anger as she slides back to put space between our bodies, but her eyes flash pain. Hurt. Betrayal.

"I'm so sorry, angel." I try to pull her back to me, and she finally relents. "My loyalty to him caused me to lie to you. I should've told you. *Made* time to tell you. It seemed like no big deal at first, but then I saw you at school and I couldn't not have you. I fell in love with you, and then telling you only became harder. I was a coward, scared of losing you if you knew what I had done that night. That I had kept it from you. Then the longer it carried on and you calling me a hero . . . Fuck, angel, I don't know. I have no good excuse. I fucked up, and I'm sorry."

Lana lays her head back down on my chest and releases a deep breath.

"I don't want to talk about it anymore." She sighs.

I nod but am too scared to say another word. Scared of seeing that pain and hurt in her eyes again.

Chapter Thirty-Seven

Lana

Jake wasn't kidding when he welcomed me into his home.

I haven't left his place for weeks now, and he, Hallie, and I have been living in bliss ever since. We spend every day side by side in domestic harmony. Getting up and ready for school and work, we share kisses good-bye as Jake heads off to the base, and Hallie and I go to school. Nights consist of dinner, homework, dishes, and washing, like in any normal family.

Family.

That is what we are. What I finally have. What I tried to push away after praying and hoping for this exact thing for years.

"What are you thinking about?" Jake's voice and the slide of his hands around my waist pull me from my daydreaming as I stare out of the kitchen window.

"You're home. I didn't hear you come in."

"I'm sure you didn't. I've been standing here watching you wash that plate for five minutes."

I look down to the plate in my hand and laugh as I mindlessly wipe over it again and again. "Sorry, I was distracted."

"Clearly." He chuckles. "What were you thinking about, angel?"

"You. Me. Hallie."

"Oh yeah?" He nuzzles my neck and places light kisses across the crease of my shoulder. "What about us?"

"That. We're an *us,* aren't we?"

Jake turns me in his arms to face him and lifts an eyebrow. "Lana. Are you about to run again?"

"No." I stress. "No way. It just hit me that this is the happiest I have ever been. I love you two more than anything."

Jake narrows his eyes. "And you don't think about how you could lose us one day?"

"Of course, I do." Jake raises his eyebrows. "I mean, I think about it a normal amount."

He laughs and kisses me lightly on the nose. "Well, just so you know, you mean more than anything to us too."

I smile and nuzzle into his hard chest, and he tightens his arms around me.

"Speaking of *us,*" he says. "Where is the other third?"

"In her room. She's making a card for Emily. It's her birthday tomorrow."

"She's really made a friend there." He kisses the top of my head.

"Yeah. Her mum asked about a play-date this weekend, so we're going to the park on Saturday. Her mum seems nice enough. Someone I could be friends with. It's hard to split the teacher and parent sometimes."

"It's only new, angel. I think you're doing awesome. I've never seen Hallie so happy or content."

I smile at him before stepping up on my tiptoes, wrapping my arms around his neck and kissing him hard. My tongue runs along his bottom lip, looking for instant access, and Jake doesn't disappoint.

"You guys kiss a lot." A little voice comes from the entry of the kitchen.

Pulling away from Jake, I go and check on the pasta bake in the oven.

"That's what mummies and daddies do when they love each other."

My head shoots to Jake at his flippant comment.

"Yeah, Emily says her parents kiss a lot too," Hallie says casually as she walks to the drawer and pulls out the table settings.

My eyes are wide, and Jake just laughs and winks at me as he passes. "I'm going to go take a shower and change. How long until dinner?"

I shake my head at him. "Ten minutes, so hurry."

"Yes, ma'am." He salutes me.

I quickly chop a salad while Hallie sets the table. It's not long before Jake joins us, freshly showered and sporting gym shorts and a singlet.

We sit to eat, and I can't help but smile. This is my favourite time of the day. The three of us together, chatting about our day. The good, the bad, and the in-between.

"Brad came to see me today."

"Oh yeah?" I cringe at the distaste in my tone. Since Jake told me about the fire and how he came to be there, he hasn't stopped apologising or trying to make up for it. I told him he didn't have to. That I understood. Understood his thinking. The situation he was put in.

"Yeah. He apologised."

"Again?" I scrunch my nose up. Just because I have forgiven Jake and understand what happened does not mean I want anything to do with someone like Brad.

"He seemed sincere this time. Said he's going to see someone for his *addiction*."

We both glance at Hallie to see how much attention she's paying to our conversation. Her head bops along to the tune she is mindlessly humming.

"Well, good. But that doesn't change how I feel about him."

"Fair enough." He chuckles and leans over the table to give me a light kiss on the lips.

"Hal, tell Dad about your music lesson today."

"I can play the drums," she yells in excitement.

"Oh yeah? My own Princess Rocker."

"Yeah." I raise my eyebrows at Jake. "She wants a set from Santa."

Jake flinches in his chair, and I bite my bottom lip to contain my laughter.

"I'm not sure Santa can fit it in his sleigh," Jake says, and my laughter forces its way out.

We finish dinner with the discussion of Santa—what he can and can't do, and how he manages to do it all. From Santas in the shopping malls to all the elves and the North Pole.

Once Hallie is bathed and is settled in bed sleeping peacefully, I breathe a sigh of relief.

"Full on, isn't it?" Jake laughs.

"I just wasn't prepared for the onslaught of questions. *Why? What? How?* I should've been, I am a kindergarten teacher, but man, she is so smart."

Jake laughs as he pulls me closer. "You better get used to it."

I smile up at him. "Yeah, I suppose I better."

Jake and I tidy up after dinner and get lunches and uniforms ready for the next day before we are crawling into bed, ready to get up and do it all again tomorrow.

He pulls me tightly against him. His hands roam all over my body, from my breasts, down my arms, and to my thighs.

He flips me over and within a second is on top, looming over me, trailing kisses down the same path his hands just travelled. I sigh in contentment as I run my hands over his back and down to his hard butt.

Okay, I lied earlier at the dinner table. I love our family dinners, but *this* by far is my favourite time of the day.

Epilogue

Lana

I am unsuccessful in holding back the tears as I watch Brooke and Saxon say their vows, as they promise to love one another, to support, encourage, and be there for each other. The pure love that floats around this garden is tangible, and you can't miss the way Saxon is looking down at Brooke in adoration.

There's no sign of a baby bump on Brooke in her perfect dress. It has a heart-shaped sleeveless bodice covered in diamond-encrusted lace and then flows out from her waist in long cream silk. It's elegant without being too flashy. Perfect for a second wedding.

I wipe my eyes, trying not to smudge my makeup, and Jake takes my hand in his and squeezes. I smile over at him, and he winks before our gazes go back to the happy couple.

The wedding is small and intimate, and in the most beautiful secluded garden that I had never heard of before. There isn't a long line of bridesmaids and groomsmen; only Brooke and Saxon stand with the minister in front of their closest friends and family.

"God, don't they look so ridiculously happy," Harper whispers in my ear.

"Yes. Look at the way he looks at her."

"He's not the only one who looks like that." Harper gestures over my shoulder, and I turn to find Jake smiling down at me. I giggle and knock him with my hip, and he chuckles as he wraps his arm around me and pulls me into his side.

Everyone cheers as Brooke and Saxon make their marriage official with a mostly chaste, but slightly inappropriate kiss.

Murmurs begin as the newly married couple go to sign their wedding register. I glance over to the older couple Harper told me were Nate's mum and dad, Brooke's dead husband's parents.

Apparently, as soon as they told Mark they were setting a date, he agreed they would be here, even if he had to drag his wife kicking and screaming. This was something Harper also said had to happen.

As I look over at her now though, I'm not sure. She wears a small smile as she wipes away tears from her eyes. She doesn't appear to be the witch of an ex-mother-in-law who is completely against the union as I've heard. We'll have to organise another girls' night out so I can get the finer details from Brooke on that subject.

Brooke and Saxon, who are now finished signing with her parents as their witnesses, walk down the aisle holding hands, with huge smiles on their faces as they hug and kiss and receive congratulations from all their guests.

"Congratulations, hon," I whisper, as I step forward to embrace Brooke in a hug. "You look beautiful."

She smiles and I step back and slip a beautiful gold ceramic painted horseshoe over her wrist before Harper barrels through me to offer her congratulations.

Jake pulls me tight against him as we dance at the reception. Our joined hands are lying on his chest between us, his other hand resting on my lower back as my fingers are entangled in the short hair at the back of his neck. We sway to the soft music of "The Way You Look Tonight", which the hired band plays.

"It was a beautiful day, wasn't it?" I say.

"It was."

"Well deserved."

"They sure have been through a lot," Jake agrees.

I smile as I glance around at all our friends and family dancing around. Brooke and Saxon looking into each other's eyes as if there is no one else in the room. Tate and Harper have their arms wrapped tightly around each other, laughing and giggling together.

"When will we deserve our day?"

"What?" I turn back to look at Jake who now has his serious eyes focused on me.

"When will we have our day, angel? When you will marry me?"

"Oh, I don't know, I don't know. Maybe we should wait until after the baby comes."

Jake doesn't look amused at all, and I give him a knowing smile. His eyes narrow, disbelieving. "No."

Excited adrenaline pumps through me. I've been waiting for

the right time to tell him. "Yes."

"You're pregnant?" His eyes are wide.

"Yes."

"Oh my God." He laughs as he picks me up and spins me around.

"So you're happy then?" I can't contain my huge smile.

"Angel, I could not be any fucking happier. Except . . ."

"Except what?" My elation quickly begins to fade as my heart stills.

"I want to marry you before the baby comes."

My heart rate picks back up and I grin. "Oh, well, I guess that could be arranged."

Jakes laughs again as he sways me side to side.

"What are you two so happy about?" Tate asks, as he and Harper dance up to us.

I look at Jake with wide eyes, and he just nods.

"I'm pregnant." I smile at my baby brother.

"Oh my God!" Harper squeals, untangling herself from Tate's arms and pulling me out of Jake's embrace and into a huge hug. "Oh my God, congratulations."

I laugh. "Thank you."

Jake and Tate shake hands, and the commotion on the dance floor brings Saxon and Brooke dancing over.

"What is all the ruckus over here? Pulling attention away from me on my big day," Brooke teases. Before I can even respond, she stops dancing and her mouth drops open. "Oh my God, you're pregnant."

I stand shocked, as she smiles at me.

"How did you know?" Harper pouts.

"I noticed you've had to pee a lot tonight."

Harper, Brooke, and I all crack up laughing as the boys look at each other with confused expressions.

"We should do that," Tate says to Harper, taking her back in his arms and gesturing to me.

"What?" she screeches.

"We should have a baby."

"I don't fucking think so." She frowns. "Not yet, anyway."

After more laughter and congratulations, Tate swoops me up in his arms and turns me around the dance floor before Jake can protest.

"Congratulations, Lala."

"Thank you." I smile up at him.

"Mum and Dad, and Nonna and Nonno would be so happy for you. For everything you've built with Jake and Hallie."

I give him a sad smile before resting my cheek on his chest. "You too, you know."

"I know." He pulls back to grin at me before taking us into a fast waltz.

It's not long before Jake comes to the rescue, Harper in his arms. "Be careful with her," he warns Tate. "She's carrying my baby."

Tate throws his head back and laughs before releasing me and taking back his fiancée from Jake.

Jake wraps his arms around me, moving at a slower pace that I'm much more comfortable with.

"I'm so happy. I don't know if I have ever been so happy before," he says.

"You saved me." I smile up into his warm brown eyes.

"No, angel. You saved me."

The End-

Thank you so much for reading. I hope you enjoyed Lana and Jake's story. It would be so greatly appreciated if you could spare a minute to leave a review, good or bad, on the purchasing site.
Thank you, Steph xo

Coming Soon – Whatever It Takes
Book 4 in the *Try Again* Series

Georgia and Henry's Story

Acknowledgments

I promise, I'm really going to try and keep it short this time!

Firstly, to you, the reader. I can't tell you enough how much I appreciate your support. I don't have thousands and thousands of faceless sales. I appreciate every one of them. I see your tags, I see your pimps, I see your comments about my books in reader threads. I love receiving your messages and emails, whether they are of love for my characters, or hate for all the tears I have made you cry. I love how excited you get and how thankful you are when you win one of my simple giveaways.

It's easy to follow and support the authors you know and love. But to give a new author a go and then support them through their new journey is just wonderful and it leaves me speechless every time someone takes a chance on me and my stories. So, thank you! XO

My AWESOME group of girls in *Stories By Steph*. You guys are the back bone to what keeps me going. Whether it be listening to me babble on, laughing at my lame jokes or offering your great support and advice. I never quite feel so alone in this crazy book world with you girls by my side. Love you all! XO

A special thanks to Sheryl Pike and her husband Dan. I can't thank you enough for the advice and research you helped me with. I was still looking back at your notes just last week, making sure I had everything covered. Hehe It really meant the world to me, so thank you!!

Lauren McKellar. On this, our third book together, I have run out of ways to tell you how much I adore you. This is where you would be offering great suggestions on different ways I could say it. Love, appreciate, cherish, treasure, respect, admire. In simple terms, I couldn't do this without you, and I hope I never have to. (Sorry these acknowledgements were last minute, AGAIN, and I didn't get to run them by you for editing ☹ hehe) XO

My beautiful beta readers. This story would not be what it is today without all of you. Taking time out of your busy lives to read my story and then telling me what wasn't working and giving me the tools to make it better. It's such an honor to have someone care as much as you do about your story and I couldn't do any of this without you girlies. I love you to bits. Mwah XO

My A is for F*cking Awesome girls. I have been so lucky to be a part of such a like-minded group of girls. I never feel like the unexperienced newbie I really am when I'm in there, and I appreciate all the advice and support you guys give me. Whether it be listening to a crazy rant about the Hubster or a stupid question about the industry. I admire you girls so much and your support means the world to me!!

Give Me Books PR and Kylie, for organising my Cover Reveal, Release Day Blitz and ARCs. Thank you for all the hard work you put in. I can't thank you enough for dealing with it all and making it so easy on my end!

To all the amazing bloggers who read, reviewed, shared teasers and links, and sent kind words of encouragement. I don't have the words for how grateful I am and for how much it means to me. You guys make the world go round and it still surprises me when you all offer your support and services so willingly for little old me!!

I know I am forgetting so many. Hang Le (By Hang Le) my wonderful cover artist. You make the process so enjoyable and stress free. Stacey Blake (Champagne Formats) you are so easy to work with and I never have to worry once it's in your hands. Jenny Sims (Editing 4 Indies). For anyone I have forgotten I'm so sorry, I've left this to the last minute again. Maybe I'll learn for the next book.

As always, last and most importantly, my wonderful husband. Josh, I can never come up with the perfect way to tell you how I feel. It should be easy, I should be good with the words, but the way I feel about you exceeds anything words could say.

It was easy to write Jake as a loving and devoted father because I have you. The best decision I ever made was choosing you as the father of my children. You are the best daddy I know and our girls will have the best opportunities in life because of you. Because of your unconditional love, your support, your encouragement, your role modelling and your hard work.

I can't wait for the months ahead and then to finally welcome baby number 3 into the Smith household. But after that, no more. Hehe

Josh, I am the luckiest girl ever and I'll spend the rest of our lives trying to be worthy and loving you until the end of time!!

About the Author

Stephanie is a Happily Ever After addict.

Loving mushy romance books, movies and music since she was young. Constantly daydreaming up stories and plots, Stephanie decided to put them on paper.

Living in South Australia with her own alpha male and two princesses, she spends her days reading, writing, and playing with the girls out on their property.

You'll find Stephanie lurking on all the below forms of social media, even though she hasn't mastered any.

www.authorstephaniesmith.com.au

www.facebook.com/authorstephsmith

https://twitter.com/stephwrites77

www.ingramcontent.com/pod-product-compliance
Lightning Source LLC
Chambersburg PA
CBHW020236180626
46810CB00006B/2222

* 9 7 8 0 9 9 4 2 4 2 7 3 0 *